Books by Nikki Rae

Fangirl Series

Reblogs & Hearts

Summer Tours & Hearts

SUMMER TOURS & Hearts

NIKKI RAE

ISBN-13: 9798991474146

Cover design made using Canva (canva.com) by: Nikki Rae.

Graphics designs by: Nikki Rae.

Library of Congress Control Number:

Printed in the United States of America

To all the losers, punks, nerds who always felt out of place until they found their people. This one is for you!

Laurel

Laurel leaned back against her chair rereading the blurb about her debut novel.

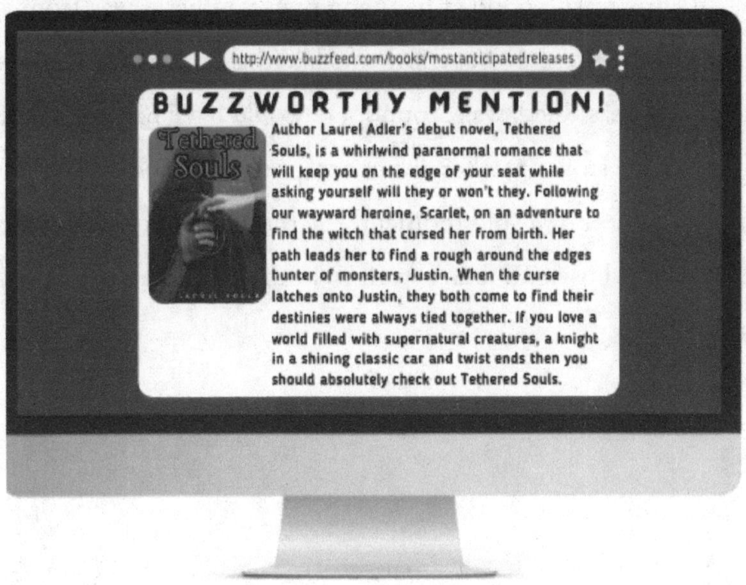

It was surreal that her book was out in the world for people to read. Her agent, Leigh Meyer, had sent her the link to Buzzfeed's article that also featured another of her clients. Leigh had a lot of buzz going for her three newest clients that all had debut or sophomore titles releasing. Laurel's phone buzzed with a new text from her debut authors' group thread.

Laurel wasn't good at handling praise, rather it was from friends or the press. It was moments like this she wished her best friend, Thomas Reed, was around. He would have had some kind of wisdom to bestow onto her about accepting the good and pushing out the doubt. For a split moment, she thought about calling him, but knew he was busy and didn't want to bother him over something so little.

She rolled her eyes thankful that neither of her friends could see her. Raelyn Jameson and Emerson Holbrook both had books releasing but had been in the entertainment industry one way or another beforehand. Raelyn had a successful series of novellas based off her husband's TV show. Her first standalone book inspired by how she met her husband, Austin Jameson. Emerson was a social media manager for a professional baseball team, Vancouver Explorers, after much encouragement from her MLB All Star boyfriend decided to write a book inspired by their happily-ever-after.

Laurel was the oddball of the group. Her debut novel was inspired by pure imagination and the desperate hope there was someone out there for everyone. It was only dumb luck that she had submitted her book to Leigh by accident. She had meant to send it to another literary agent with a similar name at the same agency. The universe took pity on her, and Leigh ended up loving her book. In a complete whirlwind of a year and half, Laurel's life changed when they sold her book to the same publishing house as Raelyn's. Now, her book was out there, and her publishers were waiting for her next book. Which was what Laurel was trying to work on when Leigh had sent her the link from Buzzfeed.

For the last three weeks, she had been locked away in her home office in Springfield, Missouri. She was known as the town recluse and was pretty sure kids in her neighbor through she was a witch. Laurel had always been content with staying in her hometown, living alone, and dreaming up fantastical worlds. Now staring at a blank document and blinking cursor, she wished she could be anywhere else but there. She had an outline for a sequel to Tethered Souls, but the words were not coming out. However, the floodgates of doubt and self-loathing had busted wide open.

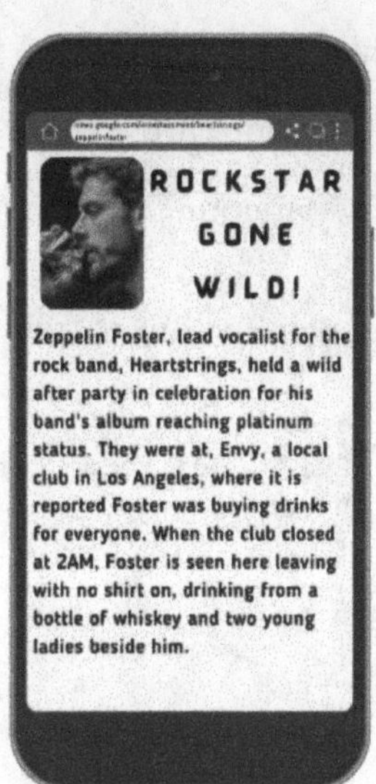

She clicked on the article. Her heart dropped when she saw the photo attached and skimmed through the article. Seeing her other best friend drunk and leaving with two girls, he could have easily been their father. She clicked out of her text group then went to Thomas's name and started typing.

The three of them have been friends since grade school. When Zeppelin had decided to pursue being a rockstar, Thomas insisted on being his manager. He attended college in California while Zeppelin played every dive bar and gig he could. They had been by each other's sides, navigating fame and fortune leaving Laurel to her books and modest life.

In moments like this she was grateful Thomas was there for Zeppelin. His wild spirit was one of the many things that attracted her to him, but he needed someone to be a voice of reason in his life.

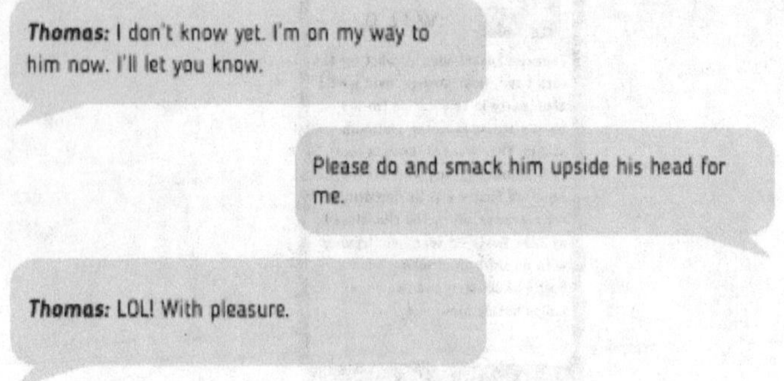

Looking at the picture of them on her desk, a familiar ache deep in her chest blossomed. Most days, Laurel preferred the solitude of writing full time. She was uncomfortable socializing with people or speaking in front of people. She hated large crowds and always found ways to seemingly disappear into the background. The only time she ever wanted to talk or hang out with anyone was with her boys or new author friends. Right now, she was missing her boys a lot.

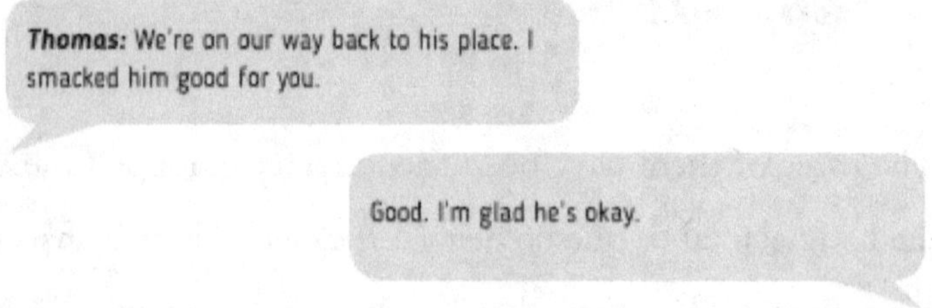

Deciding there was no way she was going to be able to concentrate on writing, she shut off her laptop and went to her second favorite spot in her home. Walking down the hall, she grabbed a bottle of water from the fridge on her way down to the basement. Turning on the string lights hung around the ceiling, her library came into view. Every wall was covered from floor to ceiling bookshelves filled with adventures, love, and heartache. It was her oasis of escapism.

Laurel went to her oversized reading chair and picked up the book she had started the night before. It was a romantasy book about a witch who ends up falling in love with a witch hunter. She had chosen it as one of her comp titles but also hoping it would help inspire her. She only made it through a chapter before giving up on reading. She couldn't focus as her mind ran through every worst-case scenario as to what Zeppelin had gotten himself into.

It was nothing new for him to be caught by the press out partying. He was your typical rockstar playing music, drinking, and sleeping with fans. There was something nagging at her to check in with him. She picked up her phone and hit his name.

"This is Zepp. Leave your details and I'll get back to ya."

"Hey, I was… um, I wanted to check in with you. I'm sure Thomas has already giving you an ear full. I just want to make sure you're okay. Call it best friend intuition or whatever, but I just need to hear from you that you're alright. Call me back."

The uneasiness in her gut didn't relax as she leaned back into her chair and closed her eyes. Deciding she needed to do something to take her mind off everything, Laurel headed back upstairs to her living room. She turned on her favorite playlist, turning it up loud and started on her weekly house cleaning.

She was in the middle of dancing with her vacuum when her phone started ringing. Her heart skipped hoping it was Zeppelin returning her call. Seeing it was Leigh, her heart slowed, and dread pooled in her stomach.

"Hi Leigh..."

"Hey, can you jump on Zoom with me? I want to check in to see how you're doing and where you're at with the next book."

"Sure, just give me five minutes to get my laptop up and running." Laurel started making her way to her office as Leigh ended the call.

She pulled up her notes and outline for her next book. Her deadline wasn't for several months, but Leigh knew she was struggling to write. As soon as her computer was on, she initiated a video call and Leigh's face appeared on the screen. Looking at her, most people figured she was a mousy, reserved woman when she was quite the opposite.

"Thanks Laurel, I'm sorry to spring this on you. Our first self-imposed deadline is coming up and I want to make sure you're on pace to hit it."

She averted her eyes to her desk, "Yeah... about that..."

"Laurel..."

"I know. I know. I have an outline and notes for a sequel to Tethered Souls." Laurel shared her document with Leigh, "It's good or it will be once I can get the words out."

She watched as Leigh read over her stuff, "You're right, it's good. There's more world building and fleshing out of the side characters from book one. I like the little love triangle that you have in here as well."

"I knew I had to stir up their relationship somehow."

Leigh looked back to her, "What's the problem then? With all of this I would figure you would have at least a quarter to a half of the book written."

It was the question Laurel kept asking herself every time she sat down to write. What was the problem? She loved her two main characters. She loved the world she built, and the love story weaved into it. She wanted their story to continue, but something was holding her back.

"I really don't know. I wish I could tell you there was a reason for me not having any of my draft written. My mind goes completely blank when I sit at my computer."

Laurel could feel the weight of her failure pressing on her shoulders. Another brick to add to the pile of failures she had over her lifetime. No real job. No husband. No kids. She was constantly reminded by her family of how they wished for more out of her life. Forget the fact that she had written a whole book that landed her a great book deal and afforded her the chance to write full-time.

"Maybe you should try a writing retreat. Go off to a beach house for a change of pace. New scenery could inspire the words for you."

Laurel shrugged, "Yeah… maybe. I'll look into it and let you know by the end of the week."

Leigh nodded, "That sounds good. You know I'm always here if you need me."

"I know and appreciate that. I'll talk to you on Friday or Saturday."

They ended the video chat and Laurel laid her head on her desk. She knew a change in scenery wasn't going to help whatever was blocking her. She had already tried going to coffee shops and the park. She thought reading more fantasy and paranormal books would help, but that wasn't the part she was having trouble with. She knew what it was even if she didn't want to admit it.

Laurel walked back down to her library and scanned over her books. She had an advance copy of Raelyn's book, Project Fanfic, that she pulled off her shelf. Romance was not a genre she typically read, but knew she needed to. With very little experience in that department herself, she found it hard to write what it was like to be in a healthy relationship. Flipping through the pages, Laurel sat back down on her reading chair and began reading Raelyn's book.

When her phone started ringing, Laurel was surprised to see she was nearly halfway through the book. Picking up her phone, she saw Zeppelin's smiling face on the screen.

"How you feeling?" She chuckled hearing him groan.

"Probably better than I should. Damn paparazzi sneaking around everywhere."

His husky voice never failed to send a wave of goosebumps down her arms, "That's what you get for being a famous rockstar and partying until the wee hours. By the way, did you card those girls before leaving with them? Pretty sure they were not old enough to be in that club."

He scoffed, "Oh for fuck sakes, not you too. I already got my ass chewed by Thomas about them. Which, by the way, they were twenty something… I think."

"You're unbelievable. Well thanks for calling me back and I'm glad you're okay." There was an awkward pause, "I'm sure you have some kind of party to head out to, so I won't keep you."

"Nope, I've been grounded for the night. Actually, I wanted to talk to you about something."

Laurel counted to ten, "My silence is your cue to continue, Zepp."

His nervous chuckle made her smile and curious as to what he would want to talk about. She and Zeppelin had weekly chats about their lives. It was the one thing she looked forward to each week. Usually, it was him talking about a new melody or lyrics he came up with. She would tell him about her writing or lack of as of recent.

"I know you've been having trouble writing and well, frankly Thomas is tired of babysitting me. We were… well, I was wondering if maybe you wanted to head out on tour with us this summer?"

She nearly dropped her phone, "W-What? Come out on tour? Really?"

"Yes really. To be honest, it would be great to see you in person again. It's been nearly a year, and I miss you. We miss you."

"I don't know Zepp. I mean, you're gonna be exhausted from performing and meeting with fans. I'll probably just be in the way."

Her chest ached as each excuse that came from her lips. She really wanted to see him again. She missed her boys a lot, but to constantly be around people without an escape was terrifying to Laurel.

"You know that's all bullshit. Maybe being out on the road will inspire you to write a great tale of a devilishly handsome performer charming his way into the hearts of millions while traveling with his band of companions." He chuckled.

"That is a good idea if I wrote high fantasy, but I don't. Right now, I'm not writing anything." She mumbled.

"Even more reason for you to come with us. You never know, maybe the music will move you to write again. Driving around the country to all kinds of cities. Kind of like when we road tripped to L.A. from Springfield."

That trip had been one of the best and worst of her life. Being in a car with Zeppelin and Thomas traveling halfway across the country had been fun as hell. Flying back home alone, after getting them all moved into their shitty Los Angeles apartment and saying goodbye had sucked.

Zeppelin's low tone caught her attention, "I'm serious Laurel. At least think about it. You can always hide away on one of the buses if you need time alone. You can work on your book, hang out with us and make fun of me from the side stage."

The butterflies in her stomach began to flutter, "That does sound like fun. I promise I'll think about it."

"Thank you. Alright, I'm off to take Thomas out to dinner. I'll talk to you later. Love ya."

"Love ya too, Zepp."

Laurel closed her eyes trying to get her heart to stop racing and her stomach to untwist. There had been a reason she hadn't seen Zeppelin in over a year. He flew out to celebrate her book being sold and after a little too much whiskey they had ended up making out like when they were teenagers. They had always toed the line between friendship and more. It was nothing for them to sleep over at each other's houses snuggling in the same bed. Anyone who saw them together always assumed they were dating, but they never were. As much as Laurel wanted to be with him, they both agreed their friendship meant more than their fleeting hormones.

She looked down at her phone to see what time it was and saw Thomas had texted her.

Thomas: For the love of everything good please come on tour with us. You'll be my hero... my savior... my sanity. Pretty please!

Like I told Zepp, I'll think about it.

Thomas: Thinking is overrated. Say yes.

LOL! That's rich coming from Mr. Sensible and Think About EVERYTHING Before Committing

I need to talk with Leigh then I'll let you guys know.

Thomas: Tell Leigh I will buy whatever she wants. Favorite flowers? Alcohol? Meal? Autographs from the band? Whatever she wants if she can get you to come with us.

I'll send her your text to make sure she knows there's something in it for her. Now, stop begging and let me think

Zeppelin

The pounding was getting louder and louder.

Zeppelin Foster groaned trying to sit up to yell at his drummer for practicing so early. Feeling his arms pinned down and excessive heat surrounding him, his eyes snapped open to an all too bright room. An all too bright room that was not his or any room he recognized. Flashes of the previous night started to come into focus through his whiskey fog hangover.

Thomas announcing their record hitting platinum. Heading out to Envy for drinks and to celebrate. Shots of tequila. Women everywhere. That is when the memory became crystal clear. Looking to his left he found a beautiful young blond woman lying on his arm with one leg draped over his waist. To the right his arm was trapped between a pair of slender legs that led up to another beautiful young woman who was resting her head on his thigh.

He carefully slipped his arm from between the woman's legs and reached for his phone on the bedside table. His head throbbed seeing all the missed calls and texts from Thomas. He was getting ready to call him when three loud knocks came from the door. The ladies on either side of him groaned but made no attempt to get up.

"Ladies, I believe that would be for me." He said, getting his arm free from the blond.

Zeppelin managed to get out of the bed without ending up on his ass and collected his clothes from the floor. Once he had his pants on, he opened the door to see Thomas standing there with his hazel eyes narrowed angrily at him.

"Let's go."

Zeppelin hung his head and followed his friend down the hallway. He pulled on his shirt and did his usual pat down when he realized he was missing something.

"Shit. I left my wallet up there."

Thomas sighed, hitting the elevator down button, "I'll go get it. You get to the car."

He stepped into the elevator with his bodyguard, Jake, whose emotionless face spoke volumes of how aggravated the two of them were at him. The familiar blacked out SUV was waiting in front of the hotel and Zeppelin immediately got into the backseat lying down.

"Jake, you got a spare set of sunglasses?" He asked as a pair of glasses landed on his chest, "Thanks."

Slipping them on, he tried to ignore the constant pounding in his head. A few minutes later, he heard the passenger door open and shut then the car began to move. His stomach lurched up into his throat and he swallowed hard to push it back down.

"What the hell were you thinking Zepp? You didn't tell anyone you were leaving with those girls or where you were going. This isn't like when you were playing bars fifteen years ago. Those girls could have taken you anywhere and done anything with you."

Zeppelin slowly sat up, leaning his head on the window, "Sorry mom. I didn't know I was grounded from having fun."

He heard Thomas scoff, "Damn it this is serious! Those girls were barely eighteen. We don't need a scandal right before you head out on tour. You need to get your head on straight and fucking grow up."

Peeking one eye open, Zeppelin found Thomas facing forward texting on his phone. Closing his eyes, he felt a firm smack on the top of his head making hit throb twice as much.

"What the fuck was that for!"

"That was from Laurel who read an article on Google news about your wild night last night." Thomas turned back around and stared out to the road ahead of them.

The mention of his best friend's name sent his heart plummeting into his churning stomach. Every week they would check in with each other about their lives. No matter where he was or what he was doing, Zeppelin always made the time to check in with her. Lately, he had been keeping their chats about what he was working on and nothing about his social life. The truth was, he was flying high with a successful music career, but never felt more alone. Even with Thomas with him, he still felt like there was something missing.

Sitting up, he watched as Hollywood's rich, and elite passed by in their sports cars. People walked in and out of high-end clothing stores or a five-star restaurant from a business lunch. Zeppelin often wondered if they felt like he did. He always thought money would make things better and all it did was make things more complicated. He never knew who was getting to know him for Zeppelin Foster the man or Zeppelin Foster the rockstar. Usually, it was the latter.

They headed out of downtown Los Angeles and headed up into the hills looking over the city. He felt his body relax finally and the pounding in his head was subsiding enough to pull down the sunglasses to look out over the city below. They drove up the long drive to his home where Thomas and the band lived with him. The thought of being in that house alone had nearly sent him into a full-on panic attack when he first purchased it. With a built-in studio and all the equipment, they would ever need, his band mates were happy to live there.

"The prodigal front man returns." Alec Braxton, the bassist, called out from the couch.

"Ha. Ha." Zeppelin walked past him into the kitchen to grab some water.

Sitting at the table were the other two members of his band, Heartstrings, Rich Roberts and Samantha Forester. Rich was shoveling food into his mouth while Samantha was tapping her drum sticks on the table.

"You look like shit." She mentioned with a smirk.

He rolled his eyes, downing the bottle of water. His empty stomach immediately churning as the water sloshed around. He went to the fridge and snagged a cold piece of pizza then headed off to his room. Zeppelin wasn't quite ready to deal with all of them yet. He needed a shower and to sober up a little more.

Entering his room, he found Thomas waiting for him and he groaned, "Look can I at least eat this nasty cold pizza and shower before you start in on me again?"

"You know where to find me."

Without another word, Thomas walked out closing the door behind him. Zeppelin couldn't remember the last time his friend had been this upset with him. Maybe in the fifth grade when they had gotten into a fight for Thomas teasing him and Laurel. Sure, they had little arguments and disagreements. Nothing they could never not work out.

Zeppelin ate his pizza and showered, feeling a hundred times better afterwards. Walking back out into the living room, he found the house to be empty and quiet… too quiet. Walking to the lower level, he found the door to Thomas's office ajar and music softly playing from it. He knocked a couple of times before pushing the door open. Thomas was sitting behind his desk with his eyes focused on his laptop and his fingers flying over his keyboard.

"Let me finish this email." He said without looking up.

Zeppelin flopped down on the small couch across from Thomas's desk and looked around at the walls.

All the Heartstrings' album covers were framed and hung in order of release. There were framed photos from tours, other artists they had met, and award shows they had attended together. There was a small collage frame with pictures of him, Thomas and Laurel from various stages of their friendship. Grade school, middle school talent show, prom and a few from Thomas and Laurel visiting one another at their colleges.

The center photo was the most recent of the three of them. It was from a party celebrating Laurel's debut novel being sold. She was holding up the first draft of her book while he and Thomas were on either side of her sandwiching her into a hug.

"I wanted to talk to you about an idea I have concerning the tour."

He looked up at his friend, "Alright..."

Thomas wrung his fingers together nervously, "I want to invite Laurel out on tour with us."

Of all the things Thomas could have said at that moment, Zeppelin hadn't seen that coming. The thought of Laurel, his Laurel, being on tour with the band, crew, groupies had his chest seizing with panic.

"W-What? You want Laurel to come out on tour with us? Why?"

"She's struggling to write her book, as I'm sure you know. I think maybe a getaway from Missouri and seeing some different cities would be good for her. Plus…"

Zeppelin knew it couldn't be that simple, "Plus what?"

"Plus, I think it would be good for you as well. It's obvious that you're not going to listen to me even though I'm your friend and manager."

"Thomas…" He started to say but Thomas held his hand up.

"Laurel always had a way of getting through to you. Whatever the reason, you listen to her and take her opinion seriously. You need this tour to go smoothly and having another friend out there with you is a good start."

Zeppelin hated to admit it, but Thomas was right. Not to mention it had been nearly a year since he last saw his best friend. Having her traveling with him could be a lot of fun and any time spent with her was good. When he was about to agree another thought popped into his head overshadowing the good reasons to ask her to come with them.

"This isn't some lame attempt of getting her to spy on me or babysit me, is it?"

Thomas laughed, "Now you know better than anyone that if I wanted someone to spy on you it would not be Laurel. If, and it's a big if, she agreed to come with us I think we would be lucky if she came off the bus."

That made Zeppelin laugh. As much as he was a social butterfly, Laurel was a hermit. She was content staying home reading or writing while he always wanted to be out at a local bar or club.

"True. I mean, I'm alright with her coming on tour if you want to ask her." He sat up, pushing himself off the couch.

"I think you need to ask her. I think she will be more likely to say yes if it comes from you. Again, you two have always had your own connection. Think about it. Either way, give her a call to let her know you're alright. She's worried."

Zeppelin nodded, heading towards the door when Thomas called out to him again.

"Zepp, the band went to check out a local band to see about them opening for you guys. I think maybe you should take the night off and relax here."

By Thomas's tone, it wasn't a suggestion and Zeppelin sighed, "Yes sir, I'll be upstairs, Netflix and chilling by myself then." He saluted Thomas who promptly flipped him off.

Heading back upstairs, he grabbed his phone from his room then walked out to the living room. He turned on the TV flipping through channels before landing on some paranormal documentary. Halfway through the program, his phone started buzzing beside him. Laurel's beautiful face was on his screen. He couldn't bring himself to answer her call, letting it go to his voicemail.

It was bad enough disappointing Thomas, but he couldn't face hearing that disappointment in her voice. She was the one person in the whole world he never wanted to disappoint, and he was sure the way his life was currently going she would be disgusted with him. Ever since he turned forty, a huge chasm had split open deep within him with an endless void.

He tried filling it by writing music and collaborating with other artists. He tried filling it with copious amounts of alcohol and wild nights with women. All it did was push the split open further and darkness filled his mind, heart and soul. He didn't want Laurel to see the shell of the man he had become. However, that was not the only thing that kept him from answering her call or asking her on tour.

He pulled up his photos on his phone, swiping through an album he had of him and her. A lot like Thomas's collage of photos, some of these were from when they were kids. A picture from their first rock concert together in high school. Endless photos of Laurel writing in a notebook and him strumming on his guitar. His favorite photo, the one he had within his guitar case safely pinned to the lid, was him kissing Laurel's cheek the day she was released from the hospital after her accident. Her smile was breathtaking and had inspired so many of the songs he had written.

Staring down at the photo now, Zeppelin's heart ached painfully within his chest. She was always the one he had loved unconditionally. The whole reason for him to become a famous rockstar was to provide her with a life that only she could be worthy of. Now, he wasn't even worthy of being in the same room as her. He had fucked all of that up by being the stereotypical celebrity. She deserved better than that. Better than him.

A voicemail notification popped up and he hesitantly hit it.

Hey. I was… um, I wanted to check in with you. I'm sure Thomas has already giving you an ear full. I just want to make sure you're okay. Call it best friend intuition or whatever, but I just need to hear from you that you're alright. Call me back.

The ache within his chest deepened. There was not a hint of disappointment in her voice, which he should have known. There was only worry and the guilt settling on his chest pressed down a little harder. He was about to call her back when Thomas walked into the room.

"We're going to release a statement tomorrow morning about last night."

"I'm sure Dani was pissed. Thanks for handling that." He was eternally grateful for Thomas always being willing to handle his publicist whenever she was angry at him.

Thomas chuckled, "Yeah, she told me she would kick your ass later. Try and stay out of trouble before the tour. Please."

Zeppelin nodded, "I will. I'm going to call Laurel and ask her about coming out with us. I figure it won't hurt to ask, and it would be nice for the three of us to hang out again."

"Great. Maybe I'll send her a few texts encouraging her to say yes."

"You mean begging her to say yes?" He laughed.

"Tomato, tamato." Thomas headed off into the kitchen before

Zeppelin heard the back sliding door open and close.

He looked down at his phone, taking a deep breath before hitting Laurel's name listening to the other line ring.

Laurel

September 1994 – 5ᵗʰ Grade

Laurel walked into her kitchen, nervously straightening out her new skort. The first day of school was always the worst as everyone around her was happy to see their friends again. All of Laurel's friends were within the pages of books she read. Currently, she had spent time with a young girl and boy around her age in a magical garden.

"Are you excited for school today?"

She looked up at her mom standing by the kitchen counter. She was a petite woman who normally was gone before Laurel woke up. Since it was the first day of school, she was still home and packing Laurel's backpack.

"I guess so." She shrugged.

"I know it's been a tough summer with your dad…" Her mom trailed off, looking down to her feet, "This is a chance for you to have a new beginning. You can be anyone you want to be."

Laurel nodded, grabbing her bag and a banana for breakfast. "I know. I love you mom." She hugged her mom tightly around her waist.

Her father had moved out just a week earlier into a home that was an hour away. Her mom had sat her down to tell her that she would be seeing him every other weekend and if she ever wanted to see him more to tell her. Laurel didn't want to see him at all but had nodded silently.

"You better get to the bus stop. Have a wonderful first day and don't forget to go to Miss Carol's after school. I have to work late tonight." Her mom kissed the top of her head, "I love you, Laurel."

Heading out the front door, she walked up the hill from her house to the bus stop. The same kids were standing there talking as in previous years. Some of her classmates were huddling together talking about their summers and the latest Teen Bop gossip. There was a couple of first graders nervously standing by their parents, looking down the street for the bus. That's when Laurel noticed a new boy sitting on the sidewalk.

His long golden hair was pushed back by the headphones covering his ears. A new portable CD player resting in his lap as he bopped his head along to whatever music he was listening to. His eyes were focused on the notebook resting on his backpack in front of him. He bounced a pencil on his lips as he read what was written on the page. He had on baggy jeans, a T-shirt with a band she had never heard of on it and a plaid shirt tied around his waist.

He glanced up at her with the brightest green eyes she had ever seen. Laurel quickly looked away to see the bus was almost at their stop. Glancing out of the corner of her eye, she watched as he packed up his stuff and trailed behind everyone. She walked behind the other fifth and sixth graders as they rushed to the back of the bus. Laurel sat in her usual spot in the middle where the wheel was and rested her bag on her lap.

"Can I sit here?"

She looked up to see the new boy pointing to the spot beside her. She nodded and pulled her book from her bag. Glancing over at him, he had one of the earphones behind his ear and the other still covering his other ear. She could clearly hear the hard beat of a rock song coming from the speaker. His eyes were once more focused on his notebook. Looking down, she was surprised to see what looked like a poem written down.

She went back to reading, letting the steady beat of the boy's music and his pencil taps pace her reading. She was reading the last page of a chapter when they arrived at Point Primary School. Placing her bookmark in the crease of the book, she slid it back into its spot within her bag. She noticed the new boy was staring at her as the bus came to a stop and they waited to be released into the school.

"Do you like Nirvana?" He asked suddenly.

Laurel shook her head, "I-I've never heard of them."

His eyes widened, "Never heard... wow. What about Alice in Chains?"

She shook her head again.

"Pearl Jam?"

"Nope." She whispered, feeling her cheeks getting warm.

He scoffed, "What kind of a music do you listen to?"

She shrugged. Her mom often listened to an easy listening station or an oldies station. Laurel was content with silence and her inner voice narrating the book she read.

"I don't really listen to music." She looked up to see the other kids getting off the bus, "We can go inside now."

He stood up stopping the older kids from trampling over them as he let her out of the seat. Once they were walking across the blacktop, they pushed passed Laurel and the new kid.

"Out of the way fartknockers."

"What a complete asshat." The boy mumbled before walking beside Laurel, "Um, can I ask you something?"

She nodded, gripping the straps of her backpack. Her stomach flip-flopped as he stepped closer to her. No one had ever talked to her as much as he had and especially no boys ever talked to her. She was perfectly fine going unnoticed by other kids, teachers or anyone. She hated being the center of attention.

"Do you mind helping me find Mrs. Gray's room? She's my teacher and I can't remember what room she is in."

Laurel's heart skipped hearing he was in the same class as she was, "Yeah. I'm in that class too."

"Cool. I'm Zeppelin Foster." He awkwardly held his hand out to her as they walked into the building.

She hesitantly placed hers within his, feeling her cheeks burning.

"L-Laurel, Laurel Adler."

Laurel

Laurel held the first photo of her and Zeppelin in her hands. It sat in a frame on her bookshelf next to some of her favorite books. Her wrist cradled to her chest from being fractured by the popular kids bullying her as Zeppelin's arm rested across her shoulders. His mom had taken the picture the first time Laurel had come over to his house to read and listen to Zeppelin play his guitar. That was the day she first heard Led Zeppelin and Nirvana leading Laurel to finding her love of rock music.

It had been a week since he had asked her out on tour. She was meeting with Leigh for lunch to discuss her plans to complete her next book and to ask about going on tour. Placing the photo back in its spot, she let out a heavy sigh.

Secretly, she was hoping Leigh would hate the idea of her going on tour with Zeppelin, especially with her being on deadline.

However, she had a feeling she would love the idea. The rope of anxiety tightened around her chest as she grabbed her backpack with her laptop and notebook, heading out the front door.

They were meeting in their usual spot off Main Street. Fangirl Diner was the picture-perfect example of a small town diner. The regulars sat at the counter, drinking their coffees and talking about the latest gossip in the local paper. Miss Mel had been the waitress there for nearly three decades and always greeted everyone with a smile. Laurel was the first to arrive and sat in their normal booth by the window. She took out her notebook, reviewing over the few outlines of ideas she had for her next project.

"Miss Laurel, how are ya on this fine afternoon?" Mel set a glass of iced tea in front of her.

"I'm doing well. How are your grandbabies?"

Mel let out a bold laugh, "Spoiled little brats, but I love 'em. The usual for you and Miss Leigh?"

She nodded and Mel was off to make their large plate of fries to split. After a few meetings in the diner, where they would get caught up in talking about her project and not eating they decided to only split an order of fries. Laurel looked out the window watching people walk down the sidewalk or in and out of little shops. Without looking down at her notebook, she wrote a few notes.

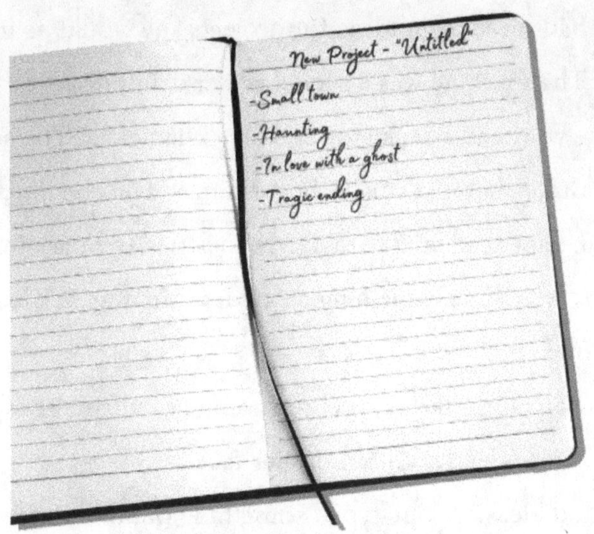

"Hey, sorry I'm running late."

Leigh slid into the booth across from Laurel, letting out a long breath.

"No worries, I've only been here long enough to order our usual."

"Fantastic. I'm starving." She pulled out her tablet, "Alright, let's start with what ideas you have for your next project, and we'll go from there."

Mel came over with a large cup of coffee for Leigh, "Here you go, hon."

"You're an angel straight from heaven, Mel." She took a sip, letting out a satisfying sigh, "I take that back. You're a goddess."

Mel's laughter filled the room as she walked back behind the counter. Laurel pulled out her laptop as Leigh took another long sip.

"Alright, let's hear what you got."

Laurel had three main ideas for projects she would be interested in writing. The first one was a sequel to her debut novel to flesh out more of the world and back stories of her characters. The second was a mystery/thriller set in a small Midwestern town. The third was a paranormal, dark academia with secret societies and dark magic. By the time she was done explaining each idea, Mel was headed their way with their fries.

"What do you think?" Laurel took a bite of a fry, already seeing Leigh's thoughts clearly written on her face.

"All good ideas…" She typed something out on her tablet without looking up at her.

Laurel leaned back, "But… there's a but coming. I can see it all over your face."

"But" Leigh rolled her eyes, "I think you need something slightly different. All the reviews for your debut have been wonderful and they've all been about the romance between the two main characters."

She turned her tablet towards Laurel reading some of the reviews, "Swoon worthy. An epic love tale. The power couple of the year."

"I always have some kind of romantic subplot in all my ideas. I balance all the lovey-dovey with a good dose of supernatural bad guys."

Laurel knew everyone loved the romance in her book. She wrote what she had always wanted in a relationship with a magical twist. She didn't care for romantic story arcs to be the central point of stories. Much like Raelyn, that is why she loved the Red Moon series. Yes, there was romance, but that was not the overall arc of their stories. It was about family, protecting the wayward souls in the world and having a safe space to be who you truly were. Plus, werewolves are cool.

"I know, but I think you should consider writing a straight up romance. Selling trends are leading towards romance, being the top leader in the next couple of years. I know you've been struggling to write, and I think maybe stepping out of your comfort zone will help."

She sighed, "Maybe you're right, but I really don't think I'll be any good at writing romance especially since I don't have it in my own life."

Leigh chuckled, "You don't have magic or werewolves in your life either, but you write about them."

"Touche." Laurel looked down at her notebook with the few notes she had written earlier.

Laurel bit her lip feeling her cheeks heating up.

"Whatever you're thinking, write it down because your face is priceless." Leigh laughed.

She made a few more notes and closed her notebook, "I'll see if I can come up with an outline and email it to you by tonight."

"Great! Now, for the next order of business… you going on tour with your bad boy BFF."

Laurel's chest ached as she looked at her agent's grinning face, "You think it's a good idea."

It wasn't a question.

"Of course I do! Visiting new cities, getting out of your office, being around new people. These are all great things. My only concerns are making sure you don't get dragged into any bad press."

"You know Zeppelin would never…"

Leigh finished off her coffee, "Oh, I know he would never purposely get you into anything. I also know that I'm going to make it perfectly clear to Thomas that if he does, I will ruin him."

Laurel pulled up Zoom and hit Thomas's name, "I'd rather be here for that than hear about it later."

Thomas's handsome face filled the screen, "Hey Laurel! Oh, and the ever-beautiful Leigh Meyer. How are you ladies? You both look fantastic."

"Stop kissing ass, Reed." Leigh smirked as Thomas's face flushed, "I know you and Foster want to take my talented client and friend out on the road with you this summer."

He nodded, "Yes, Dani thinks having Laurel with Zeppelin will keep him from doing anything dumb and I happen to agree with her. Plus, it would be nice to see our best friend again."

"You know you two could always come visit me once in a while." Laurel chimed in.

"True and the same goes for you Missy-Miss." His smiled made her heart flutter unexpectedly, "Anyway, Leigh what are your thoughts on having Laurel out with us for a couple of months?"

"I think it's great, but I have a few things to make clear with you first. If I find out that Foster has dragged her into some wild, groupie orgy that TMZ films or she gets hurt jumping into a mosh pit…"

"That only happened once when I was in my twenties." Laurel said stealing the last fry from Leigh as she went on.

"Or she ends up on every tabloid or entertainment site with her tits out or making out with the hot punk rocker, I will-"

Thomas finished her sentence for her, "You will chop off mine and Zeppelin's balls off then sauté them to feed them to us. All live on our socials."

"Don't threaten me with a good time, Reed. And yes, I will do all of that and more. Got it?"

"I accept those terms. You know we would never let anything happen to her. Zepp and I made an agreement a long time ago to always look out for Laurel's best interest."

"I'm right here, guys. Stop talking about me like I'm not even here." She grumbled.

She was grateful to all the people in her life, but sometimes they treated her like a fragile, delicate flower or a prize possession up on a pedestal.

"Sorry Laurel. All I'm saying is we miss you and will take care of you." Thomas said.

"Reed, send me all the specifics for the tour and contact information for you and Dani."

He nodded, "Will do. So does this meaning you're coming?"

Thomas and Leigh looked at her as her stomach churned with uneasiness, "I guess so. Yeah."

"Great! I seriously can't wait to see you and I'll let Zepp know."

Laurel shook her head, "I'll text Zepp to let him know. I'll see you both soon."

The video ended and Laurel felt like her fries were going to make a return visit to the plate in front of her. It was ridiculous for her to be nervous about seeing her two best friends, but her body was riddled with manic fluttering and sickening dread.

"Why do you look like you're going to puke?" Leigh asked.

"Because I'm trying not to." Laurel swallowed hard.

By the next morning, Thomas had sent them both the schedule and information for the tour. She would be flying out to Los Angeles on June 3rd, where the first show would be the next night. From there they would be traveling by tour bus to a new city every couple of days. Towards the end of the tour was a night back in their hometown of Springfield, Missouri and a two-day rock festival in Chicago. Finally, the tour would come to an end in Concord, California in the first week of August. Her deadline for her manuscript was at the end of September.

Suddenly, Laurel began panicking. She immediately picked up her phone and hit Thomas's name.

"Hey, I was about-"

"I can't do this. I can't go out on tour with you guys. I don't belong there and will stick out like a sore thumb. Not to mention I'm socially awkward and what if I embarrass you guys…"

Thomas whistled into the phone, "Whoa! Take a deep breath."

She slowly took in a breath and held it before releasing it.

"Now, listening to me very closely Laurel Adler. You are not going to stick out like a sore thumb. We have a whole crew of socially awkward people that you will fit right in with. You could never embarrass me or Zeppelin…"

Laurel felt the muscles in her shoulders and back relax as she leaned back into her chair. This was exactly why she had called Thomas in the first place. He always knew how to make all the craziness in her head go away.

"And finally, you absolutely belong out on tour with us. We've been missing the solid foundation of our group for too long." He paused, "I think once you tell Zepp that you're coming and hear how excited he's going to be then you'll start feeling less anxiety about it."

She knew he was right. Zeppelin would be thrilled about her coming out on tour with them.

"You're right. As soon as I'm off the phone with you I will text him, promise."

"Good. Honestly, it's getting hard to keep it from him. He keeps asking if I've heard anything from you. I think he's nervous that you don't want to come out with us." Thomas paused for a moment, "You do want to come with us, right?"

Her answer was immediate, "Of course I do. I'm excited to see you both."

She heard him let out a long breath, "Whew! I was worried for half a second. Text Zeppelin and stop worrying so much."

The call ended and Laurel spent the next five minutes staring down at the text thread she had with Zeppelin. She began typing a message to him.

"Hey! Guess who is coming on tour?" She deleted
the message beginning again, "OG fangirl is coming
out on tour with you!"
She shook her head, tossing her phone on the couch beside her. Why
was she over thinking this? Picking up her phone again she typed a
new message and hit send.

Zeppelin

Zeppelin was sitting in his home studio waiting for the rest of his band members to arrive for their band meeting. He was staring at the finalize set list while his mind was spiraling down into the dark abyss of doubt. Over the last month, Zeppelin had been stockpiling his fears in the back of his mind. Now, the pile had finally tumbled over making him a panicked wreck.

"Yo! Anyone home?" Rich called as his heavy footsteps descended the stairs.

Rich was the father figure of the band and took his role seriously. He was only a few years older than Zeppelin but compared to the other two they might as well have been in retirement homes. His blond hair was pulled back into a long braid down to the middle of his back. He wore his normal baggy, worn out jeans and his favorite Anime shirt.

"How you feeling?"

Rich lowered himself into one of the chairs with a soft groan, "I'm great, wonderful, amazing."

"Bullshit, but I get it." Zeppelin smiled, knowing exactly how Rich was feeling.

At a recent performance, Rich had rocked and rolled a little too hard. Not seeing he was too far over on the small stage his foot had slipped, and he fell onto the concrete floor. He had ended up breaking two ribs and fracturing his wrist.

"Doc says I'm good to go, but I'm going to try and take it easy out there."

Zeppelin looked up to the stairs when he heard the garage door shut, "Ready for the kids to be here?"

"Hell no, but here they come."

Alec's bellowing laughter echoed down the stairs. When people first saw him, they never believed he was in a punk rock band. Thick, black rimmed glasses covered his icy blue eyes, and his dyed jet-black hair was perfectly combed over to one side. He was wearing black slacks and a dark blue button down with the sleeves rolled up to his elbows. He put his messenger bag on the couch as Samantha and Thomas walked in behind him.

Sam, as she preferred to be called, was all punk rock. Her neon green pixie hair was spiked into a faux hawk matching her nails and eyeshadow. She wore a cut up Ice Nine Kills shirt that showed off all the ink that decorated her arms. She was the youngest of them and they all agreed when she joined the band two years ago that they would protect her at all costs.

"Alright Zepp, you called this meeting. Let's get it rolling." Rich said, as the others all settled into their seats.

"I wanted to make a few things perfectly clear concerning Laurel being on tour with us."

They all collective groaned. Zeppelin rolled his eyes as he began to pace hoping it would ease the nerves bouncing around in his stomach.

"Look, I know none of you would intentionally do anything to make her uncomfortable or anything. This is more for my peace of mind, and she has no idea I'm even talking to you guys."

"Because she would kill you if she did." Thomas chuckled.

Zeppelin ignored him as he continued, "She's nervous about being on tour with us. We all know how fans and the press can be with people around us. I want to make sure no one will be bothering her or trying to make any moves on her."

Sam raised her hand, "If she's so uncomfortable being out on tour then why is she coming?"

Thomas spoke up, "Her agent and I thought it would be a good idea for her to work on her next book while traveling with us. Get her out of her office and seeing the world from a tour bus."

"Wait a minute… your Laurel isn't Laurel M. Adler? The author of Tethered Souls?"

Zeppelin and Thomas looked at one another before nodding. Sam gasped then pulled out a tattered copy of Laurel's book.

"No fucking way! This is like my favorite book ever! I've read it three or four times already. Holy shit, Laurel Adler coming on tour with us. Do think she would sign my book?"

Thomas walked over next to Zeppelin, "Calm down, Sam. She's shy, but I think once you all meet her you will love her as much as we do. Also, I'm sure she would be delighted to sign your book but maybe don't go all fangirl on her when you first meet her."

Zeppelin nodded, "You guys know I'm not someone who gets all emotional, but Thomas and I agreed a long time ago to always take care of Laurel. No matter what. I'm asking for you guys to do the same if you see someone bothering her."

His band mates all looked at each other before Rich spoke up, "We got your back and hers. Don't worry, she'll be fine."

"I've got a question?" Alec took off his glass cleaning them, "Does she even like our music? Riding around on a tour bus with a band, crew and whoever else doesn't sound like a great time for someone who doesn't like us."

Zeppelin felt his shoulders relax slightly as Thomas pulled out his phone holding it up to Alec.

"This is Laurel at the last concert we all went to."

Zeppelin knew exactly what photo Thomas was showing. Laurel was in the middle of one of the largest mosh pits he had ever seen. All the men were careful around her, and she had the biggest smile on her flushed face. Zeppelin had a similar photo of her from that concert that he used as her contact photo.

"I like her." Sam laughed.

"Me too." Alec smirked as Thomas slugged his shoulder, "Ow!"

"Don't even think about it. I will personally kick your ass."

For the rest of their meeting, they went over some notes they had from rehearsals. When they were discussing the final set list, Zeppelin decided to bring up a song he was working on.

"You guys know that new song I've been toying with in the studio? I'm thinking if we work on it while on the road, we might be able to add it to the set list later on in tour."

Thomas looked up at him, "I didn't know you were working on a new song?"

Zeppelin shrugged, "It's an old song that I've been updating and setting to different styles. I think I've decided it needs to be an acoustic song. Should be easy to add it to the set list since it would only need me, my guitar and maybe Sam on her box."

She held up her drumstick saluting him, "Easy-peasy."

"I'm fine with it. It will certainly drive all the girls crazy thinking you wrote it for them. Fangirls be cray-cray." Alec chuckled.

"Great, then it's settled." Zeppelin smiled.

They all went off to their separate rooms after a late lunch together knowing it would be the last time any of them had a decent night's sleep in their own beds.

Zeppelin was sitting with Thomas outside on the back deck. They were enjoying the picture-perfect day as they always did before going out on the road. It was moments like this that made him miss the good ole days of touring hole-in-the-wall bars in their old passenger van. Thomas nudged his arm showing him a text from Laurel.

"Jake is going to go get her in the morning to meet us at the bus depot." Thomas typed a reply before slipping the phone back in his pocket.

Zeppelin looked at his own phone. Disappointment settled heavily in the pit of his stomach seeing nothing from her. Once more the fears began filling his mind at an overwhelming speed.

"Do you think it's going to be weird between us?"

Thomas leaned forward in his seat, "I think it's always awkward with us all getting together after being away for so long. We always seem to shake it off quickly and fall back into our old selves. Why?"

"I don't know…" Zeppelin shrugged, "I don't want her to feel weird around me or us. I want to make sure we're still going to be Zepp and Laurel. You know what I mean?"

"Yeah, I do. I think once we find a routine out on the road then everything will be fine. I don't think there's anything to worry about." Thomas stood up, patting his shoulder before walking back inside.

Zeppelin was getting ready to go back in when his phone buzzed. Laurel's moshing photo popped up on his screen and immediately all the nerves settled within him.

"Hey there fangirl! How are you enjoying your suite?"

"It's too much. I know it was all Thomas's doing because he's a worrier. You would have had me sleeping in your room or keeping me up all night drinking." She laughed.

"That is true. Do you want to come over here? I could send Jake back for you, but I would have to warn you that the band will be all over you like flies on shit."

Her laughter stopped, "Oh god, I'm not ready for that. Do you think…"

He waited for her to continue, "Think what?"

"Nevermind, it's dumb. I'll watch YouTube or scroll TikTok until I fall asleep."

He could hear the uneasiness in her voice, "Laurel, whatever it is, it's not dumb. What is it?"

"Do you think you could come here and stay with me? I feel weird being so close to you and not actually seeing you."

He was already heading inside to his room to grab his stuff. He put her on speaker phone as he gathered the last-minute things he needed for his backpack.

"Give me an hour and I will be there. What do you want for dinner? I'll pick it up on my way."

The sigh of relief that came through the phone made his heartbeat pick up pace.

"You're a lifesaver. Cherry flavor of course."

After giving him her order, Zeppelin texted Jake to come get him and take him to Laurel's hotel. He was about to go down to Thomas's office but then headed out the front door instead. He wanted to spend some time with Laurel by himself before he couldn't. He knew Thomas would want to tag along if he told him. He decided once he was at the hotel he would text him, so he didn't freak out.

Zeppelin nervously tapped his fingers against his leg as he rode the elevator to the fifth floor. Thankfully he was able to get through the hotel lobby without anyone recognizing him. The doors opened on the third floor as two girls stepped inside. Zeppelin pressed himself into the corner looking down at his worn Converse. Their soft giggles caught his attention as he glanced up at them looking away from him.

"Excuse me? Are you Zeppelin Foster?"

He took in a breath and slid on the invisible mask of the ever-popular lead singer of a rock band.

"Guilty as charge. How are you ladies tonight?"

They both gasped as the girl with hot pink hair dug into her purse, "Oh my god, I can't believe it's really you. Do you mind signing my magazine? We just got it for the article on Heartstrings upcoming tour. We're so excited for your show tomorrow night."

In amazement he watched as she pulled out a black marker and Rolling Stone magazine from her magical Mary Poppins bag. He took the marker and scribbled his name over the cover. He looked up at the other girl who was lifting her shirt over her head. She was wearing a black lacy bra that left little to the imagination of her perky breasts.

"Could you sign right here, please?" She ran her slender finger over her fair skin just above her bra.

Zeppelin swallowed hard when the elevator dinged for his floor, "Sure thing, sweetheart."

Carefully, he marked her skin with his signature and a small moan escaped her glossy lips. It didn't matter if he had no interest or attraction to her that moan went straight to his dick. Quickly, he handed the marker back to the first girl and made his way off the elevator.

"I hope you enjoy the show tomorrow night." He waved as the doors closed and took a moment to collect himself.

One thing he never got tired of was the endless line of women who wanted him to sign various parts of their bodies. A lot of them would get his signature tattooed and that was mind boggling. Once he felt the blood flow in his body correcting itself, Zeppelin headed towards Laurel's suite. He took a deep breath and knocked on her door.

"Hey stranger, I was starting to think you got loss."

The air he had taken in evaporated upon seeing his best friend standing before him. It had been months since he last saw her on his phone during one of their Facetime calls. She was more beautiful than he remembered wearing an old, faded Led Zeppelin t-shirt and yoga pants that clung to her like a second skin. Her long blond hair was pulled up in a messy bun with a pencil sticking out from it. Her warm honey-colored eyes were framed by her teal glasses that were on the tip of her nose.

"Zepp? You, okay?"

He smiled nodding, "More than okay, come here."

He pulled her into his arms, hugging her tightly. Tears threatened to fall down his face from the happiness radiating throughout his body. He knew he had missed her, but at that moment he realized how much he missed having her by his side.

"C-Can't... b-breathe... Zepp." She whispered as he chuckled letting her go.

"Sorry, I really missed you, fangirl."

Her cheeks turned a lovely shade of pink as she stepped aside to let him in. Once they had settled onto the couch with their fried rice and orange chicken it was like they hadn't been separated by thousands of miles for over a year. Zeppelin had bought a bottle of his favorite whiskey in case they needed some help to ease them back into being around one another. Instead, they ended up cuddled up on the floor watching an old Hitchcock movie on TV.

Zeppelin trailed his fingers down her arm as Laurel rested her head on his leg. It was a little after midnight and their bottle of whiskey was two-thirds of the way empty. As the credits began to scroll on the screen, she turned onto her back and his fingertips grazed beneath her breasts. Her shirt hitched up while she arched her back to stretch. A flash of soft skin had his fingers dancing towards her side.

"Don't even think about it." She warned.

He smirked, wiggling his fingers towards her side again, "I have the upper hand here fangirl, literally."

Zeppelin struck gently, tickling her side filling the room with her beautiful laughter. Laurel tried to wiggle her way from him, but he crawled quickly over her trapping her beneath him.

"Okay, okay, please stop!" She giggled, holding onto his wrists tightly.

He leaned over her letting strands of his hair fall in front of his face, brushing against her forehead. His hands slid down to her hips while her legs were on either side of him. The air between was charged with an electric current wrapping around them. She looked up at him with almost pleading eyes and lips begging for him to cross the invisible line between them.

"Zeppelin…" She whispered.

The way his name sounded on those lips pushed out any rational thoughts as he closed the distance between them. Everything suddenly felt right as his lips sealed over hers. He brought one hand up to cradle the back of her neck as their kiss deepened. Laurel's hand dug into his sides before sliding up over his shoulders into his hair. He was losing air and would need to take a breath, but his lips protested staying on hers.

When his lungs were burning painfully for air, Zeppelin pulled away for only a second. That second was long enough for realization to hit Laurel's eyes as they widened, and she pushed her hands against his chest.

"Zeppelin… we can't…" She stammered.

He sighed, lifting himself from her and helping her to sit up. They had this conversation long ago after prom. That was the day they had put up the invisible barrier keeping them from falling together into blissful oblivion. They were attracted to one another, but they agreed their friendship meant more than fleeing hormones driving them to sleep together.

"I'm sorry. I shouldn't have gotten carried away." He laced their fingers together, giving her hand a small squeeze, "I blame the whiskey."

She laughed, but it didn't seem to carry up into her eyes, "You always blame the whiskey. Come on, we should get some sleep. Big day tomorrow."

"Would you like for me to sleep out here?" He asked genuinely, not wanting to make her uncomfortable.

She stood, holding out her hand to him, "I think we can control our whiskey raging hormones."

He took her hand and followed her into the bedroom of the suite.

Zeppelin

April 1996 – 6th Grade

When the recess aids blew their whistles, everyone headed outside to recess. Zeppelin took his and Laurel's trays to the dirty rack before going to their usual spot by the soccer field. Their classmates were all running around on the black top playing various games. Sitting beside Laurel on the bench, he started writing down more words.

Game. Lame. Fame. Peers. Nears. Fears. Friends. Ends. Mends. Lends.

"Look who we have here."

Zeppelin felt Laurel's body tense up beside him. Glancing up, he found Andy, Brendan and Mandy walking their way. Now their group had a new member, Alyssa, who moved here last year. He also noticed someone standing behind the group but couldn't see who it was.

"What do you want?"

Andy smirked, "We're showing the new kid around and making sure he knows who the geeks are. Tommy meet the geeks."

Zeppelin recognized his new neighbor immediately. They hung out over the weekend riding their bikes down to the pond in their subdivision. He had thought Thomas was a cool guy but seeing him now had him reconsidering that.

Thomas looked uncomfortable as he stepped up next to Andy, "Hey."

"Hey, you know you don't have to hang out with these jerks. You're welcome to join Laurel and I any time."

Laurel had gripped his arm with trembling hands. This year the Jerk Squad, as Zeppelin called them, had bullied her constantly since she and Zeppelin were not in the same class. He had spent his fair share of time in the principal's office for fighting with Andy or Brendan.

Thomas gave a side glance to Andy who was waiting to see his response. He swallowed hard before speaking.

"W-Why would I hang out with geeks?"

Zeppelin rolled his eyes, "Fine. Leave us alone then."

He watched Andy lean over, whispering something to Thomas. His eyes widened and he shook his head. Andy shoved him forward towards Laurel and Zeppelin stood in front of her quickly.

"Don't." He warned.

Thomas looked back at Andy who nodded once at him. Zeppelin didn't want to fight Thomas. He honestly liked him a lot, but if he was going to do something to Laurel then he had to do what he had to.

Zeppelin was taken by surprise when Thomas shoved him to the side, "Get out of my way, g-geek." Then he snatched Laurel's book, "Only losers read."

"Hey! Give me that back!" Laurel shouted as she tried to get her book out of his hands.

The jerks were laughing and yelling out rude comments to her.

"The earth is shaking!"

"Watch out! Big Bertha is moving!"

"I don't think the blacktop can take it!"

Zeppelin could feel his anger building as his body began to shake and his hands clenched into fists. He stood up getting ready to shout at all of them when Thomas placed his hand on her shoulder and in slow motion he watched as Thomas pushed her backwards.

"He comes another Berthaquake!"

Laurel fell onto the blacktop as Zeppelin closed the distance between him and Thomas. He shoved him backwards before swinging his fist at him. Thomas dodged him before pushing him back. His blood was boiling with rage as he ran his body into Thomas's, both of them hitting the ground.

"Stop! Zeppelin, please stop!"

He could barely hear Laurel yelling at him through the pounding of his heart. He brought his fist down into Thomas's side then hit his cheek. Thomas shoved him off and pinned him to the blistering blacktop. His fist connected with Zeppelin's jaw, and he saw stars for a moment. Thomas threw his arm back right when Laurel was leaning in to try to pull him off.

The deafening crack echoed in Zeppelin's ears. He looked up into the horrified eyes of Thomas who was scrambling off him. Andy and his group had been laughing the whole time until now. Their stunned faces all staring down at Laurel on the ground. Her glasses were broken in half and blood was streaming from her nose. Zeppelin's heart stopped seeing her unmoving.

"Laurel! Laurel, wake up!" He yelled crawling over to her, "Go get the recess aid!"

Thomas hurried to his feet and ran off. Zeppelin looked for Andy and his goons, but they were running off towards the main door where classes lined up at. Zeppelin lifted Laurel's head carefully and rested it on his lap.

"Laurel, please open your eyes. Come on, for me, please." He begged as tears freely fell down his cheeks.

Soon, the recess aid had the principal and nurse out on the blacktop. He refused to move until he knew she would be alright. When Laurel's eyes fluttered open seconds later, Zeppelin took his first breath of air in minutes. The recess aid helped the nurse get

Laurel to her office while the principal walked him and Thomas to the office.

Sitting across from Mr. Cason, neither of them spoke as he asked them what happened. He called their parents and was suspended from school for one day. Thomas's aunt was first to arrive, and Zeppelin noticed he flinched when his aunt marched him out to their car. Within minutes, his mom signed him out in the office, and they had a tense, silent car ride home.

Zeppelin immediately went to his room, knowing it was best to let his parents cool down and talk before telling them his side of what happened. He knew they would listen to him completely before giving him the do better, be better speech. However, he was surprised when his mom knocked on his door only after a few minutes.

"There's someone here to see you."

They walked into the living room where Laurel and her mom were sitting with his dad. Laurel looked different without her glasses, and he decided he liked her better with them. Her nose was slightly swollen, and dark rings were already forming beneath her eyes. The two of them stood when they saw him walk in and Laurel gave him a small smile.

"Thank you, Mrs. Foster for allowing us to see Zeppelin for a moment." Ms. Adler said with a similar smile to Laurel's.

"Please call me, Kim. It's no problem." His mom looked at him with a hint of a smirk on her lips.

"Zeppelin, I wanted to come here and say thank you. Laurel told me what happened and how those kids have been bullying her for years now. I'm going to the principal tomorrow to speak to him about it. I appreciate you protecting my daughter from them. It takes a special strength to stand up to others."

Laurel's mom looked over to his mom, "Your son is a wonderful young man, and no one will be able to tell me otherwise."

"We like him most days." His dad chuckled.

Laurel closed the distance between them, throwing her arms around his neck and hugging him tightly.

"Thank you." She whispered as he wrapped his arms around her.

"You're welcome." He whispered back.

After they left, he sat with his parents explaining everything that happened. He could see the mixture of pride and disappointment on their faces. In the end, they simply told him to keep doing what he was doing for his friend. Regardless of what they had told him he was going to anyway.

The next day, Zeppelin spent mostly in his room working on the homework he would be missing in school that day. Once that was finished, he decided to make sure his room was clean and picked up around the house for his mom. He was getting ready to clean his dad's studio space when someone knocked on the door.

Thomas was standing on his porch, his head hung low. Immediately, he felt the anger from yesterday burning across his skin.

"What do you want?"

"I wanted to come over and say I'm sorry. I should have never wanted to hang out with Andy and his goons." Thomas said never looking up.

Zeppelin sighed, "I don't need your apology. You should apologize to Laurel. You broke her nose and her glasses. Not cool."

Thomas finally looked up, "I went to her house before yours. I'm going to be mowing lawns until I raise enough money to pay her mom back for her glasses. I talked with Laurel for a couple of hours after apologizing."

"She forgave you?" He asked stunned.

"No one is more surprised than me. I really thought she would punch me in the face. You know, an eye for an eye or whatever." He paused, rubbing his hand over the back of his neck, "She said she hoped you would be able to forgive me so we could all be friends. I'm kind of hoping the same thing."

Zeppelin stepped outside and they sat on the porch, "If Laurel forgives you then so do I. However, you have to promise me something."

"What? Anything?"

"If you're going to be friends with Laurel then you have to be willing to stand up to the jerk squad. They always bully her about everything. Her books, her glasses, her looks. You have to help me protect her from them or anyone trying to hurt her. You promise?"

Zeppelin held out his pinky finger to Thomas. He hooked his

with Zeppelin's and smiled.

"I promise."

"Good, now get out of here. I'm trying to suck up to my parents by cleaning the house and they're going to be home soon." Zeppelin chuckled.

Thomas started to walk back to his bike before turning around, "See you tomorrow?"

Zeppelin nodded, "See ya tomorrow."

7

Laurel

Laurel woke up alone in her hotel bed. A note folded on the nightstand beside her that she didn't read until after she had ordered room service and taken a shower. She sat on the balcony, eating some peanut butter toast with banana and opened the note.

Laurel,

I'm sorry I had to leave early this morning. I didn't tell Thomas I was going to see you and he had a meltdown. I thought it would be best to smooth things with him before you joined us. Jake is going to come get you to bring you to the bus depot. It was good hanging out with you. I didn't realize how much I needed that and you. Order room service and enjoy your morning. Jake will be there around 1pm.

Love ya,

Zepp

She looked down at her phone to see she still had a couple of hours before she needed to be ready. Laurel went back inside, placing his note in her journal for safe keeping and grabbing her laptop. She was looking over the notes she had made at the diner with Leigh a month earlier.

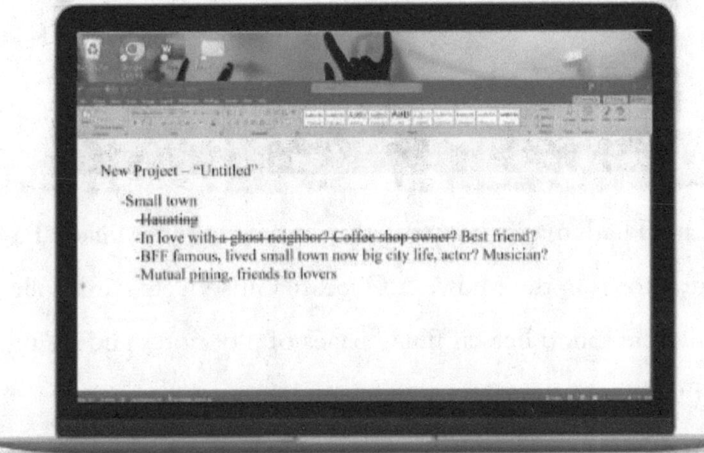

She read her notes out loud and her stomach tightened. They were a little too close to her own life for her comfort. The whole reason she began writing paranormal/fantasy romance was to escape her real life. The thought of writing a story even close to reality made her heart thump wildly in her chest. Laurel pulled up a new document and began writing new notes.

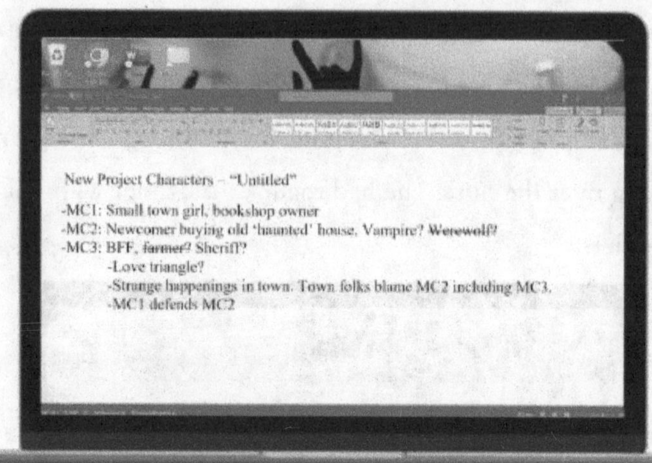

Laurel had images immediately popping into her head of a small rural town in the Midwest. Gilmore Girls meets Amityville. Suddenly, she found herself filling pages of plot notes and losing track of time until there was a knock on her door.

"I'm so sorry… I'll only be a minute."

She opened the door to see Jake standing there chuckling, "It's alright. Thomas thought you might have been distracted since you didn't answer his texts."

Guilt immediately filled her chest as she saw his messages.

Laurel typed a quick reply before tossing her phone into her backpack and grabbing her suitcase. Jake was scrolling through his phone when she walked out of the bedroom. She did a quick walk through of her room to make sure she got everything of hers. Passing the couch, she found Zeppelin's flannel from last night that she had stolen while they were watching TV. She slipped it on and headed towards the door, not missing the curious look from Jake as they walked towards the elevators.

The ride to the bus depot was silent except for the country music Jake was playing. Any time she had seen him, he was always a man of few words and all business. She found it endearing to see a small glimpse into something personal as to what music he liked. She typed a note on her phone to ask Zeppelin and Thomas about him.

When they arrived, there was a caravan of vehicles surrounding four tour buses with the band's likeness on them. Seeing Zeppelin's larger than life, handsome face on the side of the bus was surreal. She noticed a lot of the people standing around were documenting the big kick off with pictures and chatting with crew members as marked by their tour shirts.

"Don't worry, we're driving around to the back entrance where Thomas will meet you. Zepp is running on his own time as usual." Jake explained.

Relief washed over her for only a moment as they drove past the large crowd. They circled around to the back of the building through a guarded fence and waiting outside the entrance was Thomas. Zoom calls and pictures taken for his social media did not do justice to the man waiting with a wide grin for her.

Thomas had always been a tall and lanky kid even through high school and college. When he moved out to L.A. with Zeppelin is when her friend started to finally blossom. His curly chestnut hair was pushed back behind his ears and his hazel eyes were covered by a pair of dark Ray Bans. His white button down stretched across his broad chest and shoulders perfectly highlighting his well-toned body. His dark jeans covered his long legs ending in a pair of dark brown boots. He always looked like he was modeling the next wave in business casual fashion.

Maybe it was because she hadn't seen him in a year except on her phone or laptop screens, Laurel's heart skipped as she opened door and was immediately enveloped into the strong embrace of her best friend.

"Never again are we going this long without seeing each other.

Promise me that, sunshine?" He whispered.

She chuckled at his nickname for her as a few happy tears fell down her cheeks, "Promise. I've missed you, Thomas."

He chuckled, hugging her tighter before letting her go. Jake handed her backpack to her and then took her other suitcases off towards the building. They walked behind him and into a large waiting area where Laurel recognized the other band members of Heartstrings. Even though the band had been around for over a decade, she had not truly met or talked with any of the other members. When Thomas went to introduce her, Laurel found herself fangirling internally.

"Hey guys, I want you to meet Laurel." They all turned to look towards them, "Laurel this is Rich, Alec and Sam."

She shook their hands, "It's great to meet all of you. Regardless of Zepp being in the band, I love your music, and it has gotten me through a lot of all-nighters writing."

"It's lovely to meet the legendary Laurel Adler. Zeppelin and Thomas have talked about you like you're a mythical creature of the likes of a rare unicorn." Alec pulled the back of her hand to his lips.

Thomas growled lowly beside her, "Alec…"

Laurel couldn't help the giggle that escaped her lips as he winked at her. Rich pulled him back by the collar of his shirt.

"Ignore him, he's an attention whore. It's nice to meet you. Zeppelin and Thomas speak highly of you."

"I'm sure it's exaggerated especially it came from Zepp." She laughed.

Sam was the newest member of the band, only joining within the last couple of years. Everything about Sam is what Laurel had always wanted to be. Confident, loud, and punk rock. She stepped in front of her with arms crossed over her chest.

"I have three questions for you."

Laurel nodded, "O-Okay."

"First question, what are your thoughts on large group hang outs?"

"I tend to stick to myself or people I'm most comfortable with. I also tend to blend in with the crowd going completely unnoticed." She paused taking in Sam's emotionless expression, "In other words, I hate them."

Sam's lips twitch slightly upwards, "Question two, what is your favorite book?"

"I have two, one classic and the other a series of books that inspired me to write my debut novel. First, Little Women, because the bond and journey of the sisters. Second, is An Ember in the Ashes by Sabaa Tahir."

An eyebrow arched at her response, "Last question, do you like coffee?"

This was always a controversial question for her as a writer, published author, and avid reader.

"No. I can't stand the taste nor smell of it." Sam was about to say something, but Laurel held her hand up, "However, I can make incredibly good, strong coffee. Just because I don't like doesn't mean I won't make it for those who do."

Sam took a step closer to her, letting her arms fall to her side. Her face to still void of any emotion until a wide grin broke over it. She pulled Laurel into a tight embrace.

"I can't wait to be best friends with you. It will be nice to have another female to hang out on the bus with that has no interest in going out and mingling. We can discuss books and drink anything that isn't coffee. Also, I love your book! It's one of my favorites and I have read it a few times."

For the first time since agreeing to go out on tour, Laurel felt hopeful and excited for the adventure that would come.

It was a half-hour later that Jake came to get them to put them on the buses. Laurel still hadn't seen Zeppelin and was getting worried especially after their night together. Maybe things were weird between them again like a year ago when they were celebrating her book or the infamous prom night where a lot of things had changed between them.

Thomas walked her to Zeppelin's bus, "After our last tour, Zepp decided he wanted his own bus. It's smaller than the others, but there is a single bed quarters and then a set of bunk beds. You can have your choice of where you'd like to sleep. I usually ride with the band or crew, but tonight I'm going to be on here with you and Zepp."

"Awe a sleep over like old times."

Walking onto the bus was like walking into a small apartment on wheels. There was a long bench couch along the right side of the bus and across from it were a couple sets of booths and tables. There was a small kitchenette and one bathroom that was only slightly better than an airplane bathroom. There was a small walkway with a bunk bed on either side and storage above them. At the end of the bus was a small bedroom with a queen-size bed, a built-in dresser and TV. Deciding she didn't need an entire room; she placed her backpack on one of the bunk beds.

"Zepp just arrived, so I'm going to go meet him. The band will have to do some press before we leave. Jake is going to stay with you in case you need anything." Thomas pulled her into another tight hug, "I'm happy you're here with us."

"Me too. Now go before Zepp gets himself in trouble." She pushed Thomas away as he chuckled and watched him jog down the steps off the bus.

For the next hour, she unpacked a few comforts from home onto her bunk. Her favorite pillow and fuzzy blanket. She had a few of her favorite books and her e-reader that she placed on the small shelf within the bunk. A small stuffed wolf that Raelyn had given her for their favorite TV show.

She decided to set up one of the tables as a makeshift desk when two loud, familiar voices were getting closer outside the bus. Hearing Zeppelin and Thomas laughing together filled her heart with an overwhelming amount of joy. As soon as they were both on the bus, Laurel threw her arms around each of them hugging them both.

"Hey fangirl!" Zeppelin chuckled, placing a tight arm around her.

"I think she missed us." Thomas joked wrapping his arms around all of them for a group hug.

Laurel hugged them both tighter, unable to get out what she was feeling. After so long of feeling discontent or lost, she finally felt like she was home. The drive to the venue was short and filled with them catching up. She couldn't remember the last time she had laughed so much. As they pulled into the entrance, Laurel found herself staring out the tinted windows. The parking lot was already filled with cars and trucks. People were playing Heartstrings music from the stereos and tailgating with people around them.

"Is it always like this?"

Zeppelin slipped his arm around over her shoulders, "Yep, they rock out before, during and after. We have some of the best fans in the world."

Laurel looked up to see his heart melting smile as his eyes scanned over all the fans. The love he had for them shining brightly as he turned to face her. That same love never fading as his smile spread wider across his face.

"Meet us as soon as the bus stops and don't leave Laurel's side. I'll call the venue manager and have words with them about their staff. Thanks Jake."

They both turned to Thomas, whose face was flushed with anger.

Zeppelin leaned forward, "What's up?"

"Apparently some of the newer staff thought it would be alright to invite their friends to the concert. They let them in backstage and now a crowd of people have been escorted outside the entrance we are to go in at. Jake is going to meet us and get Laurel to the green room while you and I distract the crowd to another entrance."

Laurel reached out gripping Zeppelin's hand on instinct and watched as Thomas' eyes snapped down at them. Zeppelin pulled her into his side, holding her tightly against him.

"I think it would be better if we all pushed through the crowd together. Put Laurel in the center and the three of us surrounding her."

Laurel shook her head, "No way. What if they try to grab at you or worse?"

He scoffed, "I've been in worst situations, right Thomas? Remember that night in Germany where the fans nearly tipped the bus over."

"What?!" She had no memory of either of them telling her about that.

"I can't believe I'm about to say this, but I think you might be right, Zepp. However, I want you to be towards the middle as well. I'm going to text Jake to get some crew to help him."

Zeppelin chuckled, "I'm sorry could you say I was right one more time so I can record it."

Thomas promptly flipped him off then continued to type his text. Laurel smacked him hard on the arm making him finch.

"Why didn't you guys tell me your bus almost flipped?"

"Ow." He rubbed his bicep, distracting her for a moment, "I'm sorry fangirl, but Thomas and I made a deal a long time ago. Anything we feel would be more harmful than good for you was to stay between us. Now ninety-nine percent of the time we tell you everything, but sometimes it's not worth worrying you."

She turned away from him, crossing her arms over her chest with a huff. His long, muscular arms wrapped around her and pulled her back against him.

"Don't be mad. We do it because we love you with all our hearts."

Leaning her head back, Laurel caught a glance of Zeppelin's puppy eyes and pout. Immediately, her body melted into a big pile of goo against him. He smiled victoriously before letting her sit up.

"You both are lucky I love you." She mumbled.

The bus came to a stop as Jake jogged up the steps, "Ready?"

Laurel took a nervous breath in then nodded as they made their way into the venue.

She spent a lot of time in the green room with the band and other members of the crew who were not actively working to set up the stage. She found that she and Sam had a lot in common including the love of a certain werewolf show. Talking to Sam was like talking with Raelyn or Emerson and she was grateful for that. When it was time for the VIPs and Meet and Greets, Laurel decided to hang out on the side to watch them.

She was amazed by how attentive and sweet Zeppelin was with

each fan. Even the ones who were overly excited and talking at hyper speed. He smiled for every photo taken and signed everything placed in front of him, including body parts. As fans passed by her unnoticed, she chuckled listening to them fangirl about meeting him.

"If only they knew that he still sleeps with his stuffy." Thomas murmured beside her.

"Or that he sleeps with the light on after watching anything remotely scary."

"Oh, that's right, I forgot about that." Thomas started laughing, "Do you want to watch the concert tonight or would you rather chill in the green room or bus?"

Laurel thought for a moment before smiling, "Can I buy a tour shirt to wear?"

Thomas rolled his eyes, "I can give you a tour shirt to wear, yes."

"I'll stay and watch the concert. I may leave to head back to the bus before the end of it to avoid the crowd."

He nodded, "Smart. Okay, let's go pick out a shirt for you to have."

After a brief squabble about who was going to pay for the merch she picked out, Laurel ended up with a couple of T-shirts, a pack of vinyl stickers, a trucker hat and a hoodie paid for by Thomas. She went into the private bathroom within the green room and changed into one of her new shirts.

Looking in the mirror, she let out a soft chuckle, "Welcome back teenage Laurel."

She braided her hair off to one side over her shoulder and put on the trucker hat backwards. She bought one t-shirt a size bigger and tied it off to the side then rolled the sleeves up, tucking them under her bra straps. To finish off her outfit was her well-worn, favorite bubble gum pink Converse. When she walked back out to meet Thomas, he was staring at her with wide eyes.

"How is it that you still looking like a teenager when the rest of us look like we're one step into the old folks home?"

She laughed, "I may have a baby face, but my body says not to rock out like we used to, or I'll throw your back out."

Laughing they walked out towards the side stage. Laurel could hear the crowd before seeing them. Pulling out her phone, she took a picture of the setting sun behind the sea of people waiting to hear their favorite band. The two opening acts were local young alternative/punk rock bands that Laurel ended up looking up on Spotify. As the stage went dark and the finishing touches of the set were in place, the crowd began to chant.

Heartstrings! Heartstrings! Heartstrings!
Laurel jumped when Zeppelin's voice filled her ears suddenly, "This moment never gets old."

He kissed her cheek then walked out onto the stage strumming the first notes of their song, *Into the Fire*. The beat of her heart matched the speeding beats of Sam's drums. She had forgotten how much she loved watching Zeppelin perform live. His energy pulsated throughout the crowd with every song he performed. That same energy was coursing through her own body as she headbang and rocked out from her spot beside Thomas.

The lights were down as the spotlight was on Zeppelin at his mic stand, "How we doin' tonight?" The crowd screamed in response.

"I asked, HOW WE DOIN' TONIGHT!"

The roar of the crowd was nearly deafening, and Laurel noticed the wide grin on Zeppelin's face.

"That's more like it! On behalf of the band, we wanted to say thank you for coming out to the show tonight. Concerts on warm nights are what make summer the best time of the year. Speaking of summers, let's head back to summer of 2000 with No Quiet Songs!"

Laurel started jumping up and down while holding onto Thomas's shoulder. This was her favorite Heartstrings song and the one she rocked out to the most to at home. When Zeppelin went into the second verse, she started singing out the lyrics with him.

'Cause you were mine for the summer

Now we know it's nearly over,

Feels like Saturday sunshine

But I always will remember

You were my summer love

You always will be my summer love

Having the time of her life, Laurel didn't realize she had stayed for the whole show. Her throat was raw from singing and shouting. Her muscles aching from moving them in ways she hadn't in years. Her ears ringing from the loud guitar solos and drumming. A layer of sweat and blistering heat covered her skin. As she walked back to the bus with Thomas, she never felt more alive in her life.

"The band have a few special meet and greets then we'll be hitting the road to Irvine. You should have enough time to shower before we leave."

Laurel jumped up, wrapping her arms around Thomas's neck to hug him, "Thank you for convincing me to come out on tour with you guys. This is exactly what I needed and I'm so happy to be here."

His arms tightened around her, "We're happy to have you with us, especially me."

He slowly lowered her feet to the ground again, staring down at her. His hazel eyes darkened, filling with what she could only describe as desire, making her head swoon. The only other man to ever look at her like that was Zeppelin. She didn't know how to feel about feeling something more than friendship with him. Her heart was torn into equal parts of excitement and fear. His eyes darted down to her lips for a moment before he took a step back.

"I-I should get back with the band." He murmured before letting her go, walking back towards the venue.

Laurel took her time in the small shower on the bus as thoughts of the night played out like a movie in her mind. Questions popped into her mind as she rinsed herself off.

Did Thomas have feelings for her?

Did she have feelings for him?

How do her feelings for Zepp fit into all of this and vice versa?

That is when a switch went off in her brain. Suddenly, ideas were flowing in her mind as she hurried to take her shower. Not even bothering to get dress, Laurel wrapped her oversized towel around herself and grabbed her notebook from her bunk. Turning to a blank page she began writing every plot point or character detail her mind conjured. It was only when she heard a group of people approaching the buses when she realized she was still sitting in only a towel.

"Crap." She looked out the window to see Zeppelin standing with two girls talking to them.

Thomas was approaching them with a stern look on his face, "Alright ladies, our leading man here needs his beauty sleep."

"Awe come on, Thomas. I think these ladies will help me get the best sleep of my life. Am I right ladies?"

Laurel could tell Zeppelin had been drinking and her heart sank hearing how different he was from the Zeppelin she knew and loved.

Thomas pulled him aside, "You do remember our best friend is on that bus right now. I'm sure she doesn't want to hear you fucking two groupies."

She was thankful for Thomas at that moment because she surely did not want to hear that. Looking at Zeppelin, she watched as he shook his head as if that would help sober him up.

"Ladies, I'm so sorry. Maybe another time we can have our one magical night together. Thank you for coming out to the concert. I love you both for that."

As Zeppelin leaned in to give each girl a hug, Laurel made her way to her bunk and quickly put on her pajamas. She climbed inside and closed the curtain shutting her light off. She heard both of her friends get on and Thomas was laying into Zeppelin for nearly screwing up having her on tour with them.

"Fuck Thomas, I said I was sorry. You of all people know I need to let off some steam after a show. What am I supposed to do? Suddenly become a monk or priest."

"I know, but you can't be getting drunk and fucking groupies on the same bus where Laurel is. If you want to let off steam, then get a hotel room and let Jake know where you'll be. Meanwhile, I'll hang out with our best friend and make her feel like she apart of this tour instead of ignoring her for some ass!"

Laurel closed her eyes as the door to the bedroom slammed shut and she could hear Thomas getting in the bunk across from hers. Turning away from the curtain, she allowed the tears welling up beneath her eyes to finally fall.

Zeppelin

The first month of touring was always the hardest for Zeppelin. Getting back into the rigorous routine of performing multiple nights a week and living on the road. Mentally, touring was demanding from all the VIPs, meet and greets and numerous interviews in each city. Most nights he would return to the bus and pass out from exhaustion instead of hooking up with fans.

After that first night, arguing with Thomas, he tried not to hook up with anyone. As his body adjusted to the lack of sexual release except for when he was in the shower or in the morning when he woke up. The past week, he had spent time adjusting mentally to having his rockstar mask on more than usual. Zeppelin found himself finally relaxing as he hung out with Laurel and Thomas on his bus.

They were a couple of hours from their next city, Las Vegas, and Zeppelin was watching Laurel bopping her head along to music playing in her headphones as she wrote on her computer. Thomas was sitting across from her scrolling on his tablet. Her feet were propped up on Thomas's seat, tapping against the side of his leg. Zeppelin's stomach twisted uncomfortably seeing them together.

Something had changed in the last few weeks that Zeppelin couldn't put his finger on. Laurel and Thomas had always had their own unique friendship, but Zeppelin never felt jealous of them until now. He shook his head, trying to ignore his unsettling stomach. He focused on the song he was working on inspired by his best friend after his first show.

"Zepp?" Laurel's concerned voice brought him out of his thoughts, "You alright?"

He pushed his lips into a wide smile, "Of course, why wouldn't I be?"

She shrugged, "I don't know… you've been unusually quiet since getting on the road."

"Shh, don't jinx it. He's been well behaved and I'm enjoying taking a break from putting out Zeppelin fires."

Zeppelin rolled his eyes, "It's called job security."

They all shared a laughed, however Laurel's penetrating eyes were staring into his. She tilted her head to side and his smile faded for a moment. She was the only person in the world who could break down his walls with a single glance.

"I promise, everything is fine. I'm focused on a new-ish song I'm writing."

Laurel slid over and patted the seat beside her, "Let's see if I can help any. Like the good ole days when we would sit outside for hours."

A genuine smile crossed his face as he sat next to her. He pulled his acoustic guitar onto his lap and began strumming a few notes trying to get a feel of the kind of melody that fit with the lyrics. He was thinking of an acoustic ballad as he sang the lyrics.

Roses are always red,

Skies are always blue,

I love beautiful fangirls,

But not as much as I love my girl

He glanced over at Laurel, whose nose was scrunched up. Zeppelin chuckled knowing that look all too well, "Not it?"

She shook her head, "Definitely not."

Zeppelin wondered if she would recognize the song. It was one he wrote in middle school, and she had helped him back then. When he asked his mom to mail out one of his old notebooks with the original lyrics in it he had decided to start rewriting it.

At first, Zeppelin was going to have it be dedicated to their fans, but now that Laurel was there with him all he could think about is making it her song again. He tried a more upbeat melody as she grabbed his notebook reading the lyrics.

Oh, darling fangirl, my girl

Your spirit like wildfire on a summer day,

You're like a soothing wind on a warm evening

"Nope. This needs to be more like 'Always Stay Loving'. Put some twang into it."

She continued to read his lyrics as he started strumming, filling the bus with a slow country melody then an idea struck like lightning. He pulled his notebook back in front of him and began writing notes next to each section of lyrics. Once he was done, Zeppelin leaned over kissing Laurel's cheek.

"You're a genius, fangirl!"

The smile and blush spreading across her face erased any worries he was having about their friendship changing. He glanced over at Thomas whose eyes were darting back and forth between him and Laurel. When his best friend's eyes met his, Zeppelin recognized what was flashing in them as he averted them back to his tablet...

Jealousy.

Immediately there was a palpable tension between them. Zeppelin had always counted on Thomas being the one guy he would never have to worry about liking the same woman. Thomas' ex-wife, Whitley, had originally wanted to hook up with him, but after a few late nights with Thomas they were inseparable. Until Thomas was always on the road with the band and Whitley turned out to be a possessive and crazy.

Zeppelin tapped Thomas' leg with his foot and when he wouldn't look up, he knew it wasn't good. He moved back over to the couch and the tension faded as Thomas went back to joking with Laurel. Zeppelin took out his phone sending a text to Thomas.

Zeppelin scoffed trying to focus on his song but decided to catch a quick nap unable to stand the obvious tension coming from Thomas. As he lay on the bed, all he could think about was Laurel falling for Thomas before he could ever get the chance to tell her how he felt. He made a promise a long time ago that he wouldn't pursue Laurel until he was the man who could take care of her one hundred percent.

Financially, he could do that for her. Physically, he would lay down his life for her. Emotionally, he was still the young, wild Zeppelin who loved to get in trouble and wasn't ready to settle down. Having Laurel on tour opened his eyes to having the best of both worlds. Settling down and traveling the world together. He could care less about the groupies and parties, the drinking and drugs. He and Laurel were always able to create their own chaos.

When he felt the bus stop, Zeppelin made his way to the front of the bus to catch Thomas. Peering out the window, he found him walking with his arm around Laurel's shoulders towards the venue. Zeppelin's veins burned with anger taking off after them.

"Yo, Thomas! Wait up!"

Thomas tried to keep walking however Laurel slipped from his arm to wait for Zeppelin. He wedged himself between the two of them placing one arm around Thomas' shoulders and his other hand on the small of Laurel's back.

"Laurel, do you mind if I steal our good ole buddy here?"

If she could feel the charged energy between him and Thomas, she never let it on.

"Absolutely. I'm going to hang out with Sam and talk about the latest book she read. I'll met up with you guys later."

They watched her walk beside Jake before disappearing into the venue. Thomas shoved Zeppelin hard enough to make his intentions known.

"What the hell is your problem Zepp?"

"My problem! What the hell is yours?" He shot back.

Thomas stood at his full height, nearly three inches taller than Zeppelin, "I don't have a problem except for your possessiveness over Laurel. You do remember she's my friend as well, right?"

Refusing to back down, he got right into Thomas' face, "Is that all she is to you? You know how I feel about her, and I get the not so sneaky suspicion that you want her all to yourself."

"Oh, my fucking god, Zeppelin." Thomas let out a laugh, "Are you really that insecure about yourself? You can have any fucking woman you want and usually you'll have two or three of them at a time. I show a small bit of interest in one woman, and you immediately go into a jealous temper tantrum. Grow up."

Before he knew what he was doing, Zeppelin shoved Thomas as hard as he could knocking him to the ground. He pushed him back down as he tried to get up and pinned him to the asphalt.

"You could have any woman you want if you'd only put yourself out there. Instead, you hide behind your tablet and spreadsheets. I seem to remember back in the day you fucking around with a groupie or three so don't you fucking dare judge me. We made a promise a long time ago to protect Laurel at all costs. I was honest with you from the get-go how I felt about her and what I promised her father. All of sudden, now, you want to be with her."

"Hey! Break it up, you two."

Zeppelin was suddenly being lifted off Thomas. Rich's voice breaking the intense moment.

"You're lucky there was no one out here yet, but me. Get your acts together and walk it off." Rich turned to Zeppelin as Thomas walked towards the buses, "What the hell was that about?"

"Nothing." He huffed.

"Bullshit, but you know what I don't care. Leave your drama on the bus. We have two nights of shows to put on and we're counting on you to be on your fucking A-game."

He was still steaming but let out a shaky breath with a nod, "Alright, alright. I'll go cool down then meet you guys for rehearsals."

Rich slapped his back, "Ten minutes."

Zeppelin walked into the venue and went straight into the green room restroom. Splashing water on his face, he looked up into the mirror. His hair created a curtain in front of his exhausted eyes. He tried to relax his aching jaw, flexing his fingers against the sink, he splashed more water on his face. The anger was building fast, and he needed to let out before he went to face everyone. He took one look at the brick wall next to him before throwing his fist into it.

The pain was nearly blinding as currents shot up from his knuckles through his arm into his elbow. As fast as the pain traveled his arm came the numbing sensation of the tips of his fingers tingling. Looking down at his hand, he knew instantly he had broken at least one knuckle if not two.

"Fuck." He breathed before washing his hand off in the sink.

Zeppelin quietly made his way to the first aid tent and was able to get his hand wrapped well enough for him to play. The paramedic told him to get to the hospital as soon as he could for x-rays, and he lied saying he would right after the show. It wasn't the first time Zeppelin played with broken bones and probably wouldn't be the last if things kept going the way they were with Thomas. The only one to notice his hand was Rich earning him a slap to the back of the head before rehearsals.

As they waited to go out on stage for their set, Zeppelin looked all around for Laurel and Thomas. They were not in their usual spots and suddenly he felt like he was going to throw up.

"Laurel is working on her book in the hotel and Thomas was on the bus last I saw." Sam said before running out to her drum set.

Zeppelin shook his head, closing his eyes and letting the roar of the crowd wash over him. Right now, he couldn't afford to think about Thomas or Laurel or anything else. The first beats from Sam rumbled within his chest and the crowd grew louder covering his body in goosebumps. When he opened his eyes, walking out to center stage, he was rockstar, Zeppelin Foster, and let the music take him away from reality.

For two blissful hours, Zeppelin put all the anger, frustration and pain into his performance. This had been one of the best crowds they had ever performed for and when they were taking their final bow he wished Laurel had been there. After the VIPs and meet and greets, the band headed out onto the Vegas Strip to celebrate. Once they were settled at their first club, five or six groupies joined their table. Two young ladies were doing shots off one another in front of him and all he could think about was Laurel being alone in her hotel room.

"Ladies, as entertaining as your performance is…" They giggled making bile rise to his throat, "I think I'm going to have to take my leave."

His band mates' heads shot up as he untangled himself from the women on either side of him.

"Dude… are you alright?" Alec asked, taking his spot before the question was out of his mouth.

Zeppelin rolled his eyes, "I'm good. I'll see you guys at rehearsal tomorrow."

He met Rich's knowing smile, "Smart Zeppelin, see you tomorrow."

Jake was waiting for him at the entrance of the club, "Early for you, ain't it?"

"Not feeling it tonight. I'm heading back to the hotel." When Jake began to follow, he stopped him, "I'm good on my own. I swear, I'm going straight to the hotel."

Jake nodded, returning to his spot beside the SUV they were renting. Zeppelin enjoyed walking down the Strip and people either did not recognize him or were too intoxicated to notice him. True to his word, he walked into the hotel lobby and headed for the elevators. He hit the floor for his suite and thanked whatever god that was listening for the ride up being lonely. When he stepped out of the car, he headed towards his room before stopping in the middle of the hallway.

Laurel's room was in the opposite direction near Thomas' room. He hadn't seen either of them since arriving earlier in the day. Jake had told him that he had moved his stuff to the band's bus and had been there all night. For a split second, Zeppelin worried that Thomas would leave as the band's manager. They needed him for a variety of reasons, but mainly for his sensibility and caring nature. He knew he had to make things right between them, but not until tomorrow.

Turning around, he headed towards Laurel's room. He stood in front of her door for a solid two minutes running a hundred different scenarios in his head.

What if Thomas is in there and things get dicey again between us?

What if they're making out or fooling around in there?

What if he told her about his feelings for her or my feelings for her?

What if she chooses him?

He knocked on her door before he lost his nerve too. The door opened and every scenario vanished as she stood in front of him.

"Hey Zepp, everything okay?"

He nodded, the exhaustion of everything that happened in the day hitting him at once, "I'm good… just needed a quiet night in but didn't want to be alone."

Her soft smile made his knees wobble as she stepped aside, "Well come on in. Doesn't get any quieter than a manic writer listening to her headphones and typing furiously."

He chuckled, "Sounds perfect to me."

After tossing his jacket and boots off to the side, Zeppelin flopped down onto the couch. Laurel had her notebook open on the floor with her laptop and several other sheets of paper. There was every color pen, highlighter and sticky note spread out as well. She put away her headphones and turned her music on softly in the background.

"Are you sure everything is okay? There's nothing you want to talk about?"

Her question shot a cold chill down his spine. Maybe Thomas had told her everything and now he needed to come clean once and for all.

"Y-Yeah, why? Does it seem like I need to talk about something?"

Laurel knelt beside the couch, taking his wrapped hand into hers, "Your busted hand is a pretty good clue. What happened?"

He flinched as she unwrapped it seeing the swollen knuckles for the first time since cracking them against concrete.

"I was feeling some big feels, as the kids say, and took it out on a wall in the bathroom."

"Zeppelin Foster…" She gently ran the tips of her fingers over his hand, "We should go to the hospital and get it x-ray."

He shook his head, "I'll be fine, plus it's not the first time I've played with a broken hand before."

Laurel sighed as he watched the memory from their childhood flash before her eyes. Right before their 8th grade talent show, the same bullies who always picked on Laurel had decided to make life hell for her. After school, Zeppelin decided to put them back in their spots and ended up breaking his hand with a right hook to the kid's face. Of course, he had gotten into trouble with his parents, but they were proud of him for sticking up for Laurel.

"Were you defending me this time?" She asked, bringing the back of his hand to her cheek.

He slipped his hand beneath her chin, their eyes meeting, "I will always defend you, but not this time it was plane ole male stupidity."

Her laughter filled the space between them, but never quite reached her eyes, "Well do you want to watch terrible TV or rent a movie?"

Zeppelin looked down at her stuff on the floor and shook his head, "Nope, I think I rather watch the mastermind of the writer in her natural habitat."

"Seriously? I'll have plenty of time to work on my book. I don't have to work it on now."

She went to clean up her stuff when he reached over and stopped her.

"How about a compromise? I'll order some late-night snacks and you can work until they come. After that we can eat, chat or watch bad hotel TV."

"Deal. If by snack you mean a late-night dinner because I forgot to eat tonight. Not that I couldn't afford to skip a meal or twelve."

He hated when she put herself down but chose to ignore it as he tossed her the menu, "Pick whatever your heart desires and I'll have the same."

After ordering their food, Zeppelin relaxed on the couch and watched as Laurel worked on her book. He was fascinated by her dedication and focus. She would type several pages then refer to notes she had written down in her notebook.

His favorite moments were when the light would obviously go off in her head and a wide, giddy smile would spread across her face. She would hurriedly scribble down whatever scene her brain had conjured then go back to her notebook to find the perfect spot to place the note in. Sometimes she would let out a little squeal of excitement or do a little victory dance in her spot. Even after their food had come and been eaten, Zeppelin continued to watch her work until he could no longer keep his eyes open.

Laurel

May 1998 – 8th Grade

It was the perfect spring day. The sun was shining, birds were chirping, and a cool breeze was blowing. Laurel closed her eyes enjoying the peace and quiet of her and Zeppelin's favorite spot.

"Damn it!"

Zeppelin's growl broke her moment of tranquility, and she peeked open one eye.

"What?" She watched him crumble up another page from his notebook.

"I have the perfect melody, the perfect flow of notes and music, but the lyrics…"

Laurel sat up crossing her legs in front of her. Picking up one of the many balls of paper she read over some of his lyrics.

Oh, special fangirl, my girl

Your soul like fire on a hot day,

You're like a cooling wind on a hot evening.

"What's wrong with these?" They weren't horrible, but not the best either.

He stared at her for a full ten seconds before answering, "They're terrible. I thought you were a writer?"

She crumpled the paper again, throwing it at him, "I am a writer and the first rule in writing is all words are good words. In my professional opinion, these aren't bad."

Laurel snatched his pen from his hand along with his notebook, "You just need some different word choices." She began replacing a few of the words.

Oh, darling fangirl, my girl

Your spirit like wildfire on a summer day,

You're like a soothing wind on a warm evening

"Try this." She handed him the notebook, "Maybe this will jump start your pea sized brain."

He stuck his tongue out at her before reading what she wrote.

"You know the thing that sucks about being friends with you? You're always right." A slow smiled spread across his face, "This is good. This is really good. Okay bring your adorable butt over her and help me write this."

She moved beside him as he picked up his guitar and started playing the first notes of his original song.

Over the next couple of weeks Laurel helped Zeppelin write and compose his song. He was playing it for the entire school at the 8th grade talent show. By the night of the show, Zeppelin had the music and lyrics memorized.

Laurel and Thomas had to be at school after Zeppelin's rehearsal to help collect show tickets. They met with Mrs. Carlton to get set up for people to start arriving at six o'clock. They would chat and smile, joking with the little kids who came to see their siblings. When a familiar high pitch giggle filled her ears, Laurel cringed watching Mandy and her squad of girlfriends approaching the table.

"Did you see Zeppelin is performing?"

Laurel's ears perked up hearing her best friend's name.

Mandy smiled widely, "Between you and me that's the real reason why I'm here. Honestly, musicians are way hotter than jocks."

Her fists clenched at her side as Thomas placed his hand on her back, "Ignore them."

"I bet by the end of this summer, Zepp and I will be the new hot couple of SHS. Only the best are worthy to have me as their girl."

"Ticket. Please." Laurel asked through her gritted teeth.

Mandy rolled eyes, handing her ticket over, "Here you go. I guess this was your only talent. Manual labor to those better than you."

Thomas gripped her elbow, "It's not worth it. Remember, we're here to support Zeppelin."

"Soon, Zepp won't need your support. I'll be with him, and he'll forget all about you losers."

Mandy and her friends walked past the table before Laurel could unleash her rage on the snotty blond.

"I really hate her." Thomas scoffed.

She nodded in agreement but something Mandy had said was nagging at her.

Soon, Zepp won't need your support… he'll forget all about you…

The gym lights dimmed and their music teacher, Miss Gillam, took to the stage. Quite a few of their classmates were dancing to popular songs from their favorite bands. A group of drama kids did an improv act that had everyone laughing. Andy, who had a noticeably black eye and swollen nose, demonstrated his *awesome* basketball tricks. Finally, the last act of the night was Zeppelin.

Laurel and Thomas were sitting next to their families and Zeppelin's parents in the second row. She narrowed her eyes at the back of Mandy's head when she began clapping loudly. Zeppelin walked out on stage with his guitar and stared out at the audience. His eyes were wide, and his hand was gripping the neck of his guitar tightly.

Mandy shouted out, "Go Zepp! You got this babe!"

Laurel watched as he shook his head then looked over at Mandy in front of her. Immediately her heart swan dived into the pit of her stomach. His beautiful smile was point right at the one person who made her life a living hell.

"This song is dedicated to my number one fan. This is Fangirl, My Girl."

As he began strumming the first notes of the song, tears began pooling within her eyes. She watched as Mandy was swooning over every word they had written together. He was at the bridge of the song and finally walked over to their side of the stage. His fingers dancing over the strings and his long hair was hanging low over his face.

Even though her heart was shattering in a million pieces, Laurel couldn't help the pride swelling in her chest. He was born to perform in front of people and have adoring fans as beautiful as Mandy was. When he sang the last lyric, she stood up clapping and cheering with Thomas joining in beside her. Zeppelin's smile was brighter than the spotlight on him and made her knees weak. Miss Gillam came back out on stage thanking everyone for coming and the gym lights came back on.

"Come on girls, let's go meet Zeppelin in the hallway and tell him how amazing he was." Mandy flipped her hair over her shoulder, walking towards the gym entrance.

Thomas leaned over, "How much you wanna bet he ignores them and comes looking for us?"

"I don't know, you know how much Zeppelin loves attention from the opposite sex." She saw a glimpse of his golden-brown hair as many of the girls from their class surrounded him, "Let's go wait for him outside."

She followed their families outside to their cars. Her mom had to leave for work and Thomas' aunt needed to get home to his cousins.

Mr. And Mrs. Foster offered to take them out for a celebration dinner and to have them home by ten o'clock. Zeppelin finally walked out of the gym about a half hour later with his guitar case in hand.

"So, what did you guys think?"

Zeppelin's parents pulled him into a family hug, "Sweetie, you were amazing up there."

His dad nodded, "I'm proud of you, Zeppelin. Now, let's go celebrate with burgers and milkshakes."

"Yes! I'm starving!" He slung his arm around her shoulders, "What did you think of the song?"

She forced her lips into a grin, "It was great. One day it may even be number one of TRL."

His green eyes searched hers before he smiled, "You really think?"

She nodded, not trusting her rollercoaster of emotions to speak. They drove to Zeppelin's favorite hole in the wall diner off Main Street and sat in a corner booth. She sat in between her two best friends, barely touching her food Miss Mel brought out as her stomach twisted into knots. She listened to Zeppelin talking with his dad on how to improve his song and possibly recording it in his studio. His mom was fussing over Thomas being too skinny and making sure he got enough to eat.

Laurel felt at home and out of place all at the same time. The only thing she wanted to do was go home, bury herself under a mountain of blankets and cry until exhaustion took her. She was staring down at her plate when a french fry hit her in the chest.

"I missed." Zeppelin chuckled.

She looked up to see him aiming once more at her chest. The fry flew through the air and right down her V-neck shirt.

"Score!"

"Zeppelin Dean Foster!" his mom yelled, making his cheeks go bright red.

He smiled bashfully, "Sorry mom, but it was necessary. Laurel was lost in her own thoughts, and I had to bring her back to reality. It's my sworn duty as her best friend."

She rolled her eyes at him, "I'll remember this the next time I need to smack you with one of my flip flops."

They finished their meals and headed towards Laurel's house. She and Zeppelin were sitting next to one another in the back of his parents' van. Thomas and Mr. Foster were in a deep conversation about how touring was back when he was in a band while Mrs. Foster was singing along to the radio.

"Did you like my dedication?" Zeppelin asked, bumping his shoulder into hers.

She nodded, "Yeah, it was really sweet. I bet your number one fan was over the moon to hear her song."

The piercing ache in her chest was making it hard to breathe. Even if Zeppelin didn't see her the way she saw him, Laurel couldn't believe he would ever like someone as vile as Mandy Parks.

"So, you were over the moon? Here I thought you were in the second row for my first ever performance."

Her eyes snapped up to him, "Me? I wasn't talking about me. I figured the way you had looked at Mandy when she called out to you that it was for her."

"You're joking, right?"

She searched his face to see if he was playing with her, but was met with the serious, piercing stare that bore into the depths of her soul.

"It wasn't for Mandy?" A spark of hope ignited within her.

Zeppelin slipped his arm around her shoulder, pulling her into his side, "Hell no. Why would I ever want that nasty girl as my fan? Ew." He whispered.

That spark turned into an ember flame filling her heart with pure joy, "You looked right at her…"

"I was looking at you, Laurel. I was freaking out and when I heard Mandy's screeching my eyes landed on you. You have always been the one who brings me back from my own self-doubt." He undid her seatbelt along with his and pulled her even closer to him, "You will always be my number one fangirl and my girl."

She buried her head into his chest so he wouldn't see the tears of happiness falling down her face, "Damn right I am." She whispered.

Zeppelin laughed, hugging her tightly to him and holding her until they arrived at her house. That night she dreamed of her best friend performing in front of thousands of people and her being in the front row rocking out.

Zeppelin

Over the next week, Zeppelin and Thomas were able to keep things civil between them. Though Zeppelin knew everyone around them could feel the rift that had wedged itself between them, especially Laurel. She tried her best to be neutral, which usually meant she avoided everyone. Tomorrow's show was going to make that impossible for her to do.

Zeppelin stared out the window of his bus at the familiar exit ramp names. Small towns that littered the highway leading to his hometown. This was the one show he was supposed to look forward to the most and yet he was sitting alone on his bus with dread pooling in his stomach. Laurel had decided to ride with Thomas on the band bus.

This will be great research for my book if I ride with them.

He hadn't questioned her at the time, but as they drove into Springfield, Missouri, his mind was slipping into the darkness of doubt. Now he wondered if she and Thomas truly had something going on between them. Realistically, Zeppelin knew he had no right to be angry or jealous, but that didn't keep him from feeling exactly that.

He was grateful when they pulled into the hotel parking lot, and he could retreat to his room. What he hadn't been expecting was his family waiting for him when he opened the door. When he saw his mom, Zeppelin dropped everything in his arms and scooped her up into them.

"I missed you, sweetie." She whispered.

"Missed you, momma." He was on the verge of tears but held strong knowing it would make his mom crying as well.

"Son, you're looking good for being on the road." His dad pulled him into a tight hug.

Zeppelin chuckled, "Thanks dad, I promise to clean up before we go out to do anything."

"Where's Thomas?"

He grabbed his stuff from the door, setting it in the bedroom suite, "He's helping Laurel get settle." He felt his parents' eyes on him

"Laurel? Why didn't you tell us Laurel was on tour with you?"

He took a seat on the couch beside his mom, "It was Thomas's idea. He knew she was struggling with her new book and thought a few months of touring would spark inspiration for her."

"How is she handling tour life?" His dad settled into the chair in front of him.

"As well as my introverted best friend can. You should have seen her on the first night of the tour. She was rocking out from the side stage. I think I awakened her inner punk rock girl… again."

His mom leaned in, "Have you told her about…"

"Mom…" He groaned.

"What? I was just wondering if you had told her how you feel finally. This is the first time you two have seen each other in a year, right?"

He leaned forward, kissing his mom's cheek, "I'm going to take a shower then we should grab Thomas and Laurel to have dinner."

Before either of his parents could say anything, Zeppelin walked into the bedroom suite and shut the door. After taking a long, hot shower, he put on his favorite jeans and dark gray Henley. He opted for his Chucks rather than his boots and felt more like plain ole Zeppelin. He grabbed his sunglasses and baseball hat in case he needed them.

When he opened the door to the suite, the room was filled with Laurel and his mom's laughter. He found them sitting on the couch looking down at his mom's phone. His dad and Thomas were on the balcony having a tense conversation undoubtedly about him. He decided to spare himself the aggravation and sat in front of his two favorite ladies.

"What's so funny?"

Laurel's head snapped up first with a bright grin on her face, "Mom was showing me the newest tenants of our old treehouse."

Looking at the screen he immediately busted out laughing. There were three little red foxes playing on the latter while two older foxes watched from above.

"Reminds me of the time the three of us tried to sneak out there at midnight and dad was waiting for us inside." Zeppelin handed the phone back to his mom.

"Steven knew you three were up to no good…" His mom's eyes looked past him as his dad chuckled.

"And I was right, but you guys ended up letting the old man have a fun night camping with his favorite kiddos."

Thomas swung his arm around Zeppelin's dad shoulders, "Only because we wanted to hear stories from your wild touring days and knew mom wouldn't let you tell us in her presence."

His dad shushed him as they all began to laugh. The tension that had been building up in Zeppelin's shoulders and chest slipped away as the warmth of being surrounded by family covered him. Letting out a long breath, he noticed Laurel watching him then her cheeks blooming a rosy pink when he caught her. He smiled softly then stood to offer his hand to help her up. As they walked down the hall to the elevators, she never let go of his hand, squeezing it tight. Then he noticed her doing the same thing with Thomas' hand and jealousy raged in his chest once more.

Dinner ended up being a big surprise party for Zeppelin and Thomas at their favorite restaurant. His parents along with Laurel's mom and Thomas' aunt who raised him rented out the whole place. His band mates were huddled near the small stage where Zeppelin got discovered. A lot of their friends from high school had made the trip into town to see the show and reconnect with them. It was an eclectic gathering of old baseball teammates of Thomas'. Laurel's agent, Leigh, was chatting with her and a few of her book club friends. While old band members from his early days of pursuing music were milling around stage.

"Zeppelin Foster, as I live and breathe."

The voice sent chills down his spine. Turning towards the bar he found one of only three people he wished he would never see again. Her bleached blonde hair was pulled up into a high ponytail and her icy blue eyes were locked on him. Obnoxious red covered lips pulled into a toothy smile that was obviously for show.

"I see you made something for yourself, Mandy." He flashed his own fake, charming smile back at her.

Her eyes rolled, pulling a beer from the ice chest, "Actually, I did. I went to community college, got a degree in business admin and bought this little gem last year."

Zeppelin was surprised by the revelation, "Wow, your parents must be proud. Well, thanks for the beer…"

"You know we should really hook up while you're in town. Talk about the good ole days and catch up."

He nearly choked on his beer. Last he had heard, Mandy was Mrs. Andy Smith, number two of the three he wished to never see.

"I believe your husband would not approve of that…" He leaned in over the bar, "And I wouldn't go near you with a ten-foot cattle prod."

Zeppelin leaned back as someone took his hand, "Hey, Thomas is looking for you."

There had never been a moment more than that one that he was thankful for Laurel. The corner of her lips pulled into a smirk as she looked past him at the bar.

"Hiya Mandy, how's the little ones and Andy?"

Zeppelin slipped his arm protectively around Laurel's shoulder, narrowing his eyes on Mandy. Thankfully, she was smart enough to realize she was outnumbered and played nice.

"They're great. I should get back to work."

Once Mandy was on the other side of the bar, Zeppelin pressed his lips to Laurel's temple whispering, "My hero."

She laughed, "I should have told you that she would be here. She's the reason why I don't come here anymore. Andy and Brendan are always drinking here."

Once the drinks were flowing and music playing, Zeppelin relaxed and had more fun with his two best friends than he could remember. It was early the next morning when the three of them piled into Zeppelin's suite and crashed.

It was nearly noon when Zeppelin woke up in his suite, alone. A note left on the coffee table with Thomas' handwriting.

He crumpled the note, tossing it into the waste basket and slowly started getting ready for his day. Jake was waiting for him in the lobby to take him to the venue wearing a particularly dark pair of sunglasses.

"Wait… I missed you cutting loose last night?"

Jake smirked, "I have no idea what you're talking about."

"Well damn Jaky-Poo, proud of you." Then a fearful thought popped into his mind, "Please don't tell me you hooked up with the blonde running the bar."

He shook his head, "Oh no. Even if Laurel hadn't warned me, I wouldn't have never gone near that."

Zeppelin slapped his back, "Good man, now let's go."

The crowds were already gathering at the venue entrance. A sea of brightly colored hair and black outfits brought pure joy to his heart. One thing he loved the most about music was how it always brought people together. Among the punks and elder emos were their kids, business people, scientists, doctors and so on. The job titles, annual income, or neighborhood status didn't matter here. Once they were in their seats and the music blaring, they were all the same.

Heading into the green room, he found Sam and Alec chatting over their catered lunch while Rich was chatting with his parents. Scanning the room, there were two people noticeably absent, and the tension tightened around his chest like a vice. Trying to play off his discomfort, he grabbed some light snacks and water before joining his parents' conversation.

The band headed to the stage for their sound check while their VIPs watched from the pit. He was half ass playing the songs as his mind was frantically running rampant with wild theories of where Laurel and Thomas were. As they paused for Alec to make an adjustment, Zeppelin heard Laurel's giggle echoing from above them. With all the noise around them, no one else noticed it.

His eyes drifted up above the mix tables to the spotlight hubs. There he could make out, Laurel burying her face into Thomas's chest as her body shook with laughter. His arms slid around her as he joined her laughing fit. Laurel playfully pushed Thomas away, but then settled beside him looking down at her lap. She held up a perfectly made paper airplane then sent it soaring into the air. It flew over the seats towards the pit and landed at the edge of the small group of VIPs.

Zeppelin looked back up to her and their eyes connected. They were wide and her lips were in a perfect O as if she had been caught by her parents. He didn't need to see her cheeks to know they would be bright red, and she averted her eyes back to her lap.

"Earth to Zepp…" Rich patted his shoulder, "You good?"

He shook his head trying to refocus his mind, "Yeah. Yeah, I'm good."

He started the song back up again, glancing back up to see Laurel and Thomas now making their way across the walk and back down to the ground. Finishing sound check, Zeppelin made his way back to his bus to calm his raging emotions coursing through his body before their show. He didn't see Laurel or Thomas before his set and any thoughts of them vanished once he was on stage in front of thousands of people screaming his name.

Their show had been one of the easiest performances they had. The hometown crowd was amazing, his bandmates were all fantastic and he was riding the after show high. He was still riding that high when he stepped off the elevator and headed towards his suite. Suddenly, he was crashing hard as he spotted a familiar couple standing in the hallway in a tight embrace. He was unable to look away as Thomas's hands cupped either side of Laurel's face and his lips pressed against her forehead.

Zeppelin darted back towards the elevators until he heard two doors latch shut. His heart thumbing in his ears and his blood flowing like raging lava in his veins. He was pissed. He was sick with jealousy. His chest throbbing as his heart cracked from the overwhelming betrayal he felt from his friends. Taking a few steps towards his door, Zeppelin turned on his heel and made his way down to Laurel's room and knocked on her door.

"Zepp? Everything okay?"

He wrinkled his nose as Thomas's cologne hitting him in the face, "Where were you tonight? I didn't see you at the show?"

She stepped aside to let him walk in, "I was there for the first half then I came back here to work on my book. Watching tonight sparked an idea for a scene I needed to get down before I forgot it."

Zeppelin stood in the middle of her suite taking it all in. Nothing seemed to be out of place other than the blanket laid out on the floor with all the hotel pillows against the couch. There was a box of pizza next to it with a few empty beers.

"With Thomas?"

There was a long sigh from her, "Yes with Thomas. He didn't feel like hanging out at the venue, so we hung out here."

"Is that all you did with him?"

The question was out of his mouth before his rational filter could catch it. The moment he saw the anger in her eyes fade into sadness he immediately regretted saying anything.

"What do you think we did, Zeppelin?" She snapped, walking to the blanket and sitting down on the floor.

"I don't know, Laurel. All I know is that I feel like I'm suddenly the awkward third wheel with you two. You're hanging out all the time, cuddling together in the rafters and kissing foreheads in hallways."

The growl that rumbled from her lips annoyed him and turned him on at the same time. She grabbed the papers spread out and started to organizing them.

"Really? Is that any worse than what we've done in the past? What is this really about?"

He sat opposite of her in the chair, "Is there something between you two? Are you… are you…" He couldn't push the words out that he was screaming in his head.

"Spit it out, Foster!" She yelled.

"Are you two friends or more?"

Her head lifted slowly as she study him for a minute. He knew Laurel could see through all his bullshit and walls. She could see the jealous, insecure, little boy sitting before her.

"We're friends. That's all."

Once again, his mouth was faster than his brain as he scoffed, "Friends like normal friends or friends like you and I are friends?"

Zeppelin swore her eyes flashed red as she stood from the floor, "You know what Zeppelin, fuck you. I get to be friends with whoever I want, however I want. You don't get to hide me away as your ego boost any time you feel less than perfect. If you don't like me being friends with Thomas the way I'm friends with you then maybe I should stay in Springfield. While you go off touring the country and fucking every girl you possibly can!"

She stormed off to her bedroom and slammed the door. Zeppelin hung his head into his hands. He crossed a line and now fear gripped his heart that he wouldn't be able to come back from it. When he went to stand, he noticed his name on a sheet of her notes. Sitting in the spot where she was, he picked it up reading what she had written.

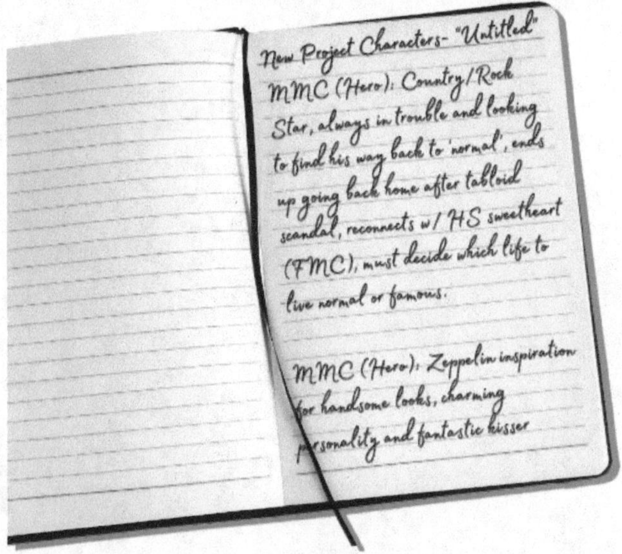

He couldn't help to read through a few more sheets of her notes before gathering them all and securing them in her bag. He cleaned up the rest of the suite, wrote a note to Laurel slipping it in her bag with her notes and turned off the lights, leaving her suite to go to his own.

Laurel

Laurel held Zeppelin's note as the bus cruised down the highway. They were headed to Chicago for a three-day rock festival. There were several bands playing that she would love to see including Heartstrings, but Laurel could not find it in her to be excited. The argument with Zeppelin in Springfield and seeing her two best friends fighting like Neanderthals was weighing heavily on her.

It was bad enough dealing with Zeppelin's on again, off again feelings. Now, it was directly affecting their friendship with Thomas, and she hated it. However, the worst part was that she hit a wall with her book. The words had been flowing from her for a week and now it was an empty well. She needed to find her flow again, her inspiration. Unfortunately, as he had admitted himself, her inspiration was being a complete asshole.

The bus came to a stop and Laurel slipped Zeppelin's note back in with her writing notebook. She could hear Jake walking back towards her bunk.

"Are you chilling on the bus or would like to go explore the venue?"

She smiled, "Will you protect me from my two best friends that are acting like toddlers?"

Jake laughed, "Absolutely, it would be an honor and a privilege. I'll meet you outside, take your time getting ready."

Laurel watched him walk to the front of the bus and down the steps. She grabbed her favorite hoodie stolen from Zeppelin and her Converse, slipping them on her feet. Looking in the bathroom mirror, she decided to braid her hair off to one side and put on her Heartstrings crew hat on backwards. Placing her notebook and laptop in her backpack, she headed out to find Jake.

She enjoyed hanging out with him. They had a lot in common, much like her and Sam. They walked around the venue, grabbing some much-needed greasy food and sitting out amongst the fans. Laurel watched as a group of girls walked past in their Heartstrings tour shirts and wild color hair. She had always wanted to cut loose and have brightly colored hair. At first, it was that her mom would never let her dye it then it was she's an adult and had to look like one. She watched the girls walk off towards the seats longing for a small taste of their youthful freedom.

"Do you think I would look okay with wild color hair?"

Jake looked at her mid bite into his hot dog, "You're asking me?"

She rolled her eyes, "No, I'm asking my imaginary friend beside you."

He swallowed, clearing his throat, "I mean… sure. I don't think the color of your hair will take away from you being pretty."

"Awe, you think I'm pretty?" She chuckled.

It was his turn to roll his eyes, "Yes, I think you're pretty. The question is, do you think you would look pretty with wild color hair?"

Laurel shrugged, "I don't think it will hurt. I'm not all that pretty to begin with."

Jake scoffed, "Well I know two men who would disagree with you. However, my two cents is there's only one way to find out."

"Jake, are you encouraging me to let loose and dye my hair?"

He smiled, "Hell yeah. You only live once, might as well live life to the fullest. Come on, we can ask the stylist what colors she has for Sam. I'm sure you'll be able to find something you like."

Jake threw out their trash and Laurel hooked her arm through his, "You are officially my new favorite guy."

They walked back to the dressing rooms and found Crissy. Laurel was surprised that she had so many different colors set aside for Sam.

"You never know what that girl is going to want to do to her hair. So, what color you thinking?"

Laurel looked at the different shades of greens, her favorite color, then the blues and purples. She finally settled on a bubblegum pink.

"How long will it take?" She asked, as Crissy wrapped a towel around her shoulders.

"About an hour probably a little sooner since your hair is all natural and blond."

Jake walked over, looking down at his phone, "I'm going to check in with Zeppelin and Thomas. They both have blown up my texts. Just text me whenever you're done, and I'll make my way back here."

"Sounds good. Thanks Jake." Laurel smiled as she slipped off her glasses.

"Can't wait to see the new, wild Laurel." He laughed, taking off into the hallway.

An hour later, Laurel didn't recognize the woman staring back at her in the mirror. Crissy had gone above and beyond all her expectations. Her blond hair faded into a light pink getting brighter and brighter until it was the perfect bubblegum color at the ends.

"I love it."

"Yay! Now it will fade fairly quickly but I can always pick up this color again or we could do a little mix match with another color. Maybe a pale green. Do you want me to braid again for you?"

Laurel nodded and watched in amazement as Crissy's fingers weaved her hair into the perfect fishtail braid over her shoulder. Laurel placed her hat backwards on her head and smiled brightly at herself in the mirror.

"You are truly the picture of a punk princess." They were laughing as the door opened and Jake appeared.

"Whoa, Laurel you look fantastic! You definitely have to go show off your new self."

She hugged Crissy, "Thank you so much. I needed this little change."

Crissy gave her an extra tight squeeze, "Anytime honey. Now go off and rock out. The guys will be here any moment."

Laurel hooked her arm with Jake's, "Do you think you could find us a safe and close spot to watch the concert?"

"I know the perfect spot, but first you forgot your phone on the bus. It's been going off like crazy."

She looked at her texts to see several from Zeppelin and Thomas then three from Leigh.

"Shit, I forgot I had a Zoom meeting with my agent. Alright, let's head somewhere quiet so I can get my ass chewed."

Jake chuckled, leading her towards the green room. She could hear some of the band joking around inside. Before they approached the door, Jake took her down a small hallway where there were some small conference rooms.

"Should be quiet in here and I'll keep anyone from bothering you. By anyone, I mean the idiots you call best friends."

Laurel pushed herself on her tiptoes, kissing Jake's cheek, "You are officially my hero, and I shall name my main character hero after you."

She watched as his cheeks turned a rosy hue before she stepped inside the room and set up her laptop. She hit Leigh's name and immediately her face popped up on her screen.

"You're late…" Leigh paused then a wide smile spread across her face, "Oh my god, I love your hair! It's about time you let loose some of the spunky personality."

Laurel chuckled, "Now you know why I'm late. By the way, I'm sorry for being late. I know you had back-to-back meetings with Raelyn and Emerson."

Leigh waved her hand in the air, "No worries, it worked in my favor. Raelyn was the easiest meeting, and Em was settling on a title. Which is a good lead way into your book and this amazing new concept."

As Leigh was talking, Laurel pulled up her email and sent the first fifty percent of what she had of her manuscript.

"Check your email."

She waited to see Leigh's eyes light up, "You little minx… damn, you've been working hard these last few weeks. I can't wait to read this. Have you given any thought of a title?"

She shook her head, "No, right now I'm calling it Project Rockstar."

"Perfect!"

"Wait, what? What do you mean perfect?" Laurel asked.

"Raelyn's book is called Project Fanfic and Emerson's decided to call hers Project Sportballs to go along with Raelyn's. We are going to do a whole series with the three of you and possibly another debut author I just signed with. Project Rockstar will fit perfectly into this fangirl series."

Laurel wasn't completely sold on the idea especially if her book was going to be put with Raelyn's and Emerson's. Both their manuscripts were phenomenal. Right now, hers was still on the hot mess express.

"If you think it's best then I guess I'm alright with it."

Leigh smiled, "Okay, enough business. I want to know how life has been on tour. Don't you dare leave out any juicy details."

"The tour has been…" Laurel paused trying to think of the perfect word, "fine."

"Fine?"

Her sharp blue eyes bore into Laurel's, "Yeah, fine." She pulled her bottom lip between her teeth.

"Spill. Now. Please let me know if I need to come out to your next city and kick Thomas's perky little ass."

She chuckled softly then proceeded to tell Leigh everything that had happened between her and Zeppelin then her and Thomas. By the time she was done, Leigh was sitting with a mug of coffee in her hands tapping her nails against it.

"Let me get this straight. You have not one but two incredibly attractive and charming men fighting over you?"

"In a weird, awkward nutshell that contains my two best friends since grade school. Yes." Laurel started fidgeting with her braid.

Leigh calmly placed her mug on her desk then looked straight into her camera at Laurel, "Have a threesome and cut the sexual tension brewing between you three."

"WHA-" Laurel coughed hard on the word trying to choke her, "Are you crazy!?"

Leigh nodded nonchalantly, "It has been said, but seriously you're living out every pop/punk girly's dream. Forget being an adult, forget living in your little protective bubble and leap off the edge into wild oblivion."

Laurel took out her pen and notebook, "That's a good line, definitely going to work that into my book somehow."

"Thank you, but I mean it. How often are you going to be able to live wild and free on tour with a rock band?" Laurel was about to answer when Leigh held up her hand, "Don't answer that. Look, I'm going to let you go and start living vicariously my spicy rockstar fantasies by reading your manuscript. I'll give you my thoughts in a couple of days."

"It's not spicy." Laurel commented.

"Well, that's my first note and complaint. We need spice in this story. All the romance girlies love their smut especially in a rockstar romance. Raelyn is the woman to speak to about it. Now, go. Run wild and have some fun."

Laurel waved goodbye then shut down her laptop. Once she had her things collected, she found Jake talking with Thomas in the hallway.

"Jake, I'm the one who told you to stay with her and keep any suspicious people away from her. I didn't mean me."

Laurel let out a soft laugh, "It's fine Jake. I'm done with my meeting."

Jake nodded, taking his hand off of Thomas' chest, "Just let me know if you want me to bounce him."

"I literally make sure you get paid. I could conveniently forget to pay you." Thomas threatened with a smirk playing on his lips.

He walked up to her and immediately took her backpack off her shoulder to carry it, "Hey, I wanted to make sure you're alright. I heard that Zepp might have stuck his big foot in his mouth last night."

"Yeah, I'm fine. Zeppelin was being Zeppelin. Nothing to worry about and nothing a little cold shoulder treatment won't cure."

They started walking back towards the green room that was unusually quiet as they walked inside.

"Where is everyone?"

Thomas set her stuff down and sat on one of the couches, "A lot of the bands are doing press for the festival then they have rehearsals."

"Really? Could you show me where they are? I would like to see what it's like for my book." she asked standing in front of him.

The hair on her arms stood up as she watched his eyes travel up her body. Suddenly, the room was stifling, and she took Zeppelin's flannel off to tie around her waist.

"I could, but first I wanted to ask you something." Thomas stood from the couch, his lean body nearly against hers.

Normally, Thomas was the one she always felt comfortable with. Never had there been the tension that pulled her to him like it did with Zeppelin. She noticed the few days stubble growing dark on his strong jaw. How his eyes were not the normal bright hazel, but a dark amber. The way his button-down shirt stretched as his chest expanded and his bicep flexed.

"O-Okay, what?"

His long fingers ran down her arms and gathered her hands into his, "I would like to take you on a date tonight. There is something here, I can feel it and I think you can too. I want to know if it's something I should pursue or if I'm just being an extra lonely, divorced guy who needs to check his emotions at the door."

"Thomas, I don't know…" Every part of her was screaming yes except the one that matter most, "What happens if we go on a date, and it gets weird between us as friends. Your friendship means more to me than some fleeting attraction."

"It can't hurt to try though. If anything, we'll find out that we're great for one another romantically or have a fun night out as friends. Come on, one date and I promise it will not change anything between us unless it's to go on another date."

Her heart was hammering against her chest as he laced their fingers together. She couldn't think of a reason why not to go out with Thomas other than she didn't want to hurt Zeppelin. Frankly, that was not a good enough reason to say no.

"One date, but can it be after the concert? Jake has picked out the perfect spot to watch the show from the crowd."

"Damn, I'm starting think Jake has a better chance with you than me." Thomas chuckled, "Sure, after the show. I will meet you out by the bus." He leaned down a pressed his soft lips to her heated cheeks, "See ya later."

Thomas dropped her hands and headed out of the green room. Immediately, her hand went to her cheek touching the tingling spot from where his lips were. She took a deep breath before heading out to find Jake waiting for her in the hallway.

"Everything okay?" He asked.

She shrugged, "Honestly, I have no fucking clue. All I know is I'm ready to go rock out to some good music."

He held his arm out to her, "Then let me lead you to your perfect spot. Just promise me you won't go moshing tonight. I've heard stories about you getting yourself into mosh pits."

"Spoil sport." She laughed, "For you, I promise no moshing tonight."

Laurel couldn't remember the last time she had this much fun. True to his words, Jake had the perfect spot down in the pit section where she could see the whole stage and still have space from everyone. A few Heartstrings fans recognized him, and he graciously took selfies with them. She made a mental note to add a handsome, charming bodyguard to her story.

When Heartstrings took to the stage, her body began buzzing. She would never get tired of watching Zeppelin command the crowd from the stage. Performing was like breathing for him and she was in awe of him. A sharp pain pierced through her chest as she remembered who was waiting for her after the show. The guilt was cold and heavy on her chest making it difficult to breathe for a moment.

Looking back up to the stage, she found Zeppelin's piercing stare on her. Alec was leading into the bridge of the song as Zeppelin was frozen in place. His eyes wide and mouth opened into a perfect circle. Rich bumped his shoulder and suddenly Zeppelin was back to performing. The way he was staring down at her filled her body with a heat she hadn't felt in a long time.

Laurel pushed herself up to yell into Jake's ear, "I think I'm all rocked out. Could we go back to the bus?"

He nodded, taking hold of her hand and leading her back towards the VIP entrance. Once they were near the buses, she stopped to hug Jake.

"Thank you for everything today. I meant it when I said you were my hero."

He shrugged bashfully, "No big thing. Always here for you.

Enjoy your night." He headed back towards the side stage.

Thomas was sitting on the bus stairs when she walked up, "Do you mind if I change really quick?"

He shook his head and stood up so she could get on the bus. Heading to her bunk, Laurel grabbed one of the only nice blouses she brought with her and her toiletries. Quickly changing and freshening up, she walked out of the bus bathroom finding Thomas sitting at one of the tables nervously bouncing his leg.

"Alright, I'm all yours for the evening." She smiled, watching a bright smile spread across his lips.

They walked to the main entrance of the venue where an Uber was waiting for them. There were plenty of things to do in Chicago on a Saturday night, but when they pulled up in front of a Pinball Bar she couldn't contain her excitement.

"I love pinball!"

Thomas smiled, "I know. Come on, I'm thinking you can get the high score on at least four or five machines."

He had been right, in the two hours they were there drinking beer and laughing, Laurel managed to get the highest score on four machines before they had last call. As they stepped outside, Laurel shivered from the cool breeze. She rubbed her arms wishing she had remembered her jacket when suddenly she was blanketed in warmth. Her nose filled with the clean scent of Thomas's cologne as he wrapped his button-down shirt around her shoulders.

Laurel slipped her arms into the sleeves and looked over stunned at the sight before her. Thomas stood in a pair of dark jeans and black t-shirt. His hair was falling in front of his handsome face as rain gently began to fall on them. For the first time, she saw him as the truly handsome man he was and not only her best friend. Her fingers flexed desperate to brush back the strands of dark curls and to feel the rough stubble beneath her fingertips.

When she was about to give in their Uber pulled up and Thomas opened the door for her. The ride back to the venue was torturous. Every bump and touch between them were magnified to a million. She gripped the sleeves of his shirt to keep them to herself. The last time Laurel had felt anything close to this was with Zeppelin the night before the tour started but she was used to it with him. Not with Thomas and now she wanted to know if maybe the tension between them was real. There was only one way to find out and the thought of it made her stomach clench.

The rain was still lightly coming down as they walked from the entrance to the buses. It was a little after one in the morning and the crew was putting away the last items to get them back on the road. She stopped outside the bus door, turning to Thomas.

"I had an amazing night, Thomas. Definitely one of the best dates I've had in a long time."

He smiled, taking her hands in his, "I'm glad. Maybe, we could do this again in the next city."

She looked down at their hands for a moment knowing there couldn't be another night like this again. She opened her mouth to speak when the rain started pouring down on them. Laurel let out a small yelp trying to pull away from Thomas to get on the bus.

His arm slipped quickly around her waist, pulling her flesh against his firm body. Before she could say anything, his lips crashed against hers. The rain and the world around them seem to go in slow motion. His hand cupped the back of her neck as the tip of his tongue swiped across her bottom lip. Deepening the kiss, Laurel gripped his hips allowing the flames of desire to rise within her.

Rather it was because they were both lonely or they truly had feelings for one another, Laurel didn't care. At that very moment, all she knew was she wanted to be with Thomas in every way possible. As quickly as their kiss had started, Thomas pulled away from her.

"I told you it was real." He kissed her again, "Goodnight Laurel."

She sucked in a breath, "G-Goodnight Thomas."

Laurel watched as he walked towards the band bus and only once he was out of sight did she finally push her legs to move to get on Zeppelin's bus. She was soaked to the bone, shivering and yet her body felt like it was on fire. In a daze, she went through the motions of drying off and getting changed into comfortable clothes. Her mind was racing with memories from the night and what ifs.

The driver called back to her, "You all good?"

"Yeah… I'm good…" she mumbled, "I think so."

The bus roared to life and the familiar vibrations of heading back out on the highway. She was staring down at her notebook before she picked up her pen and began writing new notes for her main character.

Laurel pulled out her laptop, getting ready to turn it on when suddenly everything began spinning. The loud crunch of steel bending and smashing together rang in her ears. Rain began to hit her skin like razors, and everything was turned upside down. Her head was pounding and there was something searing against her abdomen. When she tried to open her eyes there were flashes of oranges and yellows. She squeezed them shut again before trying to yell out.

"H-Help… HELP!"

The pressure against her skull felt like it was going to pop at any moment. She opened her eyes once more only to find the same oranges and yellows in front of her. The immense heat rolling against her before the throbbing in her head was too much for her to take. Closing her eyes slowly, she tried to call out to the one person who always came to her rescue. The one who time and time again had saved her.

"Zep… Zeppelin… help…me."

Zeppelin

July 2000 – 11th Grade

Zeppelin watched as white, puffy clouds passed by his airplane window. His dad and mom were in the seats beside him reading or sleeping. His dad's old bandmate had invited them back to New York for his new band's first concert. For the last week, Zeppelin had spent time meeting a lot of his dad's old friends and talking music with some underground rock legends. It had been an amazing trip, and he couldn't wait to get back home to tell Laurel and Thomas all about it.

He watched as the plane descended through the clouds and busy Kansas City airport came into view. Zeppelin gently shook his dad awake before his mom smacked him with her book.

"Spoil sport." She whispered, making him laugh.

After three and half hours on a plane and nearly three hours driving to Springfield, it was nearly nine o'clock at night when Zeppelin's parents turned onto their street. All he could think about was getting into his bed and sleeping until mid-afternoon the next day.

"Hmm, Thomas is waiting on the porch." His mom pointed at his friend sitting at the top of their stairs.

He hadn't told Thomas when they would be home, "Huh. I wonder if him and his aunt got into another fight."

Lately, his aunt had been pressuring him not to apply for college and staying in Springfield to help her with his middle school cousins. Many nights Thomas would randomly show up at his bedroom window and sleep on Zeppelin's floor. Never once did his parents question or ask why Thomas would be at the kitchen table the next morning. When his dad parked the car, he noticed the dark circles beneath Thomas's eyes.

"Dude, you look like hell. Everything okay?"

Thomas shook his head, looking down at his feet. Zeppelin's stomach twisted getting a sickening feeling that something was seriously wrong.

"Thomas, what is it?" His dad asked, placing a hand on his friend's shoulder.

"It's Laurel…" He swallowed hard, "A couple of days ago she was driving to Branson for a weekend writing trip by herself. She… she was in an accident with a semi-truck."

Zeppelin's world began to spin. Laurel, his Laurel, was in an accident and he wasn't there to protect her. The ground beneath his feet felt like it was tipping to one side, and he found himself reaching out for his dad's arm.

"Zeppelin!" He called out, catching his arms to hold him up, "Let's get your both inside and Kim will check in on Tricia."

Zeppelin and Thomas followed his parents inside to their living room. Thomas told them how the truck driver fell asleep and swerved into the side of Laurel's car. It had sent her rolling down an embankment before crashing into a large tree. The driver was able to get to her just as the car had caught fire, pulling her out and called 911. She was at Springfield Medical Center in the ICU with a severe head injury and several broken bones in her right arm and leg.

"Will she…" Zeppelin choked on the question he was trying to ask, unable to even think about not having Laurel in his life, "Will she be okay?"

Zeppelin's mom walked into the living room, "The doctors are hopeful that she will. Tricia said we could come by and sit with her tomorrow. They are only allowing family in the see Laurel right now, but we could come and sit in the waiting room."

He clenched his jaw, "I need to see her now." Zeppelin got up, grabbing the keys to his truck.

"Zeppelin they won't let you in honey. Visiting hours are over." His mom stepped in front of him as tears fell free down his cheeks.

"Then I'll sleep in my truck if I have to. Mom, she's," He let out a shaky breath, "she's everything to me. I need to see her for myself to believe she is truly okay."

"I'll go with him, mom." Thomas walked over beside him, "I'll make sure he doesn't do anything stupid."

She took a deep breath, "I know I won't be able to talk you out of it. Please be careful."

"Yes ma'am." They both said before each of them kissing either side of her cheeks.

Zeppelin took off like a bat out of hell when they hit the off ramp for the highway. His only thought was to get to Laurel. When they stepped foot inside the hospital the guard told them that they had to leave and come back in the morning. After Thomas pushed him towards a nearby bench so his mouth wouldn't get him in trouble they sat in silence.

He didn't know how long they had been sitting there, but the same guard came out with some coffee and sandwiches for them.

"Who are you guys wanting to see so badly that you'll camp out on this bench?"

Thomas took one of the sandwiches setting it next to him, "Our best friend, Laurel Adler, is in the ICU. We've all been friends since grade school and close like family."

The guard handed Zeppelin a cup and sandwich, "Let me see what I can do."

"Thank you." He called out, "Also, I'm sorry for getting in your face."

The guard chuckled, "Apology accepted." He walked back inside, leaving the two friends to drink their coffees.

It was nearly midnight when the guard came back outside, "Come on you two."

They threw their trash in the bin next to the main entrance and followed the guard to the fourth floor. He nodded at the nurse sitting behind the check-in desk. She gave Zeppelin and Thomas a pointed look as they walked by.

"No trouble from either of you or I'll throw you out myself."

The guard chuckled, "Don't doubt her, I know she can do it."

They both silently nodded in agreement as the guard led them down a hallway to room 1424. Laurel's name was written on a chalkboard outside her room with Nurse Megan beneath it.

"Nurse Megan was at the desk?" Thomas asked.

"Yep, don't piss her off or I will never hear the end of it at home." He opened the door, "You both can sit with her."

Zeppelin held his hand out to him, "Thank you, truly. We appreciate you doing this for us."

He shook his hand, "Sometimes, the family you choose means more than the family you didn't." With that he walked back towards the nurse's desk while they both stepped inside Laurel's room.

Nothing could prepare him for the sight before him. Thomas pulled one of the chairs near her bedside as Zeppelin stood frozen near the door. Her head was wrapped with gauze covering her dirty, blood-caked hair. Her broken arm and leg had a cast on them and her normally pale skin seemed translucent beneath the lights.

"She doesn't even look like Laurel." He said softly.

"I know. It's weird to see her laying her without a book or notebook in her hands."

Zeppelin finally pushed his feet towards her bed and sat on the opposite side of Thomas. There were cuts along her left arm and hand that had been recently cleaned and bandaged. He gently took her hand in his and pressed it to his forehead. Her skin was cool against him. He tried to push down the sob threatening to come from his chest but allowed it to freely fill the silence in the room. The guilt of not being there to protect her rushed out of him in another agonizing cry. Thomas's arm slipped around his shoulder over his chest hugging him from behind.

"She's going to be okay, Zepp. She's tough and will pull through."

Zeppelin grasped his friend's arm as tears streamed down his face. They sat like that for what seemed like forever until finally Zeppelin had no more tears to shed. Thomas decided to check with Nurse Megan to see if it would be okay for them to sleep out in the waiting room. He shook his head as Thomas opened the door.

"I can't leave her. I'll be fine right here."

For the next few days, Zeppelin only left when Tricia came in to sit with her. When they moved her from critical to stable condition they moved her into a regular room. The doctor was hopeful that she would soon wake up and the real challenge would begin. Zeppelin had decided to go home, shower and change while they moved her.

His parents had been by the hospital to check in on him several times.

He decided to bring the nurses some coffee as he walked past their desk towards Laurel's new room. When he walked inside he was surprised to see an older man sitting beside her bed.

"Who the hell are you?"

The man looked up, "I should ask you the same question, son."

Zeppelin set his guitar case down, "I'm Zeppelin Foster, Laurel's best friend. And you?"

"Johnny Alder, her father."

Immediately, Zeppelin was on edge. The man sitting there had abandoned her. Casted her aside like she was nothing.

"You got some nerve being here now." His jaw ached from how tight he held it.

Mr. Adler looked away, "You're right. Tricia told me about you and Thomas. Said you two have protected my little girl since you guys were kids."

Zeppelin sat in the chair on the other side of Laurel's bed, "That's right, we have. Did she tell you Laurel was here?"

He nodded, "Yeah, called me the night after the accident. It took me some time to get here from Vancouver."

Rage was flowing through his veins as he sat across from the man who left the greatest girl he knew behind. He placed his hand over Laurel's to give him some kind of grounding, so he didn't haul off and punch her father. The two of them sat listening to the machines monitoring her heartbeat beeping. There was so much he wanted to tell him. How amazing of a woman his daughter grew up being. How she dreamed of being a published author and how she helped him write many of the songs he was recording for demos. How she had offers from ten different colleges and had decided to stay in Springfield near her mom.

Zeppelin looked at the man who shared the same amber eyes as Laurel and adorably chunky cheeks. He recognized the pain filtering over his face as he looked over at his daughter lying in the bed. Suddenly, Zeppelin felt sorry for her dad. He missed out on truly knowing how wonderful his daughter was and would never truly know her. He looked down at her hand within his. The cuts that were bright and red a few days earlier now slightly pink. He laced his fingers with hers and spoke from his heart.

"I've hated myself these last few days for being away on a trip with my parents. I didn't have to go, but I want to have a career in music and my dad encouraged me to go to New York with him and my mom. To talk with some of his friends from back when he played. If I hadn't been so focused on my damn future, I could have been here to stop her from going on a trip by herself."

Her dad lifted his eyes to him, "You had no way of knowing."

That was exactly what Thomas, his mom, her mom and anyone else had told him. In his mind, that was only an excuse. A way to rationalize a shitty decision he made.

"I know, but that doesn't take away the feeling of guilt I have for not being here to protect her. I made a promise to her, to our friend Thomas, that I would protect her no matter what the cost. I failed her."

There was tension settling between the two of them as Mr. Adler asked, "If you truly believe that, then what do you plan on doing about it?"

Zeppelin hadn't expected him to ask that, but he respected that her dad put him on the spot. Everyone else was sympathetic towards him, walking on eggshells around him. He wanted someone to make him accountable. He didn't think it would come from the one person Laurel despised the most.

"I'm here for her because I love her. I have always loved her and will always love her. She comes first, no matter what. Nothing matters more than her. I'm going to do everything in my power to be the man worthy of protecting her. To provide her with the life she is worthy of. Only when I'm a hundred percent positive I can do both of those then I'm going to marry her." He looked her dad right in the eyes not faltering, "I'm going to marry her because she makes me want to be a better man. A better man than her father and one who will never abandon her. Ever."

Her dad flinched as if Zeppelin had hit him, but then nodded, "Good. She deserves someone who will put her above everything else. I only wish I had been strong enough to do that for her and her mom."

Mr. Adler stood from his seat and Zeppelin did the same. He

held his hand out to him and gave it a firm shake. Before taking his seat once again as Mr. Adler walked towards the door.

"Zeppelin don't mention I was here. She doesn't need that headache in her life. Promise me you'll stay true to your word and be the man I couldn't be."

"I promise." He said firmly.

Mr. Adler looked over at Laurel one last time before walking out of the room. Zeppelin let out a long, shaky breath as his hands trembled against his thighs. He crossed his arms on the edge of Laurel's bed and buried his face into the crook of his elbow. His mind was racing with wild thoughts making his heart thump heavily in his chest. He was about to get up and take a walk when he felt gently fingers weaving through his long hair.

"H-Hey, are you okay?" Laurel's raspy voice was like a choir of angels singing to his ears.

"Laurel?" He looked up to see her eyes barely opened, "Let me get the nurse for you."

Her hand weakly grasped his, "Please stay, I-I don't want you to leave. Wha… what happened?"

He brought her hand to his lips, "I promise we'll tell you everything, but please let me call for the nurse to come check on you. You truly scared the hell out of all of us."

She nodded, letting go of his hand. He called out into the hallway for a nurse and soon he was being ushered out for her doctor to check over her. Zeppelin went to get Tricia and Thomas so they could visit with her. He stood near the door as tears of happiness fell from both of them seeing Laurel awake. The doctor suggested for everyone to let her rest as she was still weak and healing.

"Could…" Laurel cleared her throat, "Could Zeppelin stay with me, please?"

Everyone looked at him, standing in the back of the room. The doctor nodded and added for only a few minutes since she needed her rest. Thomas kissed the top of her head as her mom kissed her cheek. Tricia walked over to him, squeezing his arm.

"Her dad told me everything you said."

A cold chill ran down his spine as she looked him straight in the eyes.

"Don't break her heart, Zeppelin."

"Yes ma'am."

She smiled, following Thomas out of the room. He saw Laurel watching him carefully as he sat on the edge of her bed.

"What was that about?"

He shook his head, "Nothing, just me promising to never let you drive again."

She rolled her sleepy eyes at him then patted the spot next her, "Would you lay with me?"

"Of course, fangirl." He carefully laid beside her, tucking her into his side, "Better?"

Laurel yawned, "Much. Thank you, Zepp."

He pressed his lips to her forehead, "Anything for my girl."

Zeppelin

He figured Laurel would want some space after what happened in Springfield. He had swallowed his pride and approached Thomas about riding on the band bus for a little while. In the end, it had been a blessing in disguise having way more fun hanging out with the band on the road again.

Zeppelin flopped down on the bunk below Sam's, throwing his arm over his eyes. Sam was currently showering before the bus took off while Alec, Rich and Thomas were all talking near the front. He was exhausted from performing but he couldn't remember the last time he had as much fun playing as he did the last two nights.

His mind wandered back to a couple of hours earlier, seeing Laurel out in the crowd. He had been shocked to see her amongst the fans and even more stunned at her normally golden hair turning a bright pink. If Rich hadn't brought him out of his little daze, he would have ended up staring at her for the rest of the performance. She was truly a punk rock goddess sent to torture him.

"You okay?"

Thomas's voice brought him out of his memory as he sat up on the bunk.

"Yeah, did you see Laurel today? Her hair is pink."

He noticed Thomas brush his fingertips against his lips before answering, "Yeah, I like it. Don't you?"

Zeppelin nodded, "Hell yeah. Watch out Avril Lavigne, here's come the new pop punk princess."

Thomas chuckled, sitting on the bunk across from his, "We both know she doesn't have a musical bone in her body, so I think Avril is safe."

"So true," Zeppelin looked down at the floor feeling the uneasiness pooling in his stomach, "Hey, I know I've been an asshole and I'm sorry. I seriously don't want anything to come between us and especially not Laurel. She doesn't deserve the stress of having to put up with us."

"I agree with you there." Thomas paused for a moment, "I want to be honest with you. I asked Laurel on a date tonight and she said yes. We went out to a local Pinball bar, had a fun night and I kissed her."

Zeppelin's heart dropped into his stomach, "Oh… um, okay."

His mind was screaming every foul name towards his best friend. A deep void cracking open within his chest where his heart once was.

He never thought Thomas would have the balls to ask Laurel out and now Zeppelin may have missed his only chance to be with the one person he truly loved.

"Okay? That's it? I was expecting more of a riot act than that."

Zeppelin clenched his fists barely holding on to the last bit of his will power to not go off completely on Thomas. In the end, all he wanted was for Laurel to be happy and if that was with Thomas then so be it. No matter how much it killed him. He was about to say something when Thomas' phone went off.

"Thomas Reed speaking."

Zeppelin was going to get up and grab the bottle of Jack from Alec when Thomas gripped his arm tightly. The genuine terror filling his best friend's wide eyes made Zeppelin's knees weak.

"Where are they taking her?" Thomas asked.

Her. Laurel. Something had happened to Laurel.

"Thomas, what's going on?"

He held up his finger to give him another minute, "Okay, I will have our driver take us there immediately. Thanks for the heads up, Jake."

Thomas stared at his phone; hazel eyes still wide in shock.

"Hey!" Zeppelin clapped his hands hard in front of him, "What the fuck happened?"

His stomach dropped seeing the tears falling down Thomas' cheeks, "Thomas…"

"Whoa! What the hell… holy shit, Zeppelin is that your bus?"

Alec called out from the front of the bus.

Leaving Thomas behind him, he went up to the windows and the scene before him looked like it was from a movie stunt. His bus was flipped upside down, windows broken out and engulfed in flames. The local fire department was putting the flames out as the cops diverted traffic.

"Thomas… THOMAS!" Zeppelin yelled as his friend came out standing next to him, "L-Laurel…"

Zeppelin gripped his friend's shoulders trying to get him to speak and to keep his knees from giving out.

"They flew her to Mount Sinai Hospital with second and third-degree burns. She…" Thomas finally looked at him as he spoke, "She wasn't breathing when they took her."

Zeppelin's world began to spin and the next thing he knew everything was fading around him as he fell into darkness.

***

He was sitting beside Laurel's bed, strumming his guitar when her mom walked into the room.

"Zeppelin, could I ask you to do me a favor?"

He nodded, "Of course Ms. Alder, anything."

She smiled sitting in the chair opposite of his, "The police have Laurel's car in a lot and need someone to empty it. Apparently, the…"

She paused looking at her daughter, "A-Apparently the fire didn't destroy everything completely. I… I don't think I…"

He stood up, "Don't worry about it, Ms. Alder. Thomas and I will make sure to get everything out."

She reached out squeezing his hand, "Thank you Zeppelin."

Walking out, he found Thomas talking with his mom in the waiting room. He explained that there was something they needed to do for Laurel's mom.

"I'll go sit with Tricia then. You boys be careful."

"We will." They both said, heading out to the parking lot.

Seeing the wreckage of Laurel's car was terrifying. Most of her car was burnt to a crisp, but the driver's side was seemingly untouched by the fire. There was an officer with them to make sure they only took what was Laurel's.

"I can't believe…" Thomas started to say as they opened the smashed in driver's side door.

"I know. She's definitely a lot tougher than the two of us combined."

His friend let out a half-hearted chuckle, "Agree."

Thomas went through her backseat and trunk while Zeppelin sat in the driver's seat. His heart pounded against her chest as he imagined what she had been through. Her backpack was on the passenger seat covered in charred marks, however everything inside of it was undamaged. Her laptop had been smashed when her car rolled as well as her cell phone, but he still placed both into her bag.

Zeppelin took down all the little trinkets hanging from her review mirror. A charm bracelet with charms from Zeppelin and Thomas. A set of fuzzy neon green dice her mom gave her when she bought the car. A fake lay from a Hawaiian themed school dance that Zeppelin placed on her; joking she got laid. Then something on her dash caught his attention.

Tucked away in the corner covering her RPM gauge was a photo of her and him. It was their first time at Warp Tour, and they were both sweaty, red faced and grinning like fools. Taking the photo, he ran his thumb over Laurel's face and tears sprung to his eyes suddenly. The thought of almost never seeing her beautiful face and radiant smile again was too much for him.

"Zepp?" Thomas stood next to the driver's side, "You okay?"

He shook his head, "No, no I'm not okay. This is fucked up and I can't believe we almost lost her."

***

"Zeppelin? Zeppelin, hey wake up buddy."

Rich's voice pierced through the fog of the memory. That is when everything came flooding back to him. Bus crash. Flames. Laurel. He shot up off the couch on the bus.

"Laurel! We have to get to her! I need to get to her!" He tried to push past Rich, but another set of hands pulled him back down onto the couch.

Looking over he found Alec and Sam sitting beside him. Looking around, he saw Thomas at the front of the bus on his phone. He heard the familiar hum of the motor as they cruised down the highway. Looking at his bandmates he found them all in a stage of shock or sadness. Sam's eyes were red and puffy while Alec was unusually stoic and silent. Rich was the only one who seemed to be holding it together but even his eyes were shining with tears.

"How long was I out?"

"About twenty minutes. Thomas has been on the phone with the hospital trying to get some information on Laurel."

Zeppelin rubbed his throbbing head, "I… I should call her mom.

We need to fly her up here in case…" He let out a shaky breath.

Sam squeezed his hand, "Thomas called Leigh to tell her, and she was going to call Laurel's mom and meet her in St. Louis for a flight to Chicago."

Zeppelin nodded unable to bring himself to say anything.

"I'll be calling back in exactly thirty minutes for an update." Thomas placed his phone into his pocket and ran his hand through his hair.

"Tho-mas?" Zeppelin voice crack as he stood going to his friend, "Anything?"

"All they can tell me is she is in the burn unit with third degree burns partially down her left side. She was in critical condition and there would be more of an update once the doctor saw her."

Zeppelin pulled Thomas in a hug and felt his body shaking, "We can't lose her, Zepp."

He rubbed his back finally allowing his own tears to fall freely down his face, "We're not going to. She made it out of one fiery crash, and she'll make it out of this one."

Thomas stepped back, wiping his face with his hands, "You're right. Just another badass notch on her belt to show us up."

The laugh that escaped his lips felt wrong and yet, needed.

The next several hours were a blur for Zeppelin. They made it to Mount Sinai within an hour and were all waiting in the ICU waiting room. Thomas was in constant communication with Leigh and Tricia arranging for Jake to get them from the airport. Rich and Alec went to check on the driver, who had made it out of the crash with a broken leg and few broken ribs.

Sam was sitting beside him, staring down at her hands in her lap. Every once in while a soft sniffle would come from her. He reached over, squeezing her hands.

"She's going to be okay, right?"

He nodded, "Yes. She is one tough woman, and she will be up and out of this hospital in no time."

She smiled, "Damn right she is. I'm glad I got to meet her; she's truly becoming one of my best friends."

"Hey now, no stealing our best friend."

They looked up to see Thomas sitting on the other side of Zeppelin.

"Leigh and Tricia should be here in the next ten minutes. Once Tricia is here we should be able to get a full update from the doctor."

By the time Laurel's mom and agent arrived the rest of the Heartstrings crew were spread out between the ICU and emergency waiting rooms. Jake had organized for more security to be on hand to keep fans from entering the hospital. The doctor had come out to give an update to them and take Tricia back to see Laurel.

"Well, I have some good news. Upon a better examination we determined that Laurel had second degree burns and some superficial burns. Whomever was able to pull her out as quickly as they did save her from months of recovery."

Zeppelin pulled Jake underneath his arm, "This man deserves a cape."

Everyone chuckled as the doctor continued, "She has a difficult road ahead of her, but I think with three to four weeks of recovery and therapy then weekly check-ups she will have a full recovery."

"That's wonderful news, thank you." Her mom reached out, squeezing Zeppelin's hand, "When can we see her?"

"For now, I would like to keep it just to family. Once we move her from ICU to her own room then she can have more visitors."

Zeppelin's chest tightened as he dropped Tricia's hand. She grabbed ahold it once more and reached over for Thomas' hand as well.

"I would like to make sure that these two men are allowed to go in and see her as well. They are family rather they're blood or not." She looked at them with a soft smile.

The doctor nodded, "You can give their names to the nurse to add them onto her visitor list. I'll have to ask everyone else to leave though."

"Sure thing." Thomas said, turning around and talking to Jake.

Tricia linked her arm with his, "Come on, let's see our girl."

The doctor led them to Laurel's room. Tricia stepped inside while Zeppelin's body froze seeing her through the window. Her left arm was completely wrapped and there was a cast on her right leg. Her pink hair was a tangled mess and there were patches of road rash along her skin.

"She looks a lot worse than she is. Once we're able to clean her up then she won't look as direr." The doctor mentioned.

Zeppelin could only nod as the doctor stepped away to speak to a nurse. He stared through the window trying to keep the dam holding back his tears from falling. It was when he heard a deep, quiet gasp beside him that he couldn't hold back any more.

"I should have been on that bus with her. I should have been there to protect her. I failed her again, Thomas. I fucking failed her." Tears streamed down his face as he felt a strong hand gripping his shoulder.

"There was nothing you could have done. All that matters is that we're here for her now." They stood there for a few moments before Thomas cleared his throat, "I-I'm going to coordinated with our tour manager about getting some dates moved around and lodging for the crew."

Before Zeppelin could say anything Thomas was walking away. He looked back into the room and saw Tricia looking up at him. Swallowing the large lump in his throat, he walked inside the room hit with the overwhelming memory of seeing Laurel in the hospital after her car accident their junior year.

"You know Thomas doesn't deal well with things he can't control." Her mom said.

He pulled up a chair besides hers, "I know, but neither do I. Laurel is always the levelheaded one and makes sense of the crazy."

She laughed softly, "She's been like that her whole life. I think dealing with her dad had a lot to do with it."

They sat in silence except for the machines monitoring her. Every hour a nurse would come to check on her vitals and IV. Zeppelin held Laurel's right hand, looking over every inch of her. When Tricia went to grab something to eat and check in with Leigh, Zeppelin asked the nurse if he could brush out her hair. She nodded, leaving the room to grab him one.

He needed to do something and seeing clumps of mud and asphalt in her hair was a constant reminder of what she had endured. Once he had the brush, he carefully started removing all the debris from her head. It took half an hour to get her right side completely brushed and then he moved to her left side.

His eyes traveled up her bandaged arm. Her fingertips were bright red while the rest of her hand and arm were covered. Her neck was wrapped as well with an extra-large square bandage on the side. The side of her face was bright red with some kind of ointment on it. That's when he saw her hair and his stomach clenched tightly.

Her normally long hair was now at her shoulders and singed at the ends. Streaks of burnt strands covered the bright pink. Once more, tears started trailing down his cheeks as he gently and carefully ran the brush through her hair. Clumps of hair began to come out and he immediately stopped unable to keep the sob from erupting from his lips.

"Oh sweetie, come here."

He turned seeing Tricia again and went straight into her embrace letting his guilt and shame to flow freely onto her shoulder.

The next day, they were able to move Laurel into a private room. They had her in a medically induced coma in order to treat her burns. Zeppelin never once left her side even when Tricia and the nursing staff had told him to go get some rest. He couldn't bring himself to leave her even if all he did was watch her. He also didn't trust himself whenever he saw Thomas again.

He had not seen Thomas since Laurel was in the ICU and that had his blood boiling. How could he not visit at least once and check in on his best friend. The more Zeppelin thought about it, the angrier he was getting. He looked over at Sam who was sitting in Tricia's chair and reading a book to Laurel. All his bandmates had been in to check on Laurel. Jake had not left his chair outside of her room and looked equally if not worse than Zeppelin did.

"Zeppelin?" He looked up at the door where Rich was sticking his head in, "I have your bag so you can freshen up. Do you need anything else?"

He walked over grabbing his duffel from him, "Any chance you could grab my acoustic guitar…"

Rich pulled out his guitar from behind him, "Figured you might want it."

"Thank you." He stepped out of Laurel's room, "Hey, have you seen Thomas?"

Rich looked down at his feet, "Yeah, he's been locked away in his hotel room working with venues and managers to rearrange our dates."

Zeppelin clenched his jaw, but before he could say anything Rich continued, "He's a wreck, Zepp. He hasn't slept and I'm pretty sure he's been through a bottle of Jack on his own. He's processing in the only way he can, just like you."

"I know…" Zeppelin tried to push back the anger trying to slip out, "He should be here. If he truly cares for her like I think he does then it should be him here by her bedside. The fact that he's not says a whole hell of a lot about his feelings for her."

"Cut him some slack. We all deal with stress in different ways. As much as your feelings for Laurel drive you to be the way you are, you also need to remember that you're his friend too. Try being there for him as well and not only for her."

Rich patted his back then popped his head back into Laurel's room, "Hey Sam, come grab some lunch with me and Alec."

Zeppelin walked back in as Sam placed her book on the table next to her bed, "Don't read any of it to her. I want to find out what happens." She warned.

"I promise." He managed a small smile for her as she followed Rich down the hall to the elevators.

Zeppelin sat in his chair, bringing his guitar onto his lap. He began strumming the chords to Laurel's favorite song. He specifically learned how to play "Numb" by Linkin Park just for her. Whenever she had a bad day, he would play it for her, and it never failed to bring a smile to her face. Now he would give anything to see that smile.

The sound of a muffled voice had Zeppelin's eyes snapping opening. He must have dosed off in his chair and he looked over to see Thomas sitting in the other chair. His head was down on the mattress as he spoke softly. Zeppelin set his guitar down beside him and cleared his throat. Thomas looked up with tears falling down his cheeks.

"Where have you been?" Zeppelin asked, trying to hold back the fury raging in his chest.

Thomas wiped his face, "I've been working with all the venues to arrange our next month worth of dates moved to the back end of the tour."

"That was more important than being here and checking in on your friend?"

"What? Of course not, but there was nothing I could do here. Unlike you, I can't just sit here and be brooding. There was shit to take care of and that's what I did. It's what I've always done for you, so you're welcome." Thomas snapped back, getting up from his chair.

Zeppelin blocked his path to the door, "Don't run away. If you truly care for her then you'll sit your ass back down and be here for her."

"I'm not running away, and you know for damn well that I care for her. She knows I care for her even if I don't sit here all day and night." Thomas shoved him, "Get out of my way, Zeppelin."

"I'm going to tell you the same thing I told her dad when he came to visit her in the hospital." Zeppelin pushed his finger into Thomas' chest, "I'm here for her because I love her. I have always loved her and will always love her. She comes first, no matter what. Nothing matters more than her."

"I'm doing all of this for her!" Thomas smacked his hand away, leaning in closely, "You're not the only one that loves her, Foster. Remember that."

He shoved past him, storming out of the door. Zeppelin's fists were clenched at his side as he tried to keep himself from running after Thomas and beating the crap out of him. However, with one simple groan from behind him, all of his rage cooled. He turned to see Laurel's lips parted and face scrunched painfully.

"Laurel?"

Laurel

Laurel stuck her pencil down into her cast for the millionth time trying to get the impossible itch on her calf. She growled in frustration hearing the pencil crack. Carefully she pulled the broken wood without losing a piece of it with one sliver still connecting the two pieces.

"What did I tell you about sticking things down there?"

She rolled her eyes at Zeppelin, "If I don't get rid of this itch soon then I'm going to cut this damn thing off myself."

He chuckled, bringing in a couple bags of takeout. Setting them on the couch beside her, Zeppelin grabbed the long wire hanger he had one of the crew guys straighten out for her. She slipped it along her calf and sighed in relief as the itch was scratched once and for all.

"My hero."

"Anything I can do to help the sick and lame." He ducked as she threw the hanger at him, "Hey! Is that any way to treat your hero?"

Laurel crossed her arms over her chest, "I take back every good thing I've ever said about you these last few weeks. It's not my fault I'm broken." She pouted.

He leaned over the back of the couch, hugging her from behind, "Fangirl, you know I love ya broken or not."

She leaned back then kissed his cheek, "Yeah I know. Okay, let's get movie night started before I begin the pity party. Did you text Thomas?"

Laurel felt his arms stiffen before he let go of her and made his way around to the other side of the couch.

"Uh… I forgot… oops." He shrugged flopping down next to her.

"You forgot your best friend?" She arched an eyebrow at him, "Zeppelin…"

He shook his head, "Don't start. He's probably busy anyway. He's been dealing with all the venues and managers about our rescheduled dates. Knowing him, he has his phone glued to his ear, a whiskey in one hand and his laptop with a billion spreadsheets in front of him."

She knew it was more than Thomas being busy. There had been tension between the two of them since the beginning of the tour. Since she had arrived in Los Angeles that first night. Laurel sucked in a harsh breath suddenly feeling the crushing guilt on top of her chest. It was one more thing to add to the list of things she messed up.

The tour had come to a halt since the accident. Laurel had needed at least six weeks of recovery to make sure her bones were healing properly. The cast on her arm had come off last week and the burns on her other arm were nearly healed. She had a doctor's appointment in two days to see about getting her leg cast off.

She had begged Zeppelin to continue with the tour and she would go back home to recover. He wouldn't hear of it. She would never forget the argument he and Thomas got into in her hospital room. Security had shown up warning them both to get their shit together or they would be thrown out. Zeppelin had put his foot down that he would not continue the tour until she was one hundred percent.

For the last six weeks they had been staying at the Four Seasons in Downtown Chicago. She didn't even want to think about how much money this was costing Zeppelin to have her, Thomas, the band and whatever crew that didn't fly back home until the tour resumed staying there. Every time she asked, he would change the subject or dodge answering her.

"Hey space cadet," Zeppelin snapped his fingers in front of her, "Were you listening to me at all?"

"Do I ever?"

His jaw dropped dramatically, "I'm offended. After slaving over this immaculate dinner this is the respect I get?"

She laughed, "By slave over, you took the elevators down to the lobby and met the delivery guy then rode the elevator back up."

"I also had to dodge fans and a few paparazzi that got past the guard. I could have been trampled, kidnapped, hugged to death." He handed her a container with beef, broccoli and fried rice.

"Oh, the horror…" Setting her food on her lap she picked up her phone, "You get the movie set up and I'll text Thomas since you conveniently forgot."

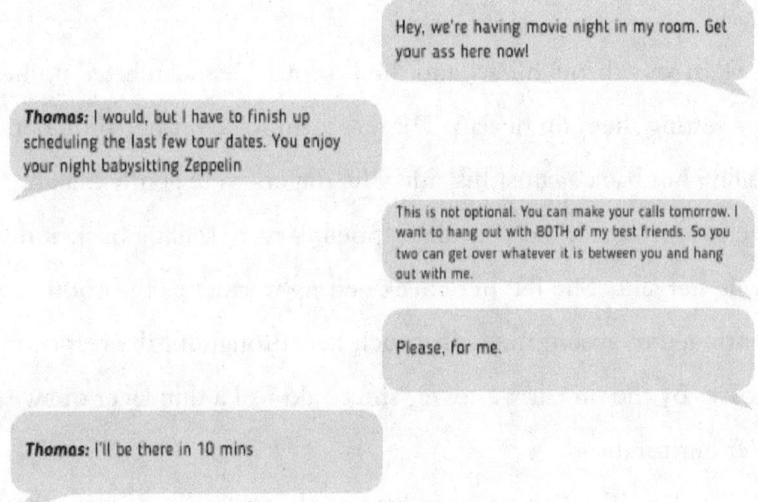

She smiled happily, "He'll be here in ten minutes."

Looking over at Zeppelin, she was surprised to see his bright eyes dark and hard looking at her. He shrugged starting the movie while taking a bite of his dinner. Sighing, she took a bite of her own food for it to sour in her mouth immediately. One thing she was sure of, she was the wedge driving their friendship apart and she hated it.

There was a knock on her hotel door about ten minutes into the movie. She paused it, looking at Zeppelin.

"Could you please let Thomas in?"

He rolled his eyes before slowly getting off the couch and heading to the door. There was no greeting, no hand slap or chest bump from them hugging. The door shut and her two best friends sat on either side of her on the couch. The tension rolling off of them tightening around her like a vice. Her stomach tightened and suddenly she found herself wishing the couch would swallow her whole.

Part way through Fast and the Furious, Zeppelin lifted up her legs setting them on his lap. Thomas' arm fell over her shoulders, pulling her back against his side. His fingers were gently making circles against her bicep while Zeppelin's were trailing back and forth along her shin. She felt her cheek getting warmer as they both continued to absentmindedly touch her throughout the rest of the movie. By the time it was over, she could feel a thin layer of sweat over her forehead.

"Alright, I'm going to say this and then you two can do whatever you want with it." She declared carefully moving her legs off of Zeppelin and back to their spot on the small table in front of the couch.

Both men sat up, concern filling their faces. She motioned to Thomas for her crutches and pushed herself up.

"You two are miserably hot and now I need a cold shower." They both chuckled as she walked towards the bedroom suite, "Will you two please figure your shit out and return my two best friends that I love."

Before either of them could say anything, Laurel made her way into the bedroom and shut the door behind her. She carefully peeled out of her comfy clothes and wrapped her cast with a trash bag to not get it wet. As soon as the lukewarm water hit her blistering skin her tense muscles relaxed. Thankfully there was a built-in seat in the shower and Laurel could easily clean herself after sitting beneath the stream for several minutes.

Sitting beneath the water, she ran her hands over her skin with her loofa. Brushing against her nipples sent ripples of pleasure down her body. Dropping the loofa, she cupped her breasts and ran her thumb over her nipples. Laurel closed her eyes, imagining Thomas's large hands covering her breasts. Kneading them and pinching her sensitive peaks. She slipped one hand down her slick body between legs. Immediately, Zeppelin popped into her mind. His long, thick fingers brushing against her clit and lazily rubbing circles against her.

The tension in her body was building as she imagined her two best friends touching, caressing, kissing every part of her body. She worked her fingers over herself wishing it was Zeppelin bringing her closer to the edge. Pressing her head back against the wall, arching her back as she pinched her nipple hard, picturing Thomas being the one doing it.

"Oh fuck…"

She moaned as waves of pleasure hit her riding out the much-needed orgasm. Laurel tried to get her breathing under control and finished up washing her body. Once she was out of the shower, looking at her flushed reflection in the mirror she let out a sigh.

"Get a hold of yourself Laurel."

With her favorite gym shorts, stolen from Zeppelin nearly twenty years prior when he came to visit her at college, and a tank top on, Laurel was ready to sit in bed to write. She ran a brush through her now collarbone length hair and clipped it back out of her face. She truly missed her long hair but if that was the only thing the fire took from her then she was overwhelmingly happy to live with it. Laurel walked out of the bathroom and yelped when she saw Zeppelin sitting on the bed.

"Holy crap Zepp! You scared the living daylights out me."

The famous mischievous Zeppelin smirk appeared on his face, "Anything to get your heart racing."

Laurel swallowed hard, "Well you may have out done yourself this time. My heart may burst out of my chest."

He stood from the bed, stepping directly in front of her. There were not many people who could make her feel small, but the six foot two, solid man before her did.

"Don't worry, I'll catch it if it does." Zeppelin stooped down and scooped her up into his arms bridal style.

"Zeppelin Foster! Put. Me. Down!"

He shook his head, his hair tickling her neck and cheek, "Not a chance, fangirl."

He placed her on the bed gently, making sure her leg was elevated and secure on the pillows at the foot of the bed. For six weeks,

Zeppelin had been sleeping on the couch in the living area of the suite. It wasn't like they had never shared a bed before, but he had insisted that she have the bed all to herself. However, tonight was the first night since the accident he climbed into bed next to her.

"Where's Thomas?" she asked, noticing his smile fade.

"We had a little chat, and he went back to his room." He answered, then his voice softened as he asked, "Could I sit here with you for a little while?"

"Of course. I'm going to try and work on my book. Is that okay?"

He nodded, "Absolutely, I'm going to work on some new song lyrics."

Laurel opened her new laptop since her previous one had been smashed beneath the bus. Thankfully, she was in the habit was saving everything on her cloud account including notes she would write in her notebook. She nearly cried seeing her destroyed notebook along with some of her favorite photos. Thomas had made sure she had a new MacBook Pro within days of the accident. Pulling up her manuscript, she read over the last few paragraphs she had written and then let the words flow through her fingertips.

She had finally reached the point in her story where her main characters were going to sleep together. She had debated on writing a sex scene or having it be a closed-door scene. She loved reading spicy, smutty romances but writing one herself was a totally different story. When she wrote Red Moon fanfiction, her smut would make her cringe sounding like a middle school boy describing sex. Even though she was told by nearly everyone who read her stories, including Raelyn, that her sex scenes were steamy and beautiful. Leaning back into the pillows, she groaned as she considered skipping to the next scene in the chapter.

"What's wrong?"

She glanced over to see Zeppelin still focusing on his notebook with the eraser of his pencil resting on his bottom lip. His eyes peeked over at her from the corner of them and he set the pencil down giving her his full attention.

"Are your characters taking the story into their own hands again?"

She chuckled, "Not yet, but the night is early."

A long time ago, Zeppelin and Laurel had decided that their friendship meant way more than fleeting teenage hormones. They also agreed to never discuss sex with one another as they never wanted to hear about the other's sex life. However, now her lack of one was directly affecting her progress to keep writing.

"Hey, what has your hamster running a wheel marathon?"

She took a deep breath before letting it all out.

"I'm to the point in my story where the main characters are getting ready to have sex."

His eyes brightened as he smiled, "Ah sexy fun times."

"Yes, and I have to decide to write all the gory details or have it be closed door for readers to use their imaginations."

"Does it make sense for you to not write it in detail?"

That was a valid question, "I think it would work either way. I know Leigh and my editors would tell me to write it out."

Zeppelin looked back down at his notebook, "Okay then, problem solved. Write the smut and please read it out loud for me to hear."

Laurel chewed on her bottom lip trying to decide if she was going change this conversation into confession hour or just swallow her doubts and skip the scene all together.

"Okay, by the adorable lip bite and worry wrinkles on her forehead. I take it the problem isn't solved. Out with it."

Confession hour, it was then.

"It's been a long time since…" she looked down unable to meet his gaze, "since, you know…"

"Since what? Since you've written smut?"

Laurel closed her laptop, "Just forget it."

She tried to put her laptop on the side table, but Zeppelin gripped her elbow gently. She wanted to do or be anywhere but where she was. One of the hottest rockstars in the world who could literally be with any woman he wanted was in bed next her. Her best friend who inspired her sexy main male character and she was too embarrassed to tell him that she was basically a virgin again.

"Oh no, wait a minute. We tell each other everything. You're obviously struggling with something, and I want to help."

"First, we don't tell each other everything. We agreed a certain topic was off limits the day after prom. Second, you can't help me with this." Her face was beyond burning hot and she wanted to crawl beneath the comforter to hide from him.

His finger slipped beneath her chin, bringing her eyes to his, "I promise to be the best friend you need me to be and hear whatever it is that is bothering you. Even if it concerns your sex life and with whomever is in it. I think as adults, we can handle it."

The sincerity in his eyes washed away the embarrassment flooding her body.

"I'm struggling to write about sex because it's been a long time since I've had any of any kind in my life."

His lips parted into a perfect O-shape, "Ohhh… I see."

Immediately her mind put the defenses back up to protect her heart, "Not everyone has people throwing themselves at them or able to charm their way in between whoever's legs they want. Sex for me has always been about intimacy first and pleasure second. I simply don't trust anyone to be intimate with them. Let alone being naked and sweaty with them."

Zeppelin's eyes darkened as his eyes traveled over her. They were piercing through the stone she had built around her and suddenly she felt vulnerable, exposed.

"First," His eyes darted back up to hers, "People throw themselves at Zeppelin Foster the rockstar and not Zeppelin Foster the anime nerd."

She laughed softly as he continued.

"Second, Zeppelin the rockstar can charm his way into bed with anyone." He picked up her hand, placing it over his heart, "This Zeppelin can't even find the balls to tell the one person he's madly in love with that she's everything to him."

Laurel's heart began pounding against her chest, "Zepp…"

"Third," He leaned in closer to her, his voice low and raspy, "If you think that I can't help you with this then you're sadly mistaken."

Zeppelin closed the distance between them as his lips firmly pressed against hers.

She pressed her hands against his chest, pushing him back, "Z-Zeppelin, we can't. You can't. I can't…"

The wicked smile that graced his lips made her thighs squeeze together. The filthy images playing out in her mind reminded her that he most definitely could, but her heart wouldn't be able to take it.

"Sweetheart, trust me, I most certainly can, and one hundred percent want too."

The last iron forged part of her will power made one last stand against him, "We agreed a long time ago that we were better as friends than more. Our friendship means more than fleeting hormones. You do remember that day at our spot?"

He finally sat back, and Laurel let out a shaky, but relieving breath. She could feel her body relaxing except for the ache growing in the lower part of her abdomen. She could deal with that later when Zeppelin went to sleep on the couch.

"Do you know how often I think about that conversation?"

His question took her by surprise, "Not really, no."

"At least two or three times a day it will pop into my mind. Sometimes, it's realizing we made the right decision because back then raging teenage hormones was definitely the driving force."

"Yes, we both were mature enough to see that then." She was curious where this was leading, "And the other times?"

He got off the bed, running his hand through his hair, "Most days, I think how incredibly dumb it was of me to let go of the chance to be with you."

"What? It wasn't dumb. You wouldn't be where you are now if we had dated then. I mean, eventually the relationship would have ended, and you would have still ended up a rockstar. You were meant to make music and perform for thousands of people. We both know, if we were together you would have stayed in Springfield for what little time we would have been together."

Many nights when she was alone in her house while him and Thomas were touring the world, she often wondered what if. What if they had still been together? What if they had been married or had kids? What if she toured with him all the time? She knew he was destined for greatness and that was simply not her.

"Do you honestly believe we wouldn't be together still?"

Laurel nodded, "I know for a fact we wouldn't be. You're a California ten while I'm a Missouri five at best. You were always meant for better, the best, and that's not me."

His jaw clenched as a low growl rumbled from him. He walked

around the bed to her side dragging the small ottoman with him. He pulled her legs over the edge of the bed, resting her hurt leg on the ottoman while kneeing between her legs. His glossy, dark eyes peered into hers while his hand slid up her thighs to her hips.

"Let's get one thing perfect, fucking clear. You. Are. Perfect."

She was going to argue with him, but he brought his index finger to her lips.

"Your time to talk is over. You're going to listen now. You're always saying I charm everyone around me, but so do you. Hell, you have both your best friends bewitched with your beauty and sass. You have us at each other's throats because we're both desperate to taste the forbidden fruit."

Goosebumps covered her skin as she tried to ignore the deepening ache in her belly, "You both are delusional."

"Damn it Laurel, what will it take for you to believe how amazing you are."

His hand traveled down her arm leaving a hot trail in its wake.

"How talented and smart you are."

Lifting her hand, his thumb made small circles against her palm. His other hand slipped beneath her chin, so her eyes were on his.

"How much I want you in every single possible way I can have you."

A gasp escaped her lips as he placed her hand over his hard length pressing against his jeans. He dragged her hand up to his chest.

"How much I love you. How I've been in love with you since the first moment I saw you at the bus stop in fifth grade. How the only regret I have in my forty years of life is agreeing to only being your friend, when I want to be your everything. How I still want to be your everything."

Tears were threatening to fall down her face, "Zeppelin, what if you get bored with me? You eventually will because I'm boring and I like being boring. My heart can't handle being a place holder for you to find the woman who is deserving of you and your wild heart."

He leaned down pressing his forehead to hers, "Oh fangirl, you're blind if you haven't seen what all those other women have been to me."

"Then tell me, what have they been other than another notch on your belt."

"Such a smart mouth." He smirked then his hands cupped her face, "They have all been faceless place holders for you. Place holders that could never fill the gaping hole in my chest that could only ever be filled by you. You are the only fangirl I want, my girl, if you'll finally set your wild heart free."

The last shred of her will power melted away as she opened the cage protecting her heart. Sealing her fate, she pressed her lips to his.

Zeppelin

Zeppelin woke up the next morning a new man. The woman he loved was in his arms after an evening of making out like teenagers. He couldn't believe after dreaming and fantasizing about this very moment that it was finally real. Laurel shifted beside him, and her hand slipped over his lacing their fingers together. All he could do was stare down at her and watch as her chest rose and fell evenly. Her cheeks were slightly flushed, and her lips parted as she took in a breath.

He leaned down, pressing his lips to her temple. He didn't want to wake her up quite yet, but he knew there were things he needed to do and a meeting with Thomas that he was not looking forward to. He tried slipping his arm out from beneath her pillow when he saw a pair of beautiful amber eyes looking up at him.

"Sorry, I was trying not to wake you."

A sleepy smile appeared on her face, "Trying to sneak out and do the walk of shame?"

He sat up, bracing himself with his arms on either side of her head. His long hair falling towards her as she laughed softly.

"No need to sneak out and no shame at all to be walked off. If anything, I want to shout from the rooftops what happened."

The sheer terror on her face made him laugh.

"Oh god… Zeppelin please don't."

He leaned down kissing the tip of her nose, "Eventually, he will find out. It's only a matter of time, especially if he gets the courage to ask you on second date and you tell him no."

Laurel pressed her palms against his chest, "I know, and I will tell him. I want to wait a little bit and keep this between us. Just until we know exactly what is happening here."

"You know my thoughts on this already." He rolled to his side of the bed, looking back at her as she pushed herself up, "However, if he asks I won't lie to him."

"Zepp…"

He stood from the bed not wanting to argue with her, "Laurel I won't go out of my way to tell him anything. I'm going to act like I normally do. Speaking of which, I have to get ready for some interviews with the band then a meeting with Thomas about the rest of the tour. After that, we're going to lock ourselves in this room and continue watching Fast and the Furious movies or making out. I'm good with both."

"Maybe we could actually watch more of the movie than we did last night."

He laughed, heading toward the bathroom, "Not likely fangirl."

It felt good to be with the band talking about the last leg of their tour and possible new music being released in the next year. More than once, Sam and Alec had asked him about why he was in such a good mood.

"Guys, I told you that the rest of being off the grind has done wonders for me."

Alec scoffed, "Yeah, seemingly overnight you have a whole new, positive, happy personality. If I didn't know better I would say your body has been taken over by aliens."

"Or he got laid." Sam called out from her spot in the interview chair.

Zeppelin glared at her, "Fuck you both."

Everyone started laughing.

"Ahh, there's the Zeppelin we know and love. Glad to have you back." Alec clapped him on the shoulder.

He shoved Alec away as he made his way over to the snack table. The interviews took a couple of hours to get through and by the time they all got back to the hotel it was time for his meeting with Thomas.

Zeppelin walked into the hotel restaurant; he saw Thomas first then was surprised to see Laurel sitting beside him. Her head was thrown back in laughter along with Thomas as he walked up to them.

"Hey guys, should I come back later?"

Laurel's cheeks went red as she looked up at him, "Hey, uh Thomas asked if I wanted to join you guys for lunch."

"I figured we could all come up with a good date to restart the tour since a lot of it will depend on Laurel's recovery." Thomas went from laughing to all business in seconds, "Let's order first then we can talk."

The waiter came over taking each of their orders. As Thomas gave his, Zeppelin slipped his hand over Laurel's thigh. She jumped slightly before narrowing her eyes on him. He gave her his famous smirk giving them a squeeze before she pushed his hand off of her. He stuck his lower lip out earning him an eye roll from her.

"Now, I know we can set a more definitely date after your appointment tomorrow." Thomas pulled out his tablet, "I was thinking we could start with our Labor Day show in Mountain View. That will give us plenty of time for travel, set up and rehearsals."

"That should be fine, I will need to double check with Leigh to see about my extension for my manuscript. There may be a day or two where I'll need to talk with my editors and get ready to focus on revisions. That is something I'll need to be back in my home office for. I'll need to focus and not be distracted by living out my punk rock fantasy life."

They all laughed, "I won't lie, it will be weird to not have you around. You should really think about moving to Los Angeles. I could always help you find an affordable place."

Something about the way Thomas was looking at her didn't sit well with Zeppelin. It stirred up something deep and dark within him that set him on edge.

"Affordable and L.A. don't go together. I'm happy living in Springfield for now." Laurel glanced over at him with a soft smile.

The jealous, protective beast that had awakened settled back into its dark hole. Thankfully, their lunch arrived a moment later. The rest of their lunch was filled with idle chit-chat and almost felt like their trio was back to normal.

Zeppelin paid for their lunches anxiously wanting to get back up to his and Laurel's room. The three of them rode in the elevator up to their floor and the tension from the night before was once again filling between him and Thomas. When the doors opened, Thomas' hand immediately went to the small of Laurel's back guiding her out. The beast was wide awake once more and growling as Zeppelin clenched his fists at his side.

"Zepp, could I talk to you for second?" Thomas asked.

"Sure." He looked at Laurel whose bottom lip had disappeared beneath her teeth, "You get the movie set up."

She nodded, heading to their room. Zeppelin followed Thomas down the hall towards his room.

"I know things between us are tense, but we can both agree that making sure Laurel is alright to come back on the road again is our top priority, right?"

Zeppelin nodded.

"Good, but I also wanted to make something perfectly clear." He rolled his shoulders, standing tall in front of him, "I'm going to ask Laurel on another date. Once the tour is over and her book is closed to being published. I'm going to ask her properly on a date and I'm hoping you will not stand in the way if this is meant to be."

He respected Thomas for telling him out right but also wanted to punch him in the face. Knowing that Laurel was his already, Zeppelin wasn't worried about Laurel choosing Thomas. He hated lying to his best friend and more so, he hated that he knew Thomas would get his heart broken. He wanted to tell him but knew it would cause more problems in the long run.

"Thank you for telling me up front. I respect that."

Thomas gave a short nod, turning to head to his room. However, Zeppelin couldn't let that be the last word.

"No matter what, Thomas, know that Laurel cares about you a lot. Rather things work out in your favor or not, don't lose what has always meant the most to her."

"What's that?"

"Your friendship. Have a good night, Thomas."

Before his friend could say anything or before Zeppelin could let the truth slip, he made his way down the hall towards his room. When he opened the door, he found Laurel leaning against the back of the couch waiting for him.

"You need to get your leg up." He motioned to her spot on the couch.

She shook her head, "What did he say? What did you say?"

He chuckled, "Sit and elevate your leg then I will tell you."

If looks could kill, Zeppelin would have met his maker. Laurel made her way around the couch and hastily put her foot up on the pillow resting on the table.

"Happy now?"

He nodded with a smile.

"Good, now tell me what happened."

He joined her on the couch, "He let me know his intentions with you and I let him know that I respected him for telling me the truth."

"And?"

"And what? That's all. We left it at that."

Was he leaving out a few minor details? Yes, but she didn't need to worry about that. This was something between him and Thomas.

"I don't believe you for a second. Now fill in the details."

He slipped his arm around her shoulders, pulling her into his side, "I could, but my counteroffer is this."

Zeppelin leaned down capturing her lips with his. Running his tongue along her full bottom lip before gently taking it between his teeth. A deep sigh came from her, and he knew his offer was accepted.

"You play dirty Zeppelin Foster."

He chuckled, "Oh fangirl, you have no idea. Now, let's get our Fast and Furious on and make out like teenagers."

Laurel smacked his chest before settling against him. No stage or number of groupies could ever give him the pure happiness he experienced at that moment.

The next morning, Zeppelin and Laurel were up early to get her ready for her doctor's appointment. He could tell by her leg bouncing that she was nervous, and he tried to calm her with a light squeeze to her thigh as they waited.

"Sorry." She mumbled looking down at her casted leg.

"Nothing to be sorry about." He brought her hand up to his lips, "Also, nothing to be nervous about. Everything is going to be fine."

She smiled, resting her head on his shoulder. When they called her name, Zeppelin watched as a nurse led her back through the doors to a room. She had insisted on her going alone and in the end, Zeppelin chose to pick his battles with her.

In the waiting room, his leg was now bouncing as he watched the seconds on the clock tick away agonizingly slow. Five minutes turned into fifteen. Fifteen turned in a half hour. When it hit forty-five minutes, Zeppelin couldn't take it anymore and began pacing along the row of chairs. When he looked at the clock again, it had been an hour, and he decided to go ask the nurse for an update.

Laurel was standing at the desk as he walked out of the waiting room. Her leg free of the plaster that had been protecting it for the last six weeks. He came up behind her, wrapping his arms around her waist properly and nothing in the world felt more right to him.

"You're whole again." He whispered into the side of her neck.

She giggled, "More or less. I will need to follow up with my primary doctor whenever I get back to Springfield and if I feel any tightness or have swelling then I need to see a doctor asap."

Zeppelin watched as she signed her last paper then turned to face him. She pressed herself up on her tiptoes and kissed his lips. Suddenly all the love songs in the universe made sense to him.

"It's nice to properly do that."

"So, I take it your cleared to travel…" He leaned in closer, wiggling his eyebrows, "and other physical pursuits."

He let out a low chuckle watching her face heat up.

"Travel yes. Other physical pursuits we'll just have to wait and see." She playfully pushed him away, "Now, can we please go celebrate with our friends."

They headed back to the hotel where everyone was waiting for them in the hotel restaurant. Thomas had rented out the private room in the back for them to have a night of fun before heading back on the road in the next couple of days. Zeppelin was hanging at the bar, watching Laurel mingle among the band and crew. He loved the fact that his music family had lovingly accepted her as one of them from the moment the tour started. Watching Laurel emerge from her introverted shell and allowing people to see her as she was, brought a genuine smile to his face.

"She's truly apart of the family now."

Thomas stepped up beside him, signaling for two more whiskeys for them.

"Yeah, she is. I'm happy she came out on tour with us. I think it really helped her to get out of her little bubble.”

His friend handed him a drink, “Cheers to that.”

They clinked glasses, letting the murmur of the room fill the silence between them. Zeppelin looked at Thomas as his eyes tracked Laurel’s every move. The emotions filling his best friend’s eyes weighed heavily on his own chest. He hated keeping the truth from him and his lips parted to set the truth free.

“There they are! My two favorite boys!” Laurel tipsily called out.

Him and Thomas looked at one another before laughing,

“Laurel, I think you’ve had enough for the evening.” Thomas took her glass filled with a Long Island iced tea, “Maybe I should get you back up to your room.”

The possessive beast within him sprang into action, “I got her. You get the rest of the hooligans to their rooms.”

Zeppelin slipped his arm around Laurel’s back, making sure his grip on her was tight. Thomas’s eyes narrowed in on him before giving a short nod.

“Okay. Goodnight then.”

“Night, night.” She blew him a kiss as Zeppelin led her to the elevators.

Laurel was a mess of giggles as they made their way down the hallway. Zeppelin was barely able to hold on to her and swipe his key card to get them inside the room. Laurel walked in on her own as Zeppelin secured the door. Turning around, he stopped in his tracks at the sight before him.

Her t-shirt was tossed over her head as she tried to push her pants down her legs. His mind kicked his ass in motion to catch her before she fell.

"Stupid pants are trying to kill me." She giggled.

"Come on slush, let's get you into bed then you can fight with your pants."

Zeppelin scooped her up fighting every urge in his body to have his way with her. Laying her on the bed, Laurel kept her hands clasped around his neck.

"My knight in shining armor." She pressed her lips against the side of his neck, "Saving me from my evil pants."

A shiver ran down his spine as her lips continued up along his jaw. His cock pressed uncomfortably against his pants pulling himself away from her.

"A-Anything to save a damsel in distress." He hooked his fingers around the waistband of her jeans and pulled them down her toned legs, "Now, get under the blanket like a good girl."

"Hmm, I like it when you call me a good girl…" She pulled the comforter over legs, "I should definitely use that in my book when my MCs have smexy times."

Zeppelin tried to contain his laughter as he pulled one of his band shirts out of his suitcase, "I'll remind you of that tomorrow. Here you can wear this."

The corner of her bottom lip disappeared beneath her teeth as she looked at the shirt in his hand. Her eyes were darkening as they connected with his, making his knees weak.

"I don't need to wear anything… remember? We're a couple now… smexy times are a must for couples, right? You don't need clothes for smexy times."

Zeppelin tossed the shirt to the end of the bed before leaning over her caging her in with his arms. His body filled with a raging desire to taste every part of her. To be able to hear her whimper, begging for him to pleasure her in every way he knew how. To touch her soft, porcelain skin with his fingertips. The thought was almost too much for him as he reigned in his impulsive lust.

Laurel deserved to be worshiped for the goddess she was. She deserved his undivided attention, his time, his everything. He didn't want to just fuck her, but to make her feel the overwhelming love bursting at the seams of his heart. For the first time in his adult life, he wanted to take things slow and make love because only she was worthy of that.

"You're right, we don't need clothes for smexy times," He chuckled, pressing his forehead against hers, "However, this between us is more than just sex. I want it to be more than just sex. I want you fully aware and present when I make love to you."

He closed his eyes praying to whatever higher being was listening that the beautiful woman beneath him would understand his true intentions through her Long Island fog. He felt her sigh then her gently hands were on either side of his face. When he opened his eyes, he knew that the universe heard his silent plead.

"You truly are the hero in my love story." She pulled his lips to hers for a slow, sensual kiss that seared her name onto his soul forever, "Could we still cuddle?"

Zeppelin smiled against her lips, "Absolutely."

He stripped out of his shirt and jeans, crawling into bed next to her. For the first time, he could properly hold her in his arms bringing one leg over his waist and held her hand within his on his chest. Within minutes, he felt her breathing even out and her body relaxed against his. Not long after, he drifted off into the best night of sleep in his life.

***

Zeppelin could feel Laurel's lips trailing down his chest and stomach. The morning sunlight making a shining halo at the crown of her head. A halo that was held up by the horns of the dark temptress taking control of his body. He was bare and ready for her to take what she wanted, what she needed from him, and he was more than willing to submit to her. Her burning dark eyes looked up at him as her lips curled into a wicked smile.

***

"Zeppelin… oh Zeppelin, wake up handsome."

Her sweet, soft voice was followed by a gently shake of his body forcing him to peek open his eyes. The room was dark except for the glow of the alarm clock on the side table. He had been dreaming, and the reality of Laurel being drunk and sleeping next to him came flooding back.

"Hey handsome," He looked over to see Laurel propped up on

her elbow looking down at him, "You must have been having a good dream from all the happy noises you were making."

A hot wave of embarrassment crashed into him as he tried to play it off, "Must have been all your talk about smexy times between your characters."

She groaned, "Remind me that Long Islands are not my friend."

"Will do." He chuckled, sitting up beside her, "What time is it?"

"A little past three in the morning. You being a human furnace woke me up, the happy noises were the encore."

He ran his hands down his face, "Well it is all your fault. I was having a lovely dream about you."

Zeppelin didn't need to see Laurel's face in order to feel the waves of insecurities rolling off of her. He missed the drunken confidence from her earlier.

"Laurel, what are you thinking? I can practically hear your hamster wheel spinning wildly out of control."

She sat up beside him, lacing her fingers with his. He noticed that she was wearing his T-shirt from earlier and a pair of his boxers as she crossed her legs in front of her. Zeppelin decided that was now his favorite outfit for her to wear and wanted to see her in nothing else.

"I was thinking about what you said earlier when I came on to you."

"Which part? The not needing clothes for smexy times?" He chuckled, earning him a gently smack.

"No, you idiot. That you want it to be more than just sex." Her voice more timid than normal, "I was just wondering if that is because you think I'm too inexperience in that area to be more of the latter."

Of all the things she could have said, Zeppelin would have never guessed that. Her inexperience was not even a thought or concern. He could care less about it. Zeppelin reached over, lifting her leg over him and settling her on his lap. His hands rested on her round hips as her hands gripped his shoulders.

"Your previous experience or lack of is not even a thought in my mind." He slipped his arms around her, locking his hands at her lower back, "I said that because I wanted you to know that this between us means more to me than my past experiences. Just like at prom eons ago, I don't want our first time to be only about sex. I want it to be about love, how much I love you and how much I want to love you."

There was still doubt swimming in her eyes. He dropped his hands beneath her ass and lifted her closer to him. A small, breathless gasp escaped her lips feeling the full effect she had on him.

"Laurel, I'm in this for the long run. You have always been the one for me and I was just waiting until I was the man worthy to love you fully. I want to take things slow and do them right because that is what you deserve."

He ran his hand up her back threading his fingers through her soft hair. Bringing her lips to his and whispering against them.

"However, that doesn't mean that I won't fuck you for hours until you're crying out my name." She let out a shaky breath, "Only means, I want to show you I love you first then we can get to the latter. Is that okay?"

She nodded as he gently kissed her lips. His will power fading fast she moaned softly pushing her hands into his hair. Then she tugged his head back and an electric current of pleasure shot down his body.

"First, you are more than worthy to love me. You have proven that time and time again, especially right now by saying you want to take things slow."

She began massaging his scalp bringing a low groan from his chest.

"Taking it slow is fine with me, however…" She pressed her forehead against his, "If there is one thing, I've learned from my wildly impulsive best friend is that sometimes you need to take a leap off the edge and dive headfirst into oblivion."

"Laurel…" He moaned as her hips slowly rolled against him, "Here I am trying to be a gentleman…"

She kissed him, "I don't need a gentleman right now. I need for the man I'm in love with to fuck me into oblivion."

Laurel

May 2002 – 12th Grade

"It's a rite of passage…"

Laurel stared up at her mom's reflection in their bathroom mirror, "Really? That's all you've got?"

They laughed, "Sorry sweetie, I forgot to get my copy of Convincing My Teenage Daughter to Go to Prom at the library."

She couldn't help the smile spreading across her face. Her mom continued to curl her long hair into perfect ribbons. There was a knock on the front door and her mom sighed.

"Finally, the reinforcements are here."

"Wait… what? Who's here?" Laurel called out before hearing Kim Foster, Zeppelin's mom, greeting her mom, "Mom? What are you doing here?"

Kim laughed, "Tricia called saying you were being as difficult as

Zeppelin is about going to prom. I decided I would come over for a full-on girls' afternoon while Steven hung out with Zeppelin in the studio."

"I would rather be with them than getting tortured with make-up and hairspray." She muttered earning her a smack on the should from her mom.

"Stop your complaining. Prom is important and I've never pushed you to go to any other dance."

Laurel sat back in her chair staring at her reflection then looking up to her mom, "I will keep my complaining to a minimum. Continue with your torture session."

If she were being honest with them, Laurel was excited about going to prom. Weeks ago, Zeppelin and Thomas had made a big production out of asking her to go with them after the spring play. They had waited for her to come out of the gymnasium entrance playing Zeppelin's recently recorded first song, Fangirl, My Girl and standing in the back of Thomas pick-up truck. Each of them was holding a poster board that said, *"Be our date? Be our date? We'll dance and eat some cake. It's been four years leading up to prom for goodness sakes. Please, be our date?"* How could she say no to the two guys she loved the most.

"Alright, Kim is going to do your make-up while I go make sure your dress is wrinkle free." Her mom hurried out of the room while Kim turned her chair around to face her.

"You're making your mom very happy by going, you know that

right?”

She nodded, “To be honest, I’m excited and nervous about going tonight.”

Kim began applying some foundation and powder to her face, “Why is that? I figured you would be fine since it’s only Zeppelin.”

Normally, she would have been, but since her accident last year something had shifted between them. Something more than their friendship and she didn’t know how to deal with it. She had always had some kind of feelings for Zeppelin, but now they were amplified by raging hormones. He was no help since her accident he was constantly holding her hand, hugging her, cuddling with her and even kissing the top of her head or temple. She wanted more, craved more but didn’t want to ruin their friendship.

“Laurel? Is everything okay between you and Zeppelin?” Kim asked concerned.

She smiled, “Yeah… of course they are. He’s been a little more protective of me since the accident. I think that’s why he and Thomas asked me to prom, so no one else would. Not that I even wanted to be asked prom or even go.”

Kim laughed as she began applying eyeshadow, “I didn’t want to go to my prom either. The only reason why I did was because Steven’s band was playing and I wanted to be a supportive girlfriend.”

“Really?”

She nodded, “I ended up having one of the best nights ever. I sang and danced with my friends then we all went out to an old abandon mansion to continue partying into the wee hours of the morning."

Laurel smiled as Kim put the finishing touches on her face before turning her around to look for herself. Her mouth dropped open not recognizing herself. Her normally pale skin now shimmered making it look almost translucent. The contrast of her pale skin was the deep green eyeshadow and dramatic eyeliner that made her eyes pop out even with her glasses on. The finishing touch was bright pink lipstick with a purple shimmer gloss over it.

"Holy crap… I…" Laurel was speechless and turned around to hug Kim, "Thank you."

"You're welcome honey. You look beautiful and with your dress I think Zeppelin will have his hands full keeping all the other guys away from you."

She chuckled, "I don't think he'll have to worry about that."

Her mom walked in stopping in the doorway when she saw her, "Oh Kim, you made my little girl look like a woman." She sniffled.

Kim threw her arm around her mom's shoulders, "Hate to tell you this, but she was already there. Now, let's get her into the dress so I can give her the present Zepp got for her."

"What present?"

An hour later, everyone was waiting for her to come down the stairs to see her all put together. Standing at the top of the stairs, she could hear their moms gushing over Zeppelin and his dad laughing.

"Stop it mom…" She heard Zeppelin say and took that as her cue to save him.

Everyone went silent as she walked down the stairs. Her dress was a satin, strapless, sweetheart A-line in a dark forest green. There was a black belt that tied into a bow on the back and a knee length slip that showed off the gift Zeppelin had gotten her. Once she was off the stairs, Laurel looked up at everyone to see smiles and tears. Their moms were of course smiling through the tears while Steven, Zeppelin's dad, snapped pictures of them.

Finally, her eyes landed on Zeppelin and all the air from her lungs vanished. He was wearing a black-on-black tux. His long golden-brown hair was tucked behind his ears except for the one piece that was always slipping in front of his eyes. His tux fit him perfectly, showing off the muscles he had gained from playing baseball. He was holding two stems of pink and red tulips, her favorite flower. He was painfully beautiful to stare at and suddenly she felt inadequate.

She was brought out of her trance when his dad cleared his throat, elbowing his son, "Say something…"

She watched as Zeppelin's eyes traveled from her feet to her eyes then a breathtaking smile spread across his face, "You look stunning, fangirl."

He handed her the flowers then slipped his hand around to the small of her back stopping when he reached her hip.

"You, uh, don't clean up so bad yourself, Zepp."

"Alright, let's get some pictures and then you two can be off. Are you stopping by to see Thomas before you head to school?" Kim asked.

Zeppelin nodded, pressing her even closer to him, "Sure are. It sucks he can't go."

"Hey mom, you think you could follow us and take some pictures of the three of us?" Laurel asked as her mom nodded.

As soon as they were done with pictures, Zeppelin led her out to his Jeep Wrangler that was decorated with streamers and balloons making Laurel laugh.

"What the hell happened to your baby?"

"I don't even want to get into it. My dad insisted I do this…" He opened her door and helped her get in, "By the way, I meant it when I said you look stunning. You're gorgeous."

Laurel felt her face heat up, "Thanks Zepp, you already know you look good, so I don't need to tell you." She chuckled.

"True but hearing it from a beautiful woman is always welcomed." He closed her door and made his way to the driver's side.

Thomas was sitting outside on his porch when Zeppelin pulled into his driveway. Thomas ran down to her side and opened the door.

"Wow… Laurel… just wow." He helped her down then twirled her around, "You're beautiful."

"Thanks Thomas and look no heels to worry about me falling over." She stuck out her foot covered by the black Converse

Zeppelin had given her.

He started laughing as Zeppelin joined them, "Good call man."

"Yeah, no more hospitals trips for Evel Knievel here."

"Where's the twins?" Laurel asked, looking around for Thomas' younger cousins.

He groaned, "They're eating dinner and watching TV inside. I needed a moment away from them before I killed them."

Laurel could see the sadness in her friend's eyes and hugged him around his waist, "I'm sorry you can't come tonight. Honestly, if I thought you could fit in my dress, I would send you with Zeppelin and I could stay with the twins."

"Ah hell no, fangirl. There is no getting out this." Zeppelin said, slipping his arm around her back once again.

Thomas laughed, "Zepp's right, plus that dress is so not my color. I'm a summer not an autumn."

The three of them started laughing as Laurel and Zeppelin's moms walked up, "Alright you three, get together and act like you actually like one another."

They posted in several poses including Charlie's Angels where Thomas and Zeppelin were the angels. Thomas hugged Laurel tightly.

"Try to have fun, but not too much." He whispered, "And seriously, you look incredible."

She smiled up at him, "Thanks Thomas."

Finally, she and Zeppelin were headed to school and the

butterflies in her stomach suddenly woke up fluttering. The parking lot was full, and Laurel felt like she was going to throw up. When Zeppelin helped her out of his truck, she wobbled on her feet slightly.

"Everything okay?" His dark green eyes filled with concern.

She took a deep breath then nodded, "Yep. I'm good."

Once they were inside, Zeppelin coaxed her into getting their picture taken before finding their group of friends. The music was loud, and people were already spread out over the dance floor. Their group of friends were near the back of the gym and consisted of a lot of band, choir and theater members. It didn't take long for Zeppelin to become the center of attention as Laurel happily stuck by her closest theater friends dancing the night away. Before she knew it, they were announcing the last song of the night.

The beginning notes of a slow, country song began to play, and couples paired off spinning around the floor. Suddenly, someone grasped her elbow and twirled her around into a set of strong arms. Laurel giggled as Zeppelin baritone voice filled her ears. He was swaying them back and forth as he held her tightly against his body. She pressed her ear against his chest listening to his steady heartbeat and the rumble in his chest as he softly sang the song.

The lyrics told a story of two people realizing there was more between them, and the narrator of the song was telling his beloved that everything had changed. She shouldn't kiss him unless she meant it. As Zeppelin sang the chorus their eyes connected for a brief second before Laurel found herself pushing up on her tiptoes and kissing her best friend.

His lips were as soft as she had always imagined. When she began to step back, his hold on her tightened and his lips were on hers. The tip of his tongue brushed against her bottom lip and she instinctively parted them for him to deepen the kiss. She ran her hand up into the soft strands of his hair and he moaned against her lips.

"Laurel…" He whispered almost pleading, "We should…"

Reality of what had happened crashed down on her and she stepped out of his arms, "I-I'm sorry… I don't know what came over me."

The DJ ended the song and announced the end of the prom. Laurel stood staring at her feet as students filed out of the gym into the parking lot. Zeppelin tried to lift her chin, but she stepped away from him again. One of their other friends came up to them laughing with her date.

"Hey, you guys are coming to the party, right?"

She looked up to see Zeppelin nod, "Sure are. We'll see you there."

Laurel began walking towards the door with Zeppelin following behind her. She got into his Jeep before he was able to help her. She couldn't bear having him touch her again. Not when her heart felt like it was shattering into a million pieces. She made the first move, but he had made the last. Honestly, she couldn't even blame him for not wanting her. He was popular even if he hung out with the not so popular groups. Girls threw themselves at him all the time and he definitely wasn't a virgin, unlike her.

Embarrassment flooded her face and sprung tears to her eyes as he got into the Jeep, "Laurel? Laurel look at me, please."

She shook her head looking out the window, "I'm fine Zepp. You can drop me off at home then go to the after party. I'll just be in the way."

He was about to say something, but a teacher motioned for him to get in the line of cars exiting the school. It wasn't until they had left the parking lot that Laurel realized they were going in the opposite direction of her house.

"Zepp, my house is the other way."

"I know." He said flatly.

She sighed, "Are you going to turn around?"

He shook his head, "Nope."

"Zeppelin, I don't want to go to a party. I don't go to parties. I'll just be uncomfortable and end up alone having to find my own way home."

It wouldn't have been the first time she walked home alone after being left behind at parties. Zeppelin and Thomas were inseparable at parties held by their baseball team. After the second time of her walking home, she told them both that she didn't want to go again.

Zeppelin pulled off into an empty parking lot, turning his truck off, "What the hell just happened? We were having a great time at prom and now I feel like I fucked something up."

Laurel closed her eyes, "You didn't do anything. I had an amazing time at prom."

"Okay, then what? Why all of a sudden do you want to be as far away from me as possible? I mean you kissed me and then you can't even look at me."

"I…I shouldn't have kissed you. I'm sorry. I know you don't see me in that way."

Zeppelin cut her off, "Um yes, I do. What makes you think that?

Her eyes snapped over to his, "What? But you were getting ready to tell me we shouldn't be kissing. Right?"

"I was going to say we should stop before I get in trouble for doing something in front of god and everyone. Laurel, the last thing I wanted to do was break the moment, but if we didn't then I would have taken it even further and that is something we can't do at school." He chuckled.

"Don't mess with me, Zeppelin Foster. I'm already an emotional basket case and embarrassed myself by kissing my best friend. Do not joke with me."

Zeppelin got out of his truck and went to her side, opening the door. There had been a million of times she sat on that very seat hugging him as he stood in front of her. This time she wasn't prepared for what he was going to do.

His hands slipped up beneath her dress grasping her calves and locking her legs around his waist. She yelled out his name just moments before his lips crashed against hers. His hands gripping her hips pressing himself fully against her. A small gasp escaped her lips as their lips parted.

"Zep-Zeppelin…"

"I have wanted you for the last year. I've never wanted someone as much as I want you. I was hoping to ask you out properly after prom, maybe… just maybe be a lucky son of a bitch and get to call you mine."

He lifted her hips as he rolled his against her making a soft moan push out from her lips, "Lucky to call you mine in every way I possibly can."

His lips lowered down to her neck as he continued to slowly grind against her building a glorious pressure in depths of her stomach, "Fuck Laurel, when I saw you tonight I couldn't breathe, I couldn't think, all I knew was that I wanted you so fucking bad."

The pressure was building greater as his pace quickened and she tightened her legs around him, "Oh god… Zepp…"

He growled against her neck, "Fuck I need you… I didn't want it to be like this, here but I need you now."

Laurel's body began to tremble as Zeppelin guided her over his hard length. She had made herself come, in the privacy of her own room, but this was different. Everything around her was heightened and all she knew was that she needed the dam to break.

"Zepp… please… more, oh god I need more." She moaned like she had fantasied about time and time again in her dreams.

He lifted her off the seat pressing her back against the side of his

Jeep. He thrusted against her hard and steady. Even through their clothes she could feel they were both close to falling over the edge. She wrapped her arms around his neck and laced her fingers through his hair.

"Fuck Laurel, I'm gonna come… come with me. F-Fuck, come now." He cried into her shoulder.

Feeling his body shaking beneath hers was all she needed for the waves of pleasure to overwhelm every sense she had. She cried out his name, not caring who could hear her and held on as they both rode out their own pleasure.

Zeppelin was breathing hard against her shoulder, "Damn it, that is not how this night was supposed to go." He chuckled.

"H-How did you want it to go?" She whispered.

He looked at her with a flush faced and eyes shining with post orgasmic bliss, "For one, we were supposed to have some liquid courage in us then be in our hotel room and naked. I mean we could still do all of that… if you want to."

There was nervousness laced between his words. Honestly there was nothing she wanted more than Zeppelin Foster naked and on top of her… inside of her. She unhooked her legs from his waist as he gently set her feet on the ground. Immediately, she wrapped her arms around him hugging him tight.

"Hugs are good. This is good. Naked hugs in bed are better."

She laughed before looking up at him, "You know I love you, right?"

"Oh, I don't like where this is going…"

"We are graduating in a few days then we have a couple of months before you move out to L.A. with Thomas and I go off to college. The chances of us keeping a long-distance relationship going at our age is not good. Especially if you become a rockstar god."

He chuckled, running his hand through his hair, "But if we're just friends then our friendship could last forever."

She nodded, "I would rather have you in my life forever as a friend than for a short time as a sexy rockstar boyfriend."

"You think I'm sexy?" She smacked his arm as he laughed, "I know you're right, but Laurel I don't know if I can go back to just being friends."

She bit her bottom lip, looking up at him, "Well sometimes friends come with certain benefits. Maybe we have one of those friendships that is closer than others." She ran her fingertips along his belt slipping it out of the buckle.

"Hmm… you know, I like the way you think. This is why you're the brains." He groaned as her hand slipped over the front of pants then he snatched her hand up placing his lips on her palm.

"This is going to be a hard line to balance, and I don't want to hurt you."

The seriousness in his tone was endearing, "I promise to let you know when it's too much for me. As long as you do the same."

He hooked his pinky with hers, "Promise and we should definitely not tell Thomas about any of this."

Laurel nodded in agreement, "Promise. Now, are we actually going to that party?"

"Hell no! We are going to the hotel room I reserved for us to chill, make out and whatever else the night may bring." He lifted her back into his Jeep.

"Sounds perfect to me."

Laurel

Had she really just said that? By the wild, dark eyes looking up at her, she had, and he was going too.

"Are you sure?" He whispered.

Not trusting her voice, she nodded.

"I need to hear you say it, Laurel. Are you sure?"

She swallowed the bundle of nerves lodged in her throat. His hands gripped the shirt of his she was wearing as if at any moment he would rip it from her body.

"Y-Yes, I'm sure."

"Good girl." Zeppelin flipped her over onto her back, resting his weight between her legs.

His lips came crashing to hers sucking the breath from her lungs. Suddenly, it seemed like Zeppelin was dominating her every sense. The last lingering smoky scent of his cologne filled her nose. His hands sliding up into her shirt leaving a scorching trail along her skin. The remnants of whiskey he had on his tongue now were on hers. The deep moan rumbling from his chest as she gripped his hair. Finally, there were his eyes as he pushed himself up, hovering over her.

Dark, filled with desire and locked onto hers. The passion in them made her core clench around nothing and desperate to feel him inside her. His thumb brushed against her ribs before following the curve of her breast. Laurel shivered as he pushed her shirt over her breasts the cool air pebbling her nipples immediately. Zeppelin's tongue darted out over his lips like his favorite meal was sitting in front of him. Even with his hungry eyes trailing down her body as he set up on his knees, a flood of insecurities washed over her as she looked up at the rock god before her.

His perfectly sculpted body was the complete opposite of her pudgy, round form. Seeing him now was a cold splash of reality for her.

"Zeppelin, are you sure you want this?"

Her words were barely above a whisper as he stared down at her. His eyes softening as he leaned over her again. His large hand slipped behind her to the small of her back, pressing against her firm to hold her place. She gasped as he slowly rolled his hips against her, sending a hot current of pleasure throughout her body.

"Fangirl, there is nothing I've wanted more in my life." He kissed below her ear before repeating the same, slow movement against her,

"I've been dreaming, fantasizing, wishing for this very moment since prom."

"Z-Zeppe-lin…" She moaned as his lips continued down her neck, sucking gently on the curve of her shoulder.

He paused long enough to pull his shirt off of her, leaving her bare except for her underwear. Once more, the shame of him seeing her ugliness push her arms to cover herself. The rush of tears to her eyes had her turning her head away. She was ruining everything she had ever dreamed of, and it was nearly too much for Laurel to take.

Zeppelin slipped his legs beneath hers on either side and pulled her up to straddle his lap. His hard length resting perfectly against her to make them both groan. He wrapped her arms around his neck and held her in place by locking his hands behind her back.

"Talk to me, Laurel. What happened to the confident, sassy woman that told me to fuck her into oblivion?"

She shook her head, "It…I…" she stammered, her words coming to her mind faster than her mouth could process.

That's when she felt it.

Her chest tightened as an invisible rope constricted around her. Her lungs crushing close, unable to take in the air she desperately needed.

No, no, no. Fuck… fuck, make it stop…

She was trying to say except nothing, but gasps of air were wheezing out of her.

"Whoa… Laurel, calm down for me sweetheart." He held her

closer, taking in his own deep breath, "Now, breath with me. Breath in and count to five."

She tried making it to three before the air rushed out of her.

"That's okay, try again. Breath in and count to five." She did it this time, "Now, breath out slowly for five."

She did it again. He repeated this for three times, and she felt her chest relaxing. Laurel could feel his hand rubbing slow circles down her spine, relaxing her further.

"Good girl." He whispered, burying his face into the crook of her neck, "That's my good girl."

A soft giggle escaped her lips, "You really love saying that to me."

"Only because I know you love hearing it." He sat back to look at her, "Are you alright?"

Her heart skipped as she nodded. There was no judgment or annoyance in his eyes. She had ruined what could have been the best night of her life and Zeppelin was only concerned for her.

"I love you."

His eyes widened then he smiled, "I love you too."

She pressed her lips to him and once more she was breathlessly falling back onto the bed with Zeppelin. He looked down at her arching an eyebrow at her.

"We don't have to do anything. I can see your mind wildly spinning out of control. There is no pressure to do anything. I've waited over two decades to be with you, and I'll keep waiting until you're ready."

Laurel ran her hands down his chest, loving that he trembled beneath her touch, "I'm sorry for freaking out…"

"Laurel Marie Adler, there is no reason to apologize. Everything that has happened and all this build up between us, I'm surprised I haven't freaked out a little."

"You only have enough blood to flow one way, and your upstairs brain is obviously deprived."

"Well, I've never…" He let out a mocking gasp then smiled, "You're probably right, but in my defense I have a beautiful, practically naked woman in front of me. I can only be an upstanding gentleman for so long before my dick does all thinking."

Laurel laughed, pulling Zeppelin down to her and kissing him.

"I panicked because you're a perfect rock god and I'm a flabby writer." She pressed her finger to his lips, "I know you don't think that's true, but it's what I believe. Years of being conditioned to think you're nothing but useless, worthless person is hard to push out of your mind. Even if I have a sexy rockstar telling me the exact opposite."

Zeppelin laid down beside her and pulled her close to him, "I hate it that you see yourself that way. I wish I could let you see what I see. To see the beautiful, talented and amazing woman I fell in love with in fifth grade."

Maybe it was because they were both nearly naked with their bodies pressed together, making the moment feel more intimated and vulnerable. She had never felt closer to him in the entirety of their friendship. She ran her fingers over his rough beard slipping her hand behind his neck. Zeppelin always made her feel bold and brave especially as she kissed him then whispered.

"Show me. I need you to show me."

There were no more words between them. His lips traveled down her neck once again, following the same path as earlier. Her hands were in their favorite spot threaded through the soft strands of his hair. Her back arched when ran the tip of his tongue over her nipple. His mouth covered it, flicking his tongue repeatedly over the sensitive nub as her body wiggled beneath him.

"Ze-Zepp… please…" She didn't know what she needed except she needed more of him.

He dragged his hand down body stopping at her panties, "If you want or need me to stop, tell me. Promise?"

She nodded, "Promise."

His fingers slipped past her panties between her slickness, "Fuck baby, you're so wet already."

Laurel dug her blunt nails into his shoulder, "All… your… fault, oh god…"

Zeppelin lazily rubbed circles against her, "I happily take the blame for this."

Laurel lifted her hips to get more pressure against her clit, "Please… more, need more."

His long, thick fingers slipped further down until pushing one slowly inside of her.

"Oh, fucking hell…" She breathed as Zeppelin chuckled.

He slowly worked his finger in and out of her then added a second finger. She flinched as pain shot through her for a split second.

"You okay?" He whispered against her neck.

"Y-Yes, please… keep going." The pressure in her belly was wonderful and she wanted more of it.

Zeppelin gently pulled his fingers from her then quickly pulled her panties down to her ankles. Laurel kicked them off not caring where they landed and spread her legs for him. He propped himself up on his elbow and ran his fingers over her again. She hadn't expected for him to bring his fingers to his mouth and taste her arousal.

"Oh, baby you taste divine. I'm so going to enjoy eating you out soon, but right now I need you to come for me."

His words nearly pushed her over the edge. He pushed two fingers back inside of her and this time all she felt was pleasure. His pace was steady building the delicious pressure in the pit of her stomach again. The sound of fingers sliding in and out of her only pushed her further to the edge.

"Fuck Laurel, you're squeezing my fingers so tight. I can't wait to have my cock inside of you. Now be a good girl and come for me."

Over the edge she went, crying out his name as waves of pleasure overwhelmed every fiber of her being. She rode out the high of her orgasm with his fingers still buried deep in her. He kissed her hard shifting his body between her legs.

"That was fucking beautiful to watch." He whispered.

She was still trying to get her breathing under control as he knelt in front of her. She watched him pull his boxers down his thighs before lifting knee to push them down the rest of the way. Laurel always knew her best friend was well endowed. She had heard the stories from several girlfriends of his in high school and the fans he slept with. She knew from seeing him in his boxers during sleepovers and even once she accidentally walked in on him masturbating.

However, nothing could compare to seeing him for herself. He was long and thick, Laurel found herself desperate to know how he tasted.

"If you keep looking at me like that I'm going to come before we even get started." He chuckled, holding himself in his hand.

His hand slid down his length as his thumb brushed across the wet tip of his cock.

"Fuck…" Was the only word that slipped past her lips.

Zeppelin reached over to the side table grabbing a small, foil package. With expertise quickness, he tore open the package with his teeth and pulled out the condom. Laurel was fascinated watching him slip it over his length.

"Again, if you want or need to stop or the pain is too much let me know."

The only noise she managed was a low moan as he rubbed the tip of his cock against her. Zeppelin held onto her thigh as he slowly pushed inside of her. Laurel's eyes shot open from the sharp pain bringing tears to her eyes that she tried to blink away.

"Breathe gorgeous, I'm almost there."

She didn't realize she was digging her nails into his forearms until she felt him trembling. Looking up, she found his forehead scrunched together and his eyes squeezed shut. His hips guided him in the rest of the way before she finally took a breath. She never felt so full, complete in her life as at that moment.

"You okay?" He breathed out.

Laurel hooked her feet behind his back, pulling him down to her and bringing him even deeper within him. She felt his moan within his chest before she heard it.

"Zeppelin?" She said quietly, "Show me what's it like to be truly loved."

His lips parted then pressed against her as he pulled out of her and slowly pushed back inside of her. The pleasure rippling over her was warm and comforting. His slow thrusts were building a whole new Laurel within her. A Laurel that was confident, bold, brave and most of all, believed she was worthy of love.

"You feel so good. Fuck, so tight and good." He grunted against her lips.

Laurel began meeting each of his thrusts, close to another orgasm, "Harder Zepp, I'm so close… oh god, I'm close."

The echoes of their skin hitting, and his small grunts filled her ears. His pace was quick and steady as he held her hips to keep her in place. Sweat was rolling down the side of his face and she could feel his legs quivering as his pace picked up.

"So close Laurel, I need you to come for me. Fuck, come for me now."

His thumb started rubbing against her clit and suddenly all Laurel could see was white spots. She could hear someone yelling Zeppelin's name in the distance that strangely sounded similar to her. Her body shook as wave after wave of pure bliss crashed over her. When she thought she was going to simply melt into a puddle of goo, she watched the most beautiful moment happen.

Zeppelin was hovering over her as he thrust harder and deeper inside of her. His teeth digging into his bottom lip before his jaw dropped open letting out a strangled cry. His body went rigid as he let loose another slew of curses shaking. He snapped his hips against her drawing out a long moan from deep in her belly and gripped her hips tightly as he rode out his own orgasm.

Then a beautiful, lazy grin spread across his face as he leaned over her, "Fuck me, I haven't come that hard since I was in my twenties."

His laughter filled the room as he caught her rolling her eyes at him. When he tried to pull out of her, Laurel tightened her legs around him.

"Not yet… feels too good."

She whined, but it was true. She didn't want to lose this feeling of being one hundred percent fulfilled and complete.

Zeppelin chuckled, "Baby, I promise there will be many, many, MANY more times we do this. In various locations and positions that will probably get us in some trouble."

Laurel relaxed her grip, "Nevermind, you can leave now." She smiled as he kissed her then pulled out of her completely.

She groaned unhappily, "Ugh, so empty now. Come back, I take back."

"You are literally going to be the death of me. We both need to clean up and sleep. Then I promise you, I will spend every night on the bus or in a hotels, balls deep in you." He stood up disposing of the condom then ducked as she threw a pillow at him.

Zeppelin held his hand out to her, helping her onto her two wobbly legs, "Now get that fine ass in the bathroom and clean up so we can get our after sex snuggle on." He smacked her ass making her yelp.

"You're intolerable." She called out over her shoulder before shutting the door.

Laurel and Zeppelin slept well into the early afternoon. After being woken up by Zeppelin between her legs, Laurel knew there was no way she could ever go back to her life in Springfield. Lucky for her, she could write anywhere as long as Zeppelin was by her side.

Zeppelin

October 1994 – 5th Grade

Zeppelin headed towards the front door twenty minutes earlier than normal. He quickly grabbed his Leggo waffle from his mom, waving goodbye.

"Hey, where are you going? You don't need to leave yet." She called out.

He paused, not wanting to make a big deal about meeting up with Laurel. He knew his mom would ask him a million questions about her.

"I'm going to work on my song at the bus stop."

She eyed him suspiciously, "Uh-huh. Don't forget we have your dad's gig tonight. I'll be waiting at the bus stop for you this afternoon."

"Okay mom, love you!"

Zeppelin rushed out of the house and headed to the clearing. He and Laurel discovered the little hideaway spot walking home on Wednesday. They had decided to meet there before the bus and walk together. As he approached the small pathway, he found Laurel looking in the opposite direction. When her head turned towards him her lips spread into a wide smile.

"I was starting to think you weren't coming."

"Not a chance." He bumped his shoulder into hers, "I wouldn't miss you listening to Led Zeppelin for the first time."

Zeppelin pulled out his portable CD player and his dad's CD with his favorite song on it. He handed her his player and headphones, hitting the track button to seven. Immediately, Laurel's head began to bop to the beat. The song ended by the time they got to their bus stop, and she went on to listen to the next song. When they arrived at school, she was hooked.

"Okay, I need more of this in my life."

Zeppelin's cheeks were hurting from the smile on his face, "I'll have my dad copy his CD."

Her smile faded, "I don't have a cd player at home."

"Well, I guess we'll need to get you one. Don't worry, you can borrow mine for now."

She shook her head, "No Zepp, I couldn't…"

"You can and you will. That's what friends do. They take care of one another." They walked into the building side by side.

Zeppelin couldn't wait for the day to end. The jerk squad had made both recesses miserable for Laurel and he almost got into a fight with Brendan after gym class for calling her Big Bertha. When they finally dismissed everyone for the buses, he grabbed Laurel's hand as they walked to the bus. He wanted nothing more than to hang out with her in the clearing, working on his song as she read her book.

"Do you think you could bring your favorite cd for me to listen to at my house tomorrow?" She glanced over at him as they sat in their normal seat.

He smiled, "Of course, though I have a lot of favorites."

"I'll listen to whatever you listen to."

Zeppelin watched her slip on his headphones, going to track seven and looking out the window. The wind from the window ahead of them blew her blond hair over her face as her head began to bop along to the beat. He found himself staring at her trying to remember every detail of her in that moment. As the bus turned down their street, he saw his mom's car waiting for him.

"Crap." He muttered.

"Everything okay?"

He nodded, "Yeah, I forgot about my dad's gig tonight. I'm sorry I won't be able to hang out."

Laurel shrugged, "It's fine. It will give me time to start learning the lyrics to your favorite song. Are you still going to come over tomorrow? My mom said if we hang out outside then she's fine with it."

"Yep, I'll be over around noon." The bus stopped and Zeppelin stepped out of the seat to let Laurel go in front of him, "I'll also bring over one of my favorite CDs, even though it will be nearly impossible for me to choose."

Laurel was laughing as they got off the bus and across the street. Zeppelin could feel his mom's eyes on them as they walked to the corner where she was parked.

"I'll see you tomorrow, Zepp. Have fun at your dad's gig." He watched as she covered her ears with his headphones and continued to walk down the sidewalk towards her house.

He turned to see his mom grinning at him, and his cheeks began to burn. He quickly got into the car and looked out the window. He didn't know why he didn't want to tell her about Laurel. They were just friends, his first friend since moving to Springfield. Every time he thought about telling her about Laurel his stomach would twist into knots and his mouth would become dry. Like now, his mom pulled out onto the main road and kept glancing over at him.

"Who were you talking to?"

"A girl from my class." He answered.

"Does she have a name?"

He could hear the glee in his mom's voice.

"Laurel. Laurel Adler."

She hummed, turning onto the highway. His dad was playing in a town called Branson for some kind of fall festival. Any time he got a chance to play, his dad always wanted him and his mom there. Normally, Zeppelin loved going and watching from the side stage. However, the last thing he wanted to do on this particular Friday night was drive in a car with his mom for an hour with nothing to escape her questions.

"Seems like you two are pretty close for you to let her borrow your CD player and headphones."

"Yep." He nodded, keeping his eyes focused on the cars speeding past them.

When his mom sighed, Zeppelin finally turned towards her.

"She's the first friend I've made since we moved. She doesn't have many friends, and three popular kids like to bully her. I hang out with her during lunch and recess. We talk about her books and writing or my songs. I wanted her to listen to my favorite Led Zeppelin song and she ended up liking the CD a lot. That's all."

"Was that so hard to tell me?" She asked, before he could answer she continued, "Your dad and I worry about you making friends. We don't want you to be buried in your lyric notebook all the time. I'm happy you found a friend."

He smiled, "Me too, mom."

"And she's very cute…"

He groaned, "Can we please listen to the radio?"

Her laughter filled the car, and she turned to radio on to a local oldies station. Once he and his mom began singing along to each song that played, Zeppelin finally relaxed. His dad had played a great show filling in for one of the regular band members who got the flu. By the time they got home, it was well past midnight, and he was beyond tired. As soon as his head hit the pillow, he fell asleep and began dreaming of a certain brown-eyed girl.

When Zeppelin woke up the next morning, his parents were already gone to their day jobs. He poured himself a bowl of cereal and watched cartoons on the TV. When he realized it was nearly noon, he rushed to get ready to meet Laurel at her house. Deciding on his favorite jeans, a Nirvana t-shirt and a flannel tied around his waist. He grabbed his backpack and was headed out his door a little after noon.

It didn't take him too long to get to Laurel's house. She was already sitting against the large oak tree in her front yard with a book in her lap. She had a couple more books on the blanket beside her and a jug of what looked like Kool-Aid with two cups next to it.

"How many books are you going to read?" he asked as she looked up at him, smiling.

"Depends on how long we hang out. I'm almost finish with this one, so I might be able to read two or three today."

He shook his head sitting next to her, "I don't doubt that you will. So, did you learn the lyrics to 'Ramble On'?"

She nodded, "I'm pretty sure I have the chorus memorize. My mom asked me what I was listening to and was surprised by my answer. She always thought I would be into country music."

Zeppelin laughed, pulling out his notebook and pencil, "I mean some country is good, like Lynyrd Skynyrd."

"Who?"

He started laughing more, "I'll see if my dad has any of their CDs. However, for now you can listen to this." Zeppelin pulled out Nirvana's Nevermind CD and handed it to her.

Her eyes widened, "Is that baby naked?"

"Sure is. You asked for my favorite CD, and this is it. If you don't like it, then I don't know if we could be friends anymore." He tried to keep himself from smiling and tightened his jaw.

"Oh…" She looked down as if the cd was going to bite her, "I'm sure I'll love it."

Zeppelin bumped his shoulder into hers, "I'm only kidding. If you don't, it's fine. We don't like the same books, but you still like me."

He noticed her eyes shot up to his and her cheeks blossomed into a rosy pink. His stomach tightened in a way that wasn't uncomfortable, but welcoming. He liked the way she made him feel.

"Of course I do, I'm not like the jerk squad and not like people because they are different." She scoffed, tucking a wayward strand of hair behind her ear.

Laurel placed the CD into the player and slipped the headphones over her ears. He could hear the first few notes of the first song playing. He decided to lay on his stomach at the end of her blanket, working on the new lyrics he wanted to add to his song.

They filled the afternoon by chatting about her thoughts on Nirvana, which was she truly liked them. She finished two books while helping him finish the lyrics to his newest song. When her mom came home, they came inside and watched one of Laurel's favorite movies, My Girl. When the movie was over, Zeppelin looked up at the clock in her living room.

"Oh no, I'm late!"

"Late? For what?" Laurel asked, as he gathered up all his things.

His parents were going to kill him. He was supposed to be home before they got home. He didn't tell them about hanging out with Laurel or leave them a note.

"I'm supposed to be home by now. I've gotta go. I'll see you at our spot on Monday." He pulled her into a hug and then went out the door, running towards his house.

Sure enough, when Zeppelin arrived home, his parents were frantic. His dad had been trying to convince his mom not to call the cops and she was crying as he walked inside.

"I'm sorry. I lost track-"

"Where have you been! You didn't leave a note or call to leave a message on the machine. We thought you were kidnapped or worst!"

His mom never yelled at him and suddenly his eyes were bleary with tears. The guilt slamming into his chest was making it hard for him to breathe.

"I-I'm sorry, mom. I was hanging out with my friend, and I thought I would be home before you guys got back." He hung his head low unable to look either of his parents in the eyes.

"Zeppelin, why don't you go upstairs and let your mom calm down." He nodded, heading towards the stairs when his dad called out, "I think it's safe to say that for now, you're grounded for at least a few days."

He nodded again not trusting his voice and headed to his room. He shut the door and flopped down onto his bed. He hated disappointing his parents and even worse making his mom cry. His own tears were falling down his cheeks onto his sheets. Zeppelin heard his door open, and the hall light shined into his room.

"I'm sorry I yelled at you." His mom's soft voice brought more tears down his face.

He tried to take a deep breath, but only a tight sob came from his mouth. His mom sat down beside him and pulled him into her arms. The safety of his mom's hug gave him the freedom to cry openly. She sat there rocking him while all his sadness and guilt flowed out of him.

"Honey are you okay?" she asked, slightly pulling away from him.

Zeppelin took a couple of deep breaths, wiping the tears from his face then nodded, "I-I think so… mom, I'm so sorry."

She hugged him again, "I know baby. I hope you know that I was honestly just scared something happened to you. You're our only child and if anything, ever happened to you…"

"Nothing ever will, I promise." He looked up into his mom's green eyes that mirrored his.

"Do you want to tell me why you didn't want us knowing about you and Laurel hanging out?"

His cheeks burned, but after everything he had put his parents through Zeppelin knew he needed to be honest.

"I like her. I didn't even know it until today, but I really like her. I guess I was scared if you and dad knew that then you wouldn't want me hanging out with her."

His mom chuckled, "Zeppelin, it's normal for you to have crushes on girls. We would never keep you from hanging out with her unless you were doing something you weren't supposed to be doing or was dangerous."

His shoulders slumped, "Oh… I really thought you would be more upset about this."

She took his hands into hers, "There are two things that upset me. One, you hid it from your dad and me. We want to know about everyone in your life, especially the ones who make you happy. Which brings me to number two, not introducing us to her. I think you should invite her and her parents over for dinner tomorrow night. That way, we all get to meet, and the parents can get to know one another."

"Really?" He was surprised to his mom wanted to get to know Laurel's mom.

"Yes, really. You can call her tomorrow morning to ask."

He hugged his mom tightly, "Thanks mom for being so cool about this."

"You're welcome. Now, I want to know everything about Laurel and how she has you so smitten."

He groaned for only a moment before grabbing his notebook. He opened to the page of his newest song and let his mom read the lyrics.

"Zeppelin, this is quite the love song for someone so young."

He chewed on his lip, "That's because I know one day, I'm going to ask Laurel Adler to marry me."

Summer Tours and Hearts

Laurel

Muscles ached that she didn't even know she had. Laurel peeked open an eye to see the sun shining brightly through the curtains. Her body felt like it was on fire as sweat rolled in between her breasts. She was trying to remember why it was so hot in her hotel room then everything came flooding back.

Telling her best friend to fuck her into oblivion. Having a naked panic attack. Making love. Zeppelin.

Looking down at her naked body, she found herself covered by a sheet and a strong arm wrapped tightly around her waist. His long, muscular legs were entwined with hers and every inch of his hard cock was snug against her ass. She closed her eyes, trying to calm her inner sex goddess from having her way with him. It couldn't be all about sex, but their feelings for one another.

On the bedside table, her phone started buzzing. When Laurel went to grab it, the arm around her tightened keeping her firmly in place.

"Nooo… five more minutes…"

Zeppelin's deep, raspy voice sent goosebumps all along her arms and legs. His voice always had an effect on her, but usually only when he was singing.

"Your morning voice is sexy." The words were out of her mouth before her brain could stop them.

His head lifted off her shoulder, "Hmm, really? Just how sexy is it?"

Be brave and bold.

Her inner goddess whispered. Laurel took his hand, running it down her body and slipping it between her legs. He took in a sharp breath before slowly rubbing circles against her. She sighed, relaxing against his body and hooking her leg over him to give him more room.

"Damn gorgeous, all this for me and my voice?" Zeppelin nipped at her neck.

"You have millions of fangirls that get hot and bothered over your voice. Should be…" She moaned, arching her back against him when he pushed two thick fingers inside of her, "Oh god… s-should be no surprise I am too. Fuck Zeppelin…"

His deep chuckle sent shivers throughout her body.

"There's only one fangirl I've ever cared about being hot and bothered by me." He pulled out his fingers and lifted himself up to rest between her legs, "You."

He slowly rolled his hips against her creating the perfect friction to make her belly tighten. He reached inside the bedside table and pulled out another condom.

"Ever the boy scout." She watched as he made quick work of rolling it down his hard length.

"Hopeful, fangirl. Just hopeful."

Zeppelin spread her legs wider, holding onto the back of her knees. She watched as his eyes took in her body before landing on his cock sliding inside of her. The collective moan for them echoed in her ears.

"Fuck me, I'll never get tired of being inside you. Like god made you just for me, perfect in every way." He pulled every inch of himself out of her before watching himself slowly push back in.

Laurel was slipping closer to the edge with each slow thrust. She loved how attentive he was and how seemingly in tuned he was with her body already. However, the slow pace was not enough for her and her inner goddess reminded her of what she needed to be.

Bold and brave.

She could trust Zeppelin to be her herself. To tell him what she wanted. What she needed and there would be no judgment from him.

"Zepp-Zeppelin…" She moaned, feeling his hands slide and gripping her hips, "Please…"

"Tell me sweetheart, what do need." His thrust was harder this time, "Tell me what you want."

Laurel locked her hands around the back of his neck, pulling his lips to hers. Before she kissed him, Laurel whispered.

"Fuck me. Hard."

She would never forget the wild passion filling the dark green eyes she loved. His lips smashed against hers before thrusting hard and fast into her.

"With pleasure."

She thought he was a wild, crazed man on stage, but the Zeppelin fucking her, chasing after his own release was a version unlike any other she had seen of him.

And she loved it.

Soon, they were both crying out each other's names as they came. Her chest was heaving to take in air as Zeppelin's sweaty hair dripped along her shoulder.

"You're literally gonna be the death of me." He laughed, pulling out of her with a groan and throwing the condom away.

"You only have yourself to blame." Her phone buzzed again with a text.

Thomas: The buses will be ready in 20 mins. Make sure you're both there.

She stared at the text, rereading it a couple of times. Something was wrong. Normally, Thomas would text her with, *good morning beautiful.* This text was cold and suddenly all her worst fears began playing out in her head.

What if he knows about Zeppelin and me?

What if the press knows and that's how Thomas found out?

What if he heard us this morning?

The last thought was impossible since his room was at the other end of the floor they were on. She looked at her other notifications seeing a missed call and voicemail from Thomas.

"Hey, I'm outside your door knocking but no one…" He was quiet as if he were listening, "Sounds like you two are busy. I'll text you."

"Fuck."

She could hear the shower going in the bathroom when Zeppelin stepped out, "What's wrong?"

Laurel opened her mouth to speak, but nothing came out. She lifted her phone up for him to listen to the voicemail. She was shocked when he shrugged his shoulders like it was nothing.

"He was going to find out one way or another."

"Zeppelin!" She yelled, "I wanted to be able to tell him myself. To make sure things aren't weird between us and make sure he's okay."

He sat on the edge of the bed, "If you think things between the three of us aren't going to be weird then you sadly living in a fantasy world. They're already tense between us all because he and I are both in love with you."

"He's not… I mean sure he has feelings for me. He always has, but love?" She didn't believe Thomas was truly in love with her.

He couldn't be… could he?

Zeppelin stood up, "You should probably shower while I pack our stuff up. I'll shower once were on the bus." Without another word, he walked out into the living area.

Laurel flopped back onto the bed wishing she could go back to three in the morning and making love with Zeppelin without a care in the world.

Taking the quickest shower in her life, she and Zeppelin met Jake in the lobby. His eyes didn't meet hers as her cheeks grew unbearably warm.

"He knows." She whispered.

Zeppelin nodded, "Yeah he does, but only because I told him when you were in the shower."

"Oh."

When they got in the SUV, Zeppelin sat in the back with her instead of his usual spot up front. His fingers were laced with hers resting on the seat between them. She glanced over at him staring out the window. He was unusually quiet and deep in thought noticing him chewing on his nails. Laurel tugged on his hand, worried that things between them were now tense.

"Are we okay?"

He smiled then pulled her to his side, "Of course we are. Let's focus on getting to the bus and on the road. We'll deal with everything else later."

Laurel was expecting Thomas to be waiting on Zeppelin's brand-new bus, but he wasn't. She gave a long hug to the driver who had been in the accident with her.

"Nice to see you up and about again, Miss Laurel." He had said before waving them off so they could get on the road.

The new bus was more decked out than his last one. The living quarters had a long couch on one side and two table booths on the other. Behind the booths was a smaller couch leading into the small kitchenette. The bathroom was a comfortable size for two people.

"Hopeful again?" she asked, smiling.

His charming smirk appeared on his face, "Always fangirl, always."

There were two bunks past the bathroom with closet space across from them. Finally, the back quarter was the master bedroom. A queen size bed was in one corner while in the opposite corner Laurel was surprised to find a full-length desk.

"Did you get this just for me?" She found all her favorite pens, highlighters and other office supplies in the drawers.

"Of course. Again, hopeful that you'll be coming out on tour with me more often."

She turned around to find Zeppelin sitting on the bed. She stepped in between his legs, leaning down to kiss him.

"How do you feel about christening this new bed?" She pushed his flannel shirt off his shoulders.

His laughter filled the room, "I think I've created a sex monster." He picked her up, tossing her onto the bed before crawling over her.

After making love and napping, Laurel found herself sitting out on the couch watching the world pass them by. Zeppelin was still sleeping, and she took the opportunity to text Thomas.

> I was going to tell you...

> **Thomas:** No need, I should have known.

> Thomas, please don't be mad at him. If you're going to be mad at anyone it should be me.

> **Thomas:** I'm not mad. I'm disappointed and don't feel like talking. See you in Mountain View.

With that she knew he would have turned off his phone. A heavy feeling was settling in the pit of her stomach, and she hated it. She hated being in the middle of two men that meant everything to her. Most of all, she hated her heart for loving them both in their own ways.

Deciding that she couldn't sit in silence anymore, Laurel grabbed her noise canceling headphones and started blaring her emo punk playlist. She let her mind wander to her manuscript and her main female character. Thinking about the tension she had built between her and the main male character. She needed a twist to cause them to doubt each other. She got up grabbing her notebook and writing down ideas of how she could shake things up.

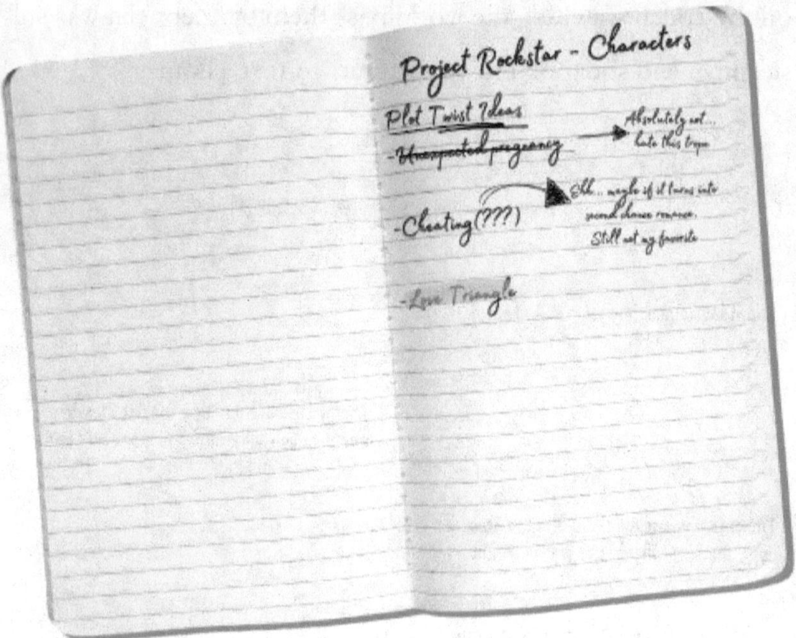

This one piqued her interest the most. Maybe it was because she was in the middle of her own love triangle, but also she really liked the trope. Looking through her list of supporting characters there were only a few choices she could make to bumping them up to main character status.

When her favorite Heartstrings song started playing she bopped her head to the music. Zeppelin's voice filled her ears and suddenly a wave of longing hit her. She looked up towards the bedroom door only to see him leaning against the frame, watching her. A soft smile was on his face as he walked towards her.

"You're adorable getting lost in your work and music."

When he sat down beside her, Laurel immediately pulled him in for a slow, passionate kiss.

"Hmm, what was that for?" He chuckled.

"I was listening to Heartstrings and missed you. Which I know sounds ridiculous…"

Zeppelin shook his head, "No, it doesn't. Why do you think I came out here? You weren't in bed, and I wanted to be next to you."

Laurel laughed, "We're kind of pathetic being so lovesick with each other."

"Nah, we're making up for lost time." He kissed her temple, "Now, tell me about what you're working on while I make coffee because I have a feeling I'm going to need the caffeine to keep up with you tonight."

Her jaw dropped, "Yeah right, more like me keeping up with you. I'm pretty sure you could go all night long or at least that's what the fansites say about you."

Zeppelin groaned, "I've told you once. I've told you a thousand times, stay off the fansites."

She laughed, "Not a chance. All of that inspirational gold is priceless."

For the rest of the night, Laurel began telling him about her idea for the next part in her manuscript. While Zeppelin played on his guitar. They ended the night in bed, snuggling and watching a movie until they both had fallen asleep.

It took them the better part of three days to arrive in Mountain View, California. Thomas had not texted or called Laurel during the whole trip. He had only reached out to Zeppelin twice strictly about tour related things. The time spent with Zeppelin was amazing, but she was missing the third person in their trio. It had always been the three of them together. With Zeppelin having a full day of press, rehearsals and the first show since the accident. Laurel was determined to talk with Thomas.

Her first stop was to talk with Jake. When he saw her coming, he tried to get away by heading towards the stage crew to help them.

"Don't even think about it, mister." She pointed her finger at him, and he stopped in his tracks, "I need two minutes of your time."

"You want to know where Thomas is."

It wasn't a question, yet she still answered, "Yes I do. It's important we talk about everything that happened."

His eyes were downcast, "You know he could fire me for telling you?"

"I promise you he won't. I will make it perfectly clear that I tortured you for the information."

He nodded, "He's staying at the Hilton. Room 1518."

She kissed his cheek, "Thank you. Do you know if he's coming back for the concert?"

Jake nodded, his cheeks a handsome rosy color, "Yes, he'll be here. If I may?" He paused for a moment, "Let him come to you. He was pretty upset a few days ago and might be better to let him process through that."

"Thanks Jake, I'll keep that in mind." She hooked her arm with his, "How about I promise not to go talk to him before the concert tonight. If I do that, then could we watch the show from our special spot?"

"Absolutely, though I would go with you regardless of whether you talk to Thomas or not. It's my job to protect you and I'm sure Zeppelin would kill me if anything happened to you."

"One day, I would love to see you cut loose and have some fun." She chuckled as they walked towards the green room.

Laurel watched Heartstrings' rehearsal from the mix area. She could tell a huge difference in Zeppelin's performance. He seemed more relaxed and freer; she couldn't help wondering if it was because they were together now. She smiled, taking out her phone and recording him on stage. His head was thrown back in laughter as Alec and he pressed their backs together playing their guitars.

In that instant, Laurel was hit with a great idea for her story. She left the mix area and headed back towards the green room. Turning the corner, her smile faded as she spotted Thomas entering the green room on his phone. She waited a few minutes to see if he would leave and decided to head back to the bus and grab her computer.

Laurel rushed back to the mix area setting up her laptop on a corner of the soundboard. Heartstrings were running through their encore set one last time before the VIPs were coming in to watch them do the last of their sound check. The scene inside her mind was coming alive on her screen. The words flowing out from her fingertips that were dancing along her keyboard. She only looked up when she heard Zeppelin's voice come through the speakers.

"You know, I miss the days of being asked about the music and not my personal life." He chuckled, "Look, all I will say is that I'm enjoying the hell out of life right now because of someone special."

"Jeez, wonder who that could be."

Laurel jumped as Jake began laughing behind her, "Damn it, don't do that!" she smacked his shoulder.

"Just too easy. Come on, we need to get to our seats."

She looked down at her laptop not ready to stop writing, "Do you think we could watch from here? I promise not to be in the way."

Laurel looked over to the sound engineers who shrugged, "Don't bother us any."

Jake smiled, "Sounds good to me. This way I won't have to jump into any mosh pits to pull you out."

"I think I'm going to save my moshing for the last show of the year. You know go out with a bang."

The absolute terror on Jake's face had her doubling over in laughter and even the engineer was chuckling.

"You'll be the death of me." Jake mumbled.

"Not the first time I've heard that today."

Laurel had written nearly a whole chapter by the time the first band went out on stage. It was then she noticed that she had never truly listened to them before. They were good mix of garage rock and punk. She made a note on her phone to look them up after the concert. Before slipping her phone back into her pocket, she noticed two unread texts.

She knew he wouldn't have his phone on him so close to show time. Laurel went to the other text and sighed.

The house lights went off and the roar of the crowd vibrated in her chest. She looked up on the stage to see Sam sitting at her drum set while Alec and Rich took to their mics. The first few notes of Into the Fire began and Zeppelin ran out on stage.

"You ready to rock, Mountain View?" He yelled out as the crowd screamed, "I can't hear you. Are you ready to rock, Mountain View!"

The crowd screamed even louder as Zeppelin started strumming on his guitar. His mouth pressed against his mic as his deep voice filled the arena.

I walked into the fire to find love

Searching for a beautiful woman in the summer of love

But I found myself so lonely and bitter,

After the breakup I felt so much better

Zeppelin took his mic off the stand, walking over to Alec's side of the stage. Leaning over the edge he sang the next verse to a group of women going absolutely feral for him. Laurel typed a note on her character sheet about playing up the charm and confidence of her main rockstar character when performing. She found herself watching and enjoying the concert more than working on her manuscript.

Their set was at the halfway mark when Zeppelin took center stage on a stool and his acoustic guitar. Sam brought out her cajon sitting off to the side of Zeppelin. She didn't remember this from any of the other concerts or during their rehearsal.

"Do y'all mind if we slow it down and I play something new for you?" The crowd cheered as he chuckled, "Well, it's new to you, but for me this song is one of the first ones I ever wrote. Enjoy."

As soon as the first few notes came from his guitar, Laurel was sent back to eighth grade. Watching her best friend singing his song for his number one fan. The memory playing out vividly in her mind as he began to sing.

Oh darling Fangirl, my girl

My shining star in the night sky,

The perfect companion to my whiskey soul.

Tears sprung to her eyes as he smiled looking right up at her.

This time, she knew it was her he was singing to.

Roses are always red,

Skies are always blue,

I love beautiful fangirls,

But not as much as I love my girl!

She felt her phone vibrate in her pocket, ignoring it the first time. She couldn't tear her eyes away from the man singing on stage. The man who held her heart within his hands. The man she was madly in love with and never wanted to leave his side again.

When her phone buzzed for a fourth time, Laurel finally pulled it out of her pocket seeing texts from Thomas.

Thomas: Laurel, please come back to the green room and talk to me.

Thomas: I don't want to make scene in front of everyone.

Thomas: Nevermind, it's not worth it. You will always choose him.

Thomas: I hope it's worth it.

Zeppelin

Zeppelin couldn't remember the last time he had felt this good after a show. The crowd had been full of energy that fueled him to play harder than he had the whole tour. He couldn't wait to see Laurel and see what she had thought about hearing her song live in front of thousands of people. He was about to head into the green room, but Rich caught him by the arm.

"We have meet and greets. After tonight's show, I'm sure there are a ton of eager fans waiting for us."

Zeppelin sighed, "You're right, come on let's see how many chests I have to sign tonight."

They both laughed as they entered the meet and greet room there was loud cheering. He was pleasantly surprised that he was only asked to sign a few chests and that most fans wanted to talk to him about the newest song they played. The last fan was leaving when Laurel walked through the door. Her arms were crossed over her chest, and she looked as if she was upset.

Immediately, Zeppelin's mind went to her being upset with him. Did she not like the song? Was she embarrassed? Had she forgotten who the song was for? A million thoughts ran rampant inside his head until he saw Thomas come in after her. He grabbed her elbow, and she snatched it away from him. She took a few steps away from him and he stepped in front of her. He couldn't hear what they were saying but the conversation looked heated.

Walking over to them, Zeppelin went to slip his arm around Laurel's shoulders when a sharp pain shot up his jaw. His mouth filled with a rusty, metallic taste and he wipe his mouth seeing a streak of red.

"What the fuck…" Zeppelin mumbled, trying to piece together what had just happened.

Looking up, he found Thomas' dark eyes narrowed on him and his blood covering his knuckles. Thomas had punched him. He had actually punched him.

"Thomas!" Laurel yelled, her panicked voice cutting through the pain radiating over his face.

In that moment, everything around Zeppelin faded and a quiet calm came over him. A steady flow of pure rage pushed his body into motion. He lunged at his best friend, colliding with Thomas and sending them sliding across the floor. He pinned him down, bringing his fist down into his stomach. A gush of air wheezed out of Thomas as Zeppelin brought his other fist across Thomas' face.

A sickening crack echoed as he raised his fist into the air again, bringing it down over and over against Thomas' body. Zeppelin's vision darkened around the edges, and everything faded around him. Only the grunts and whimpers of his best friend filled his ears. Suddenly, he felt someone tugging him back before another sharp pain spread across his abdomen.

His world began to spin as his back hit the floor and Thomas hovered over him. His head cracked against the concrete, and he felt a gush of warmth bloom over the back of it. Bright white spot filled his vision as he caught a glimpse of Laurel stepping behind Thomas.

"STOP IT! BOTH OF YOU!"

The next thing Zeppelin heard was Laurel crying out in pain. His eyes cleared, looking up into Thomas' wide, fearful ones. The overwhelming sense of de je vu hit him. They both scrambled to their feet seeing Sam cradling Laurel in her arms. Bright crimson was flowing down her chin, dripping onto her shirt and floor.

"Shit! Laurel, I didn't... I..." Thomas tried to go to her, but Zeppelin shoved him back.

"Stay the fuck away from her." He seethed.

Thomas stood tall, trying to push his way past Zeppelin. That's when Jake, Alec and Rich pulled each of them away from one another and Laurel. Zeppelin watched as Sam led her towards First Aid and he pushed Jake off him.

"Let go of me."

Jake shook his head, "Not until you calm the fuck down. You're no good to her if you're acting like a fucking maniac."

His jaw clenched, "Jake, last time, get off of me or so help me…"

Suddenly, Zeppelin was being pulled backwards by two thick arms wrapped around his chest. Glancing back, he watched as one of the other bodyguards picked him off the ground and carried him back towards the green room.

"Put me down!" He yelled, trying to break free of the man carrying him.

Rich and Alec were standing in front of Thomas as Zeppelin was dropped onto the couch. Jake stepped inside keeping one hand on the door.

"Rich, I'm going to check on Laurel. Johnny will be right outside if you need him." Jake shut the door behind him.

Zeppelin looked over at Rich and Alec as Thomas slumped against the wall, sliding down it.

"I don't know what has gotten into you two lately, but you need to fix it. Now. We can't have you two swinging at one another while we're on tour. You're fucking adults, so act like it." Rich signaled towards the door, following Alec out of the green room.

The tension filled silence was suffocating. Thomas was holding his head in his hands, while Zeppelin was rubbing his aching jaw. He was about to stand up to leave when Thomas broke the silence.

"You can have any woman you want in the world. Why her? Why did you have to want her?"

Zeppelin sighed, "You've always known how I felt for her. You more than anyone knows I've always loved her."

Thomas finally looked up as tears fell down his face, "I love her too, Zepp. I'm positive she feels the same for me."

"Yeah, well she loves me too." He paused, running his hand through his blood-soaked hair, "There's only one way to truly settle this."

"What's that?"

Zeppelin stood heading towards the door, "It's Laurel decision who she wants to be with. We have to respect whoever she chooses."

Thomas pushed himself up, wiping his face, "Either way, I can't be here right now. I can't be around you and keep myself from doing something dumb. I think it's best if I had back to L.A. now."

"If that's what you want then fine." Zeppelin walked out of the green room and headed towards First Aid.

Once he was checked out and the EMT told him he didn't need stitches, Zeppelin headed to his bus. Jake was standing near the door and stopped him when he tried to get on.

"Jake, I know she's upset but I have to make sure she's alright for myself."

He shook his head, "I'm sorry Zeppelin, she asked me to keep you and Thomas off the bus until we reach the next city. Sam is on there so she's not alone."

Zeppelin could feel the rip tearing through his heart, "Alright, I guess I'll ride with the band or crew tonight."

"Just so you know, Thomas grabbed all his things off the band bus and got a ride to the airport with one of the venue managers. Said he was headed back to L.A."

"Thanks Jake." Zeppelin headed for the band's bus but turned around after a few steps, "Hey Jake, thanks for taking care of her. I'm glad she has at least one levelheaded man to be there for her."

Jake chuckled, "No problem. I'll text you if anything changes with her."

Zeppelin nodded, then walked onto the band bus where Alec and Rich were already in their bunks for the night. His bags and some personal things were in the spare bunk above Rich. Climbing up, he quickly took off his concert clothes and pulled the blanket over his aching body. The adrenaline from the concert and anger was gone only leaving the pulsating ache in every muscle he had.

He pulled his phone out, looking at the pictures he and Laurel had taken before he went to sound check. Her bright eyes and wide smile slicing through his chest making it hurt with every breath he took. He quickly pulled up their text thread and typed out a message to her.

He turned off his phone before she could respond. Zeppelin turned off his bunk lights and shut his eyes. Finally allowing the tears to fall down his face as he faced tomorrow without his best friend and possibly the love of his life.

Laurel

April 1996 – 6th Grade

Laurel walked into the kitchen with arms wrapped around her stomach. Her mom was standing in front of the stove scrambling eggs for her.

"Mom, I don't feel good. My stomach is really bothering me."

Which wasn't entirely a lie. Her stomach had been in knots since the day before when Zeppelin was suspended for the day. The thought of facing Mandy, Andy and Brendan on her own twisted the knots tighter.

Her mom placed the back of her hand against her forehead, "You're not running a fever. I think once you're at school then you feel better. Now try and eat some of your eggs before you head to the bus stop."

She sighed, sitting at the table and pushing the eggs around her plate. Eventually, Laurel managed to eat some of her breakfast and made her way back upstairs to get ready for school. If it had been any other morning, her mom would have already been at work, and she could have missed the bus. For some reason, the universe was seemingly working her against her.

Laurel pulled out one of Zeppelin's flannels he let her borrow and slipped it over her arms. The warmth and familiarity of it eased the anxious butterflies thrashing around in her stomach. Grabbing her bag, she headed out the door with a quick goodbye. Waiting at the bus stop, she pulled out the portable CD player and headphones listening to the mix CD Zeppelin had made her.

So far, her favorite bands were Nirvana, Foo Foo Fighters and Metallica. By the time she was walking into school, her stomach had settled, and her mood was slightly brighter. It continued to be like that until lunch time.

Laurel sat at her normal table with the latest book in the Christopher Pike series she was reading. The noise in the cafeteria faded into the background as she lost herself in the story of Alisa battling evil and death. Nearing the end of the chapter, suddenly her book vanished from her hands.

"Oh look, Creatures of Forever…"

Laurel looked up at Mandy smirking as she held her book up.

"An autobiography about Laurel."

Mandy and her gang of girls all started laughing.

"Very funny, may I have my book back please." Laurel asked nicely, glancing around to see if she could find a lunch aid nearby in case she needed some extra help.

"Sure, you can have your book back." Mandy started walking over to the trash can, "Fetch."

Laurel watched as she threw the book into the trash then her friends followed her by throwing their lunches in behind it. Their laughter filled her ears drowning out the bells dismissing them back to recess. Her face bloomed with heat as she stood over the trash can and tried to search for her book beneath all the scraps of food.

"Hon, you okay?"

One of the lunch ladies stood next to her, "Yeah. My book fell into the trash."

"Oh, sweetie I'm sorry. Here, let me get it for you and see if we can salvage it."

Laurel nodded, not trusting herself to not burst into tears. Not only was it one of her favorite books in the series, but Zeppelin had surprised her with it as a belated Christmas gift.

"Here we go." She took the towel from her apron and wiped off the glops of pudding and mystery pasta sauce that were on the cover, "Oh, I think some milk soaked into the pages. You'll probably have to get a new copy, so the pages don't spoil and mold on you."

Laurel took the book from her inspecting the ruined book for herself. Opening the cover page, she smiled seeing Zeppelin's handwriting still intact and protected by the cover. It was the only silver lining of losing the book.

"Thank you…" she paused realizing she didn't know the lunch

lady's name.

"Ms. Peggy, dear." She smiled.

Laurel held out her hand, "Thank you Ms. Peggy for getting my book for me. I appreciate it."

Ms. Peggy shook her hand, "You're very welcome. Come through my line any time and I'll give a little extra or," she leaned in, "if those girls bother you then I'll make sure they won't."

She smiled, "Thank you."

When Laurel finally made it home, she was exhausted from dealing with Mandy and losing her book for good. She had spent the bus ride home listening to Metallica on repeat as loud as her ears could tolerate. Walking home, she considered going to her and Zeppelin's spot to gather herself but decided all she wanted to do was go home and bury herself in her blanket.

As she walked up to her house, she was surprised to see someone sitting on her front steps. For a moment, her heart leaped with hope that it was Zeppelin waiting for her but then fell into the pit of her stomach seeing Thomas sitting there.

"What are you doing here?" she asked, pulling her headphones off her ears.

Thomas immediately stood up, towering over her and nervously bouncing from one foot to the other.

"Your mom said it would be okay for me to wait for you out here before she left for work. She also wanted me to tell you that your key is under the mat since you forgot it this morning."

Laurel brushed past him, lifting the mat up and finding her key. "Thank you. Why are you waiting for me? Your friends tortured me enough today and even ruined one of my books, so I'm not exactly in the mood to be bullied some more."

She noticed him flinch as if she had physically hit him, causing her to pause and push back the anger trying to erupted out of her.

"I wanted to come say I'm sorry. What I did yesterday was mean, and I feel terrible for what happened." He ran his hand over his hair, "Even though I don't deserve your forgiveness, I wanted to see if I could explain myself."

He finally lifted his hazel eyes to hers and the sun made the little flecks of golden-brown shine within them. For the first time, Laurel found herself finding someone other than Zeppelin good looking and that sent waves of excitement and nervousness down her body. She sat down on the top step and motioned to the spot next to her.

"You're right, you don't deserve my forgiveness." His shoulders slump forward as he sat next to her, "Lucky for you, I believe in second chances. So, tell me why you decided to hang out with a bunch of bullies and pick on me and Zeppelin."

A small smile appeared on his face before he began explaining his side of the story.

"This is my fourth school this school year. My parents died in an accident a little over a year ago and I've been living with my grandparents until they decided that it was too much work to raise another child."

A wave of guilt washed over Laurel, humbling her anger, "Thomas, I'm so sorry."

He shrugged, "It's fine. I mean, it's not fine, but all I can do is deal with it. Anyway, my grandma convinced my aunt to take me in. My aunt is cool, and I was excited to be in a semi populate city versus the back roads out in the middle of cow fields."

Thomas chuckled, "My aunt's brilliant advice was to find the most popular kids and make friends with them. So, that's what I've been trying to do."

"Terrible advice concerning who the popular kids are in this school." Laurel joked.

"I know that now, but I really thought that was the only choice I had."

"What do you mean? You could have literally been friends with anybody else. Zeppelin and I would have totally been friends with you." She watched as Thomas chewed on his lower lip, "What?"

"When I started here I thought you and Zeppelin were the popular kids. I couldn't imagine a dude with a rockstar parent who writes music and the smartest girl in the whole grade not being the cool kids."

She broke out into laughter, "For real? Zeppelin and I are the furthest thing for being popular."

Thomas joined in with her laughing, "You'd be surprised by how other people view you guys. I thought you guys were cool. Too cool for me, in fact. I didn't think you guys would be friends with a loser like me. Not to mention you're super cute. Way cuter than any other girl in the school."

Her cheeks burned suddenly, "Not only are you delusional but you're blind as well."

"Hey!" He laughed, "My sight is perfectly fine. My judgments and sanity are questionable. Except for thinking you're cute because you are. Since I'm being totally honest here to try and win your forgiveness and friendship. I've had a crush on you since day one in English class."

Laurel shook her head, "There are way better girls to have a crush on, but I'm flattered and appreciate your honesty."

Her hands were trembling in her lap. No one had ever had a crush on her. She never wanted any of the guys in her grade to like her like that except one and he was her best friend.

"There's really not, but I won't argue with you. Honestly, I would rather be friends right now anyway. I need some friends that will have my back and sadly, I think I've ruined any chances of that happening now."

Before her brain could process what she was doing, her hand reach over rested on top of Thomas' hand, "You haven't ruined anything. You coming here, apologizing and being honest was a big step in the right direction. My vote is to add you to our little friend group."

"Really?" He asked.

Laurel nodded, "Yep, however convincing Zeppelin will be the challenge. Have you talked to him yet?"

"No, I wanted to talk to you first and apologize since you're the one who got hurt. Again, I'm really sorry."

She waved her hand, "You're forgiven, so no need to apologize any more. You should head over to Zeppelin's and talk with him."

"Okay, should I go get some kind of armor before I head over there?" He chuckled.

"Nah, he's not the fighting type… well unless provoked." They both stood up and Laurel wrapped her arms around Thomas, "Thank you for the apology. It made my bad day a little better."

He wrapped his arms around her, squeezing her tightly, "I'm glad I could make it a little better. Now wish me luck with Zeppelin."

He headed off down the street as she waved goodbye. Laurel flopped down onto the couch and pulled out her book that was starting to smell. Sighing, she ripped out the cover page with Zeppelin's note and got up walking over to the trash can in her kitchen. Tossing the book inside, she walked away before the tears could well up beneath her eyes. Laurel headed off to her room and placed the cover page in her keepsake box thankful she could save the most important part of the book.

Laurel

I saw you staring at this the last time we were at the bookshop. I had Miss Rose hold it for me until I got my allowance. The smile it brought to your face is one I want to see all the time. I like it when your happy and if vampires and demons is what makes you happy then I will buy you all the vampire books you want.

Love ya, Z

Laurel stared down at the worn and tattered cover page. The memory of Zeppelin and Thomas fighting in grade school had been etched into her memory that was until now being replaced by a whole new memory. The two people she loved the most, her best friends, her boys were fighting each other over her. She couldn't close her eyes without seeing the disdain in Thomas' eyes or the rage burning in Zeppelin's. Falling back onto the bed, she curled into a ball unleashing the tears she had barely been holding back.

"Laurel?"

Sam's soft voice pushed more tears down her cheeks. All the drama and tension on this tour was all because of her.

"Laurel, are you okay?" There was a brief paused as the bed dipped down on one side, "I mean, I'm sure you're not okay, but… I don't know. I wanted to check in on you since we've been on the road for a while."

She opened her mouth to speak, but all that came was an agonizing sob. Sam's hand ran down her back gently and soothingly. Her body began to tremble as all the emotions she had been holding back came rushing out of her.

"Shhh, it's going to be okay. I know it doesn't seem like that right now. Everything hurts and that fucking sucks. Let it hurt but then try to hold your head up one day at a time. Don't let those idiots get to you."

Laurel tried to suck in a breath to speak, "I-It's… all…my…"

"Don't you dare finish that sentence." She felt Sam move off the bed then saw her appear in front of her, "None of this was your fault. You are not to blame for those two being Neanderthals. There has been tension between the two of them for a while and this was just the tipping point."

Laurel nodded, unable to form a coherent thought together. All she could do was wallow in her own misery of possible losing the two men at the center of her world.

Arriving in San Jose, Laurel finally emerged from the private bedroom on the bus and found Johnny sitting on one of the couches. Looking up, he nodded towards her and went back to looking at his phone. There was a slip of paper on the table with some ibuprofen, a muffin and apple juice.

Laurel, I figured you would want some time to yourself on the bus. Jake is having Johnny stay behind in case you need anything and to keep those who must not be name away. If you need anything just text me or Jake. We got your back!
Sam

She couldn't help the small smile on her face. She grabbed her laptop deciding the best way to distract herself was to work on her book. Eating her muffin and happily taking the ibuprofen for her aching cheek and nose. Laurel began loading her project while checking her phone for the first time in nearly twelve hours. She should have known there would be a thousand messages for her. A lot of them from Leigh and her group chat with Raelyn and Emerson. Then she saw a text from Thomas.

Laurel wiped away the tears slowly slipping down her face. She couldn't pinpoint it, but his text broke her heart. He was already defeated like a decision had been made. She had no idea what she was going to do. Could she put her feelings aside for both of them and just be friends with them again? Could she leave with the fact that no matter what she was going to end up hurting one or both of them. At the very least, there would always be a fracture between Thomas and Zeppelin because of her.

Suddenly, all Laurel wanted to do was go as far away from all of it. To go back to the safety of her home office and keeping all the drama in her books. Clicking out of Thomas' text, she found one from Zeppelin. The crack Thomas' text created began mending as she read Zeppelin's text.

More tears fell as Laurel flipped her phone face down trying to resist the urge to text Zeppelin back. She needed to clear her head. She needed to talk everything out with someone not directly affected by what she needed to do next. Picking up her phone again, she texted the one person she knew would listen and understand completely.

She decided to try and make herself look as presentable as she could. Sitting at her desk, Laurel brushed her hair into a messy bun and cleaned the tear stain streaks on her face. She was slipping on her favorite writing hoodie when her phone began to ring.

"Hey Laurel, what…" Raelyn's eyes widened, and Laurel knew her plan to look put together hadn't worked, "What happened?"

"I look that bad, huh?" She tried to joke.

She watched as Raelyn sat in her reading chair with her cat, Cordy, laying behind her head.

"Besides the dark bruises beneath your eyes and over your nose. I'm also all too familiar with the staying up all night and crying look. I'm assuming it has something to do with the gossip blogs reporting on Zeppelin fighting with his manager and best friend."

"Damn, the media knows already. I was hoping the fans wouldn't say anything."

Raelyn chuckled, "They're fans, they'll gossip about anything. I should know."

Not only had Raelyn been a fangirl herself with her husband's TV show, but she had been on the receiving end of fandom hate when the news broke about her dating Austin.

"Was the fight about you?"

Laurel felt the tears pooling beneath her eyes as she nodded, "Raelyn, I don't know what to do." She began telling her everything that had happened while on tour between her and Thomas, and her and Zeppelin.

She hadn't thought it was possible, but she cried once more talking about Thomas and Zeppelin fighting. When she was finally done talking her throat was raw, her face crimson and her heart heavy.

"I'm so sorry Laurel."

"I've been in love with Zeppelin since we were kids, but I also think I've loved Thomas as well. I truly don't know how or even if I want to choose between them."

Raelyn spoke gently as if Laurel could break at any moment, "I don't think there is any other way through this than to make that tough decision. Which, by the way, there is a third option to not choose either of them for the sake of your friendships."

Laurel scoffed, "I'm pretty sure I would at least lose one of their friendships no matter what." She then read the texts she received from each of them.

"Oh wow…" Raelyn sighed, "I see what you mean. Okay then, play along with me for a moment."

She nodded as Raelyn continued, "Close your eyes and clear your mind."

"Raelyn…" Laurel started to protest.

Her friend held up her finger, "Indulge me. Close your eyes and clear your mind."

She rolled her eyes before closing them hearing Raelyn laugh. She imagined a blank piece of paper, counting the number of blue lines on it.

"Take in a deep breath." As she did Raelyn counted to five, "Now let it out slowly."

Laurel's shoulders relaxed and her body fell back gently into her chair.

"Now, I'm going to ask you a simply question and I want you to tell me what pops into your head immediately. No thinking, just very first thing that shows up in that beautiful mind of yours."

She smirked, "Got it."

"You hear someone outside your office door, who is leaning against the door frame?"

He popped into her mind as clear and crisp as the first snow fall in winter. Her heart skipped into a quick pace and her cheeks burned. She could imagine every detail about him from the way his hair was unruly to his clothes and even his bare feet crossed at the ankles.

Her eyes snapped opened to see Raelyn smiling from ear to ear, "I think you have your answer."

"Yeah, I saw-"

Raelyn plugged her fingers into her ears, "La la la, I don't want to know."

Laurel started laughing, "Why not?"

"And ruin the end of this epic love triangle. No thank you. I am all about the slow burn and tension. I want to see the third act climax for myself in real time."

"You do know this is not about a book, but my real life."

Raelyn nodded, "Oh yes, which makes it even better. Though, your real life would make for an excellent book. A rockstar romance, childhood friends to lovers with a love triangle." She gave a chef's kiss.

A switch flipped within Laurel's mind. Her writer's brain kicked on thinking of all the possibilities from a story like that. Images of flashback chapters showcasing their childhood friendship. Special songs and love confession performance. The tension of one of the main characters having a boyfriend/girlfriend creating the wrong place and time.

"I can see the wheels turning. I'm going to go and let you write down whatever is running through your mind before you lose it. Text me whenever you take the leap with your decision or when you have that idea fully flushed out."

Laurel smiled, "I definitely will and thank you Raelyn."

She shook her head, "No need to thank me. I'm here for you, always."

"I appreciate that. I will talk to you soon."

The call ended and Laurel wasted no time in getting all her ideas out on paper. Being so focused on the outline in front of her, she hadn't realized that hours had passed. Johnny knocked on the wall to get her attention.

"I'm going to go grab something to eat. Would you like anything?"

Her stomach growled as they both laughed, "Apparently so. Could you grab me a sandwich and a salad, please. Also, Diet Dr. Pepper would be great as well."

He nodded, "You got it. I'll be back in a bit."

Laurel went back to her outline and was about to call Leigh about it when she heard someone coming up the stairs onto the bus. She walked out of the bedroom with her notebook and laptop.

"Did you forget some-"

Expecting to see Johnny when she looked up, Laurel was surprised to see Thomas standing there.

Laurel

"Hey Laurel."

She continued to stare at him not completely believing her eyes that he was standing there.

"I thought you flew back to L.A.?"

Thomas took a few steps closer to her, stuffing his hands into his pockets, "I was going to, but as I was sitting in the airport I couldn't stop replaying everything in my head."

Laurel set her things on the table, "Yeah, my two best friends beating the crap out of each other has been playing on repeat in my head to."

"That's not what I meant." His hazel eyes locked onto hers, "I was meaning us."

Us.

The thought of her and Thomas being an *us* made her stomach twist uncomfortably. Were they an us after one date and one kiss?

"Oh…" was all her brain could manage to get through her lips.

"Did I even have a chance against Zeppelin? Or was I some kind of stand in?"

She was taken back by the question and Thomas took her silence as his answer.

"Fuck Laurel, really?" He turned away from her, threading his fingers through his hair, "I really thought that maybe, by now, you would be sick of Zeppelin's bullshit. That maybe you could see through his shit and see he's never gonna change. Not even for you."

Her hands clenched into fists at her sides, "You're one to talk!" she yelled.

Thomas slowly turned back to her, "What's that supposed to mean?"

"You're supposed to be his best friend, Thomas. You're supposed to help him whenever he loses himself. You're supposed to support him when he has a tough time."

The anger was building as quickly as the words were coming from her mouth.

"You two are supposed to be brothers! You two were supposed to protect me! Yet, who are the ones hurting me the most right now!" Laurel watched his eyes widened, "Before you go judging me, why don't you go take a good, long look in the mirror."

"Thomas," Johnny appeared behind him carrying a bag of food, "I think you should go."

"Laurel, I…" Thomas stopped as Laurel could no longer hold back the tears, "I'm sorry."

He turned around quickly walking off the bus. Laurel slumped down into the booth, laying her head on the table.

"Are you okay?" Johnny asked, sitting across from her.

She nodded, "I will be. Right now, I'm hoping you forgot my salad and brought me one of those greasy cheeseburgers."

He smirked, "You can have mine. I'll go back and get another one. I need to go check in with Jake anyway. Are you sure you'll be alright?"

"Thank you and yes, I'll be fine."

Once Johnny had left, Laurel pulled out the secret stash of whiskey Zeppelin had on the bus. In between bites of her burger, she would take a long, generous swig from the bottle. Before she knew it, her skin was warm and tingly along with a lovely whiskey fog drowning out all the thoughts inside her head.

She put the bottle back in its spot then went back to her laptop and notebook. Looking over the notes she already had and the outline she had come up with, she decided it was time to call Leigh. Laurel propped her phone up against the window and hit Leigh's name.

"Laurel? Everything okay?"

She waved, "Hi Leigh! Everything is great."

Leigh's laughter filled the bus, "Are you day drinking? Boy, tour life has changed you my friend."

She giggled, "Just needed a little whiskey-poo to take the edge off."

Her laughter faded to silence, "What happened? Which was those assholes needs his ass kicked?"

Leigh could always see right through Laurel's bullshit. She took a deep breath as the whiskey threatened to make a return trip.

"Well, I might as well tell you everything that happened because it's going to explain why I want to scrap my current manuscript for a new one I just outline."

"Come again?" Leigh asked.

Laurel started telling her everything that had happened. She told her about talking to Raelyn and how they had come up with some great ideas for a new book. Then she shared the outline for the project she wanted to write, and they discussed if it would be possible for her to finish a rough draft by her deadline.

"I love this. I love this story, the characters. Most of all, I love how passionate you seem to be about writing it." Leigh smiled, but then her eyes met hers filled with concern, "I do have a couple of concerns though."

Laurel knew she would, "Okay. Well after this story hour of bearing my heart and soul to you; I am officially sober again. So, bring on your concerns. I assume my deadline is one of them."

Leigh shook her head, "No, I have all the confidence in the world that you will hit your deadline. I can see the fire in your eyes for this new project and I can't wait to start getting chapters from you."

"Okay, then what are your concerns?"

"You being out on tour. I know it's almost over, but I'm concerned if you stay out on tour that you won't be able to focus on your book." Leigh took a sip of her coffee, sitting back in her chair.

Laurel raised an eyebrow at her, "Wasn't the whole point of me coming out on tour was to get inspiration and write my book? Now you're concerned it will be a distraction?"

"Not a distraction…" she paused, "I don't want you to be writing this amazing book and then something happen between you and those two idiots you call best friends then you lose your mojo."

"You mean if they break my heart, and I slip into a dark depression?" she asked.

Leigh nodded, "Exactly. This story is going to be very meta for you to write. Just like Project Fanfic was for Raelyn when she wrote it. I would rather you be in a comfortable and drama free space to write than the chaos of touring."

Laurel sat back fighting the urge to defend Zeppelin and Thomas and continue being on tour with them. Even though the tour had been stressful, Laurel couldn't imagine being away from either of her boys again. The time spent with them both meant more to her than anything even if they were all at their wits ends with each other. However, she knew Leigh was right.

"Okay. I would like to stay for their last show in California then I can go hide away to write my book."

"I really thought you were going to fight me more on this." Leigh chuckled.

"I pick and choose my battles; however, it's no guarantee that Zepp and Thomas won't come find me at the end of the tour. I mean, they know where I live and where I write."

Leigh rolled her eyes, "Well, you don't have to write in your office at home. I told you, if you want to write somewhere else just tell me and I will make it happen."

An idea popped into her mind bring a smile to her face, "Well… I do have one idea of somewhere I could write and still have support around me."

"Tell me where and I will book your flight right now."

After Laurel settled where she would land after the next show, she decided she needed to get off the bus and get some fresh air. She quickly changed into some leggings and a Heartstrings shirt. Walking towards the venue, Laurel could hear Zeppelin's voice coming through the speakers on stage. She walked up to the side of the stage and sat down in a seat.

Zeppelin was standing at the microphone singing the chorus of their biggest hit. His guitar was on his back as he held the mic with both hands. If you didn't know better, anyone would have thought he sounded amazing. Laurel wasn't just anyone. She could hear an undertone of stress and sadness in his voice. His body was slightly hunched in like he could curl in on himself at any moment. While he was playing his guitar solo, she could tell he was going through the motions.

"He's been mopey all day."

"Shit!" Laurel nearly jumped out of the seat when Jake's voice came from behind her, "Don't scare me like that!"

She smacked his arm as he sat next to her, "Sorry. I saw you walking over here and thought I would check in. I heard Thomas went to see you."

"It wasn't Johnny's vault. I'm sure Thomas was waiting for him to leave before getting on the bus."

Jake nodded, "Are you alright?"

Laurel looked back up at Zeppelin walking towards the opposite side of the stage she was sitting on. Her heart longed to go to him. To hug him, kiss him. To make him smile. It was at that moment something clicked, and she knew exactly what she needed to do next.

"I will be. Hey, do you think someone would be available to take me to the airport tomorrow after we land in Concord. I'm going to be headed back home and then going on a little writing retreat."

Jake pulled out his phone, "I'll take you. I'll have Johnny take my duties for the band. Just text me when you're ready to leave."

She leaned over, hugging him, "Thank you. I'm really glad I got to know you these last few months. Promise me you'll keep in touch after I leave."

"You can't get rid of me that easily. Any time you need a bodyguard feel free to steal me away from Zeppelin." He stood, giving her shoulder a squeeze then headed towards the stairs to the stage.

Laurel took one last look at Zeppelin on stage who was talking to Rich and started walking back towards the buses. She pulled out her phone and sent a text to Thomas.

She saw the read receipt, but no response came from him. Turning the corner to the parking lot, she saw Thomas was leaning against the bus. Stopping for a moment, Laurel looked at how Thomas' body language mirrored Zeppelin's. They were both miserable and she hated that she was the cause of it.

"Hey." She said as she approached the bus.

"Hey." Thomas pushed himself off the bus, "What did you want to talk about?"

Laurel motioned for them to sit at a bench near the venue, "I wanted to let you know that I'm going to be flying back home once we arrive in Concord. I'm going to go on a writing retreat with Raelyn to start my book… again."

His head snapped to hers, "When did you decide to leave? I figured you would finish out the tour."

"I talked with Leigh this afternoon. Since I'm starting a whole new project we both felt it was best for me to go somewhere I could focus fully on it." She bumped her shoulder into his, "Being on tour with my best friends and favorite band is distracting me a little."

He didn't smile or laugh, instead Thomas looked as if he was going to cry at any moment. His hands flexed over his thighs as he struggled with whatever inner battle he was having.

"I want you to know that I didn't make this decision because of what is going on between the three of us."

"Bullshit." He muttered then turned towards her, "If you're uncomfortable being around both of us then I will leave."

Laurel let out a frustrated sigh, "You know, for once, I wish you two would believe me at my word."

Thomas scoffed, "What's that supposed to mean?"

"I told you the truth as to why I'm leaving tour early and yet you don't believe me. Even when you two are being complete morons and dicks, I have never felt uncomfortable being around either of you. So, no Thomas, I'm not leaving because of all the crap between us. I'm leaving early to be with my friend and finish my book."

"I'm sorry," His head dipped down, "Everything just feels different now…"

"Now that I know you both are in love with me. Which I think you both are delusional for that."

Finally, his lips curled into a soft smile, "Yeah, well guilty."

His lips parted to say something else, but then he looked back down at the ground. Laurel placed her hand over his squeezing it.

"Spit it out."

Thomas squeezed her hand back, "You're choosing Zeppelin, aren't you?"

This was it. The moment her decision could change everything. Laurel's stomach twisted into knots, but she took a deep breath then answered him.

"Yes."

Thomas stood up, but she grabbed a hold his hand stopping him from walking away, "Thomas, please let me explain."

"No need to. It's always been you two."

She stepped in front of him placing her hands on his chest, "I love you too."

He scoffed, but she continued, "Honestly, I think I've always had underlining feelings for you since we were kids. I think all the time together we've spent on tour really showed me just how much I love you."

"But not enough to be with me."

She shook her head, "It wouldn't be right. You deserve to be loved fully and unconditionally. You deserve someone who will burn the world for you and defend you to the bitter end. You deserve way more than I could ever give you. I love and respect you too much to selfishly be with you when eventually I think it would all fall apart."

"How do you know that though? How will we ever know if we don't try?" He asked grabbing both of her hands.

"I know because my heart has only ever belonged to one person. I know that hurts you deeply, but I won't lie to you or lead you on. I'm sorry, Thomas. I hope that we can still be friends even though I know that will change as well, but I need you in my life. You're important to me, you always have been."

Thomas looked down at her giving her a short nod, "You're important to me as well and I need you in my life, but…"

She felt the tears welling up knowing what he was about to say.

"I'm going to need some time to myself to figure out how to navigate our friendships."

Tears slid down her cheeks, "I know."

His hands cupped her face as he brushed away her tears, "It won't be forever and if you need me I will always be there for you. I promise."

Laurel nodded, wrapping her arms around him tightly. They stood there for what seemed like forever just holding one another. Thomas kissed the top of her head and loosened his arms from her. His hands found their way around her face once more when a familiar voice came from behind them.

"Well, I guess Laurel made her choice." Zeppelin said before walking past them towards his bus.

Zeppelin

May 1998 – 8th Grade

Zeppelin took a deep breath trying to get the butterflies using his stomach as a mosh pit to calm down. Sitting in their normal meeting spot, he was waiting for Thomas to get there. He felt guilty not inviting Laurel, but Zeppelin wanted to surprise her at the talent show with the final rendition of his song.

He looked up to see Thomas dumping his bike next to his with his, "You do know the talent show is in a couple of hours, right?" he asked.

"Yes, which is why I told you to hurry your ass up."

Thomas sat across from him, digging into his bag and pulling out his camcorder, "Figured, I could record you then we can review it to make any changes needed."

Zeppelin smiled, smacking Thomas' shoulder, "This is why I

keep you around. To be the brains of this operation."

"Remember that when you're famous and need a manager or something." Thomas pointed the camera at him, "Alright monkey, sing."

He flipped Thomas and the camera off before pulling his guitar into his lap. Strumming his fingers over the strings and hearing the first few notes of the song, Zeppelin began to sing. The bridge of the song was always his favorite to play, to sing, to complete lose himself in. With this song, it was easy for him to drifting into the melody and forget all about the world around him. The only thing on his mind was the music and Laurel.

"Zepp, that was amazing!" Thomas exclaimed, clapping.

He felt heat blanketing over his cheeks, "We'll see, play back the video."

Zeppelin hated to admit it, but Thomas was right. The song was nearly perfect, but there were a few improvements he could make before performing it that night.

"Do you mind recording me one more time? I'm going to change something in the chorus."

Thomas shrugged then held up his camcorder again. This time, Zeppelin focused on the notes he was changing and forgot the lyrics for a moment. Remember what his dad told him about making mistakes on stage.

Act like nothing is wrong. The audience will never notice you make a mistake unless you make them aware. Miss a note or a lyric then replay the last line of music and then going into it again.

He did just that, taking a risk to look up at Thomas. He seemed oblivious to the mistake and Zeppelin continued playing. When the song ended, Thomas played back the second performance.

Zeppelin cringed, "That was terrible."

"It wasn't terrible, but it definitely wasn't as good as the first one. Go back to how you played it first and you should be fine." Thomas snapped the camcorder shut, "I need to head home to get ready. You good?"

He nodded, "Yeah, I'll see you tonight. Don't forget we're going out after the talent show."

"Got it! My aunt is all good with it." Thomas called out over his shoulder, picking up his bike and making his way back up to the main road.

Zeppelin sat against the tree mindlessly strumming his guitar. His mind was filled with his inner critic telling him how terrible he was going to be tonight. He wanted nothing more than to head over to Laurel's for one of her famous pep talks or a hug to calm his mind. Looking down at his watch, he knew he needed to head home and get ready.

He arrived at school at five o'clock for rehearsals. Miss Gillam helped him adjust his microphone and congratulated him on his song. Soon, the stage curtains were drawn, and he could hear people filing into the gymnasium. The buzz of people chatting fueled the fluttering butterflies in his stomach. Zeppelin looked around at the other students performing and wondered if they were as nervous as he was.

He peeked out from the side stage trying to locate his family. They were seated in the second row with Laurel's mom and Thomas' aunt. Two seats had signed on them saying 'reserved' that he knew were for his friends. His ears picked up on Laurel's voice immediately as his eyes looked over at the ticket table.

"Ticket. Please." She said with her eyes narrowed in on the blond in front of her.

"Here you go. I guess this was your only talent. Manual labor to those better than you." Mandy said, handing over her ticket.

Zeppelin watched as Thomas took hold of Laurel's elbow and whispered something in her ear. He was thankful that Thomas was there to make sure Laurel was okay.

"Soon, Zepp won't need your support. I'll be with him, and he'll forget all about you losers." Mandy said before her and her friends walked away from the table.

"What the hell does that mean?" Zeppelin whispered to himself.

"Zeppelin?" Miss Gillam said, "We're about to start."

He took one last look at Laurel before stepping back to his spot backstage. There were only ten performances for the talent show. Most were dance routines set to popular pop music. A group from the drama club performed a hilarious improv act. Then there was

Andy showing off his basketball skills.

"You're next Zeppelin." Miss Gillam said before heading out on the stage, "For our final performance, we have Zeppelin Foster performing an original song."

He started to walk out on the stage when his legs felt like they could give out from beneath him at any moment. Adjusting his microphone, his hands trembled, and his fingers could barely hold his guitar pick.

"Go Zepp! You got this babe!"

He looked up to see Mandy clapping while Laurel was sitting behind her with a look that could kill. He shook his head, smiling at the thought of Laurel making Mandy's head explode with her mind and pure will. Looking back down at Laurel, all of his insecurities and nervousness vanished. Everyone in the room disappeared except for her.

"This song is dedicated to my number one fan. This is Fangirl, My Girl."

Zeppelin closed his eyes and began playing the first notes of Laurel's song. He took a chance during the chorus to look out at the crowd and see everyone bopping their heads or swaying to his music. He glanced over at his parents seeing them both smiling proudly up at him and his dad wiping his eyes. Then his eyes landed on Laurel as he sang ignoring the wildly cheering Mandy in front of her.

Oh, darling fangirl, my girl

Your spirit like wildfire on a summer day,

You're like a soothing wind on a warm evening

Your soft lips,

Your caramel eyes,

Your wildfire spirit,

Your soothing being...

How could I look at another when your beautiful love is so

strong?

He began to play the bridge, closing his eyes and lowering his head. The strings of his guitar biting into his fingertips as they slid over them. The music wound around him and took him off into a world where only he and Laurel existed. An escape from the reality before them and into a dream where the only thing that mattered was them.

Going into the last chorus, he gave it his all for her. With the last note ringing out, the crowd stood cheering and applauding him. The rush from their excitement filled his whole body with an energy he couldn't describe. He couldn't help the wide smile spreading over his face as he looked down at his family and friends. Seeing the pride in their faces made his heart soar and suddenly he couldn't wait to go be with them.

Heading backstage, he tried to grab his things as quickly as he could only to stop when Miss Gillam and Mr. Cason were congratulating him on his performance. As he headed down the hallway to the gym, Zeppelin was suddenly bombarded by Mandy and her group of friends.

"Oh my god Zepp, that was an amazing performance!" She

gushed.

"Oh, thanks Mandy." He said, trying to move past her.

She stepped in front of him, "I really think one day you could be famous. Wouldn't that be awesome if you were to be a big rock star. Of course, you would need a hot wife to tour with you."

She ran her hand down his arm, leaning in towards him, "You know I'm planning on being a model or actress. We would make quite the pair together." She batted her clumpy lashes at him as her Tommy Girl perfume made him want to gag.

Trying to be polite he chuckled, "I think right now, I'm focused on making it through high school. I really need to meet up with my family and friends. See you around."

He quickly stepped away from her and made his way into the gym. Looking around, he didn't see his family or anyone in the spots they had been sitting in. Several people came up to him to tell him how much they loved his song and how talented he was. The attention was quickly becoming overwhelming, and he felt his chest tightening.

Zeppelin smiled and thanked everyone who came up to him. Frantically, his eyes were searching for any sign of Laurel or his family. He spotted the exit sign and headed out the door. The cool night air nearly made him choke as he took in as much as his lungs could handle. That's when he heard his mom and dad's voices. Looking in their direction, he found them waiting with Thomas and Laurel by their car. Taking another deep breath in, Zeppelin headed towards them.

"What did you guys think?" He called out.

His parents pulled him into a family hug, "Sweetie, you were amazing up there."

His dad nodded, "I'm proud of you, Zeppelin. Now, let's go celebrate with burgers and milkshakes."

"Yes! I'm starving!" He slung his arm around Laurel's shoulders, "What did you think of the song?"

He noticed she had been standing off to the side as if trying to disappear without anyone noticing. Her shoulders were sagging and the smile on her face didn't reach up to her eyes.

"It was great. One day it may even be number one on TRL."

Zeppelin stared into her eyes trying to see what she was really thinking. Something was off, he could feel it deep within him.

"You really think?" He asked as she nodded getting into their van.

During dinner, he kept up conversations with his dad about the improvements he wanted to make with his song and listening to his mom fuss over Thomas. However, he was keenly aware of how distant Laurel was being. She hardly spoke unless she was asked a direct question. She pushed her food around on her plate and had barely looked in his direction. He decided he had to take matters into his own hands. Picking up a fry, he threw it at her aiming for her V-neck shirt. Her eyes snapped up to him.

"I missed." Zeppelin chuckled.

He took aim once more at her chest. The fry flew through the air and right down her shirt.

"Score!"

"Zeppelin Dean Foster!" his mom yelled, making his cheeks burn.

He smiled bashfully, "Sorry mom, but it was necessary. Laurel was lost in her own thoughts, and I had to bring her back to reality. It's my sworn duty as her best friend."

Laurel rolled her eyes at him, "I'll remember this the next time I need to smack you with one of my flip flops."

As they walked back out to the car, Zeppelin pulled Thomas back behind the group, "What's wrong with her?"

"I honestly don't know. I'm sure Mandy declaring that you and her being the 'it' couple for next year didn't help any."

Zeppelin's stomach churned, "Ew. Like I would ever be with a girl like her. Do you mind sitting in the middle so I can talk with Laurel in the back?"

Thomas shook his head and took a seat in the middle row. Zeppelin slid into the back row next to Laurel who was staring out the window.

"Did you like my dedication?" Zeppelin asked, bumping his shoulder into hers.

She nodded, "Yeah, it was really sweet. I bet your number one fan was over the moon to hear her song."

There was a sharp edge to her tone. She was definitely upset, and he was only hoping that it wasn't because of him. It was now or never to let her know the truth about his song and performance.

"So, you were over the moon? Here I thought were in the second row for my first ever performance."

Her eyes snapped up to him, "Me? I wasn't talking about me. I figured the way you had looked at Mandy when she called out to you that it was for her."

There it was. He couldn't believe Laurel would ever think he would have any attraction to Mandy, "You're joking, right?"

Laurel searched his eyes for a moment and Zeppelin tried as hard as he could to make her see she was the only one for him.

"It wasn't for Mandy?" She questioned, but he could hear a small hint of hope behind it.

Zeppelin slipped his arm around her shoulder, pulling her into his side, "Hell no. Why would I ever want that nasty girl as my fan? Ew."

"You looked right at her…"

"I was looking at you, Laurel. I was freaking out and when I heard Mandy's screeching my eyes landed on you. You have always been the one who brings me back from my own self-doubt." He reached between them unbuckling her seatbelt along with his own.

He pulled her even closer to him, "You will always be my number one fangirl and my girl."

Laurel buried her head into his chest, "Damn right I am." She whispered.

Zeppelin laughed, hugging her tightly to him and holding her until they arrived at her house. That night when exhaustion pulled him under, he dreamed of performing on a big stadium stage and Laurel being the only person in the crowd.

Zeppelin

Zeppelin had seen Laurel talking with Jake during soundcheck. She looked almost as miserable as he felt. It took everything he had to not rush over to her and pull her into his arms. Rich was talking to him about a change in the set when he caught her heading back towards the parking lot. He went back to trying to focus on rehearsals but made the decision he could not go on stage tonight without talking to her. He needed to know where they stood and that eventually everything would be good between them.

The moment soundcheck ended, he rushed off stage towards his bus. When he reached the gate leading out, he watched as Laurel wrapped her arms around Thomas. His feet suddenly fused with the ground beneath him. They stood there in a long embrace with Thomas pressing his lips to the top of her head. Zeppelin rubbed his chest as a deep ache rippled across it. Thomas got to her first and she had made her decision. The deep ache quickly turned to a burning fury. He forced his feet forward, heading straight for them.

"Well, I guess Laurel made her choice." Zeppelin said before walking past them towards his bus, "Congrats to you both. I hope the two of you will be happy together."

"Zeppelin, wait…" Laurel called out.

He kept heading towards his bus. His anger mixing with agonizing heartache, making it hard for him to breathe. He ran up the bus stairs and headed straight for the private room. He stopped immediately as Laurel's floral smell hit him with the force of a hurricane. He tried to take in a breath only for his lungs to seize and burn in his chest.

"Zep-" Laurel's voice cut off as he crumbled to the ground, "Zeppelin!"

She tried sitting him up, but he pushed her away, "Go. G-Go away. It h-hurts too much."

He heard her swear under her breath as he closed his eyes. He could feel her arm slip beneath his head while another tightened around his waist. Zeppelin swore his heart was literally ripping in half within his chest and let out a strangled sob.

"Zepp, look at me. You're having a panic attack, and I need you to focus on me."

"No… no…" He shook his head.

He couldn't focus on her, it hurt too much. She had chosen Thomas over him. Everything he had desired for his future was slipping away and he didn't see the point for him to keep going. Zeppelin felt Laurel place his hand over her rapidly beating heart. Her chest expanded as she took a deep breath then collapsed slowly as she let it out.

"Zeppelin, you have to breath with me." He felt her take a deep breath again, "Breath with me." She whispered as she let out her breath.

The next time she took a deep breath, he did as well. His chest burned as the cool air hit his lungs. Then he let it out slowly. Laurel pressed her forehead against his and entwined their legs together. His body was fully pressed against hers and immediately began to calm down within her presence.

"That's good. Can you open your eyes for me now?"

Zeppelin slowly lifted his eyelids and saw Laurel's dark eyes staring back at him. She smiled softly before hugging him tightly against her.

"You scared me for a second." She whispered.

"S-Sorry." He buried his head into the crook of her neck taking in her scent for the last time, "I'll be fine. You should go."

Laurel pulled away from him slightly, "I'm not leaving."

Zeppelin pushed himself up, resting his back against the bed, "Laurel, I'll be fine. I'm sure you and Thomas want to spend time together."

His stomach lurched up into his throat thinking about Thomas and Laurel being together. He didn't know if he would ever be able to see them together without wanting to vomit.

"Thomas and I have already talked. You're the one I need to talk to. First, you need to get some water and maybe a snack. You're paler than normal." She chuckled.

She stood up, heading toward the kitchenette. She held out a protein bar and bottled water for him. He took the bottle, pressing it against the side of his face. If he tried to put anything in his stomach it would come right back up and couldn't have that hours before a show.

"Look, we don't need to talk. You obviously made your choice and that's fine."

She sat cross legged in front of him, "How do you even know what choice I made?"

He gritted his teeth to keep from snapping back at her, "It was pretty clear when I walked up on you and Thomas outside."

"We were hugging, Zepp. We've hugged each other a million times over the last twenty or so years. We're friends, remember?" Laurel crossed her arms over her chest, "Maybe, if you had stopped and talked to us before storming off then you wouldn't be sitting here assuming shit."

Zeppelin pushed himself off the floor, heading towards the front of the bus, "I'm not assuming anything. I know what I saw, and it was much more than a friendly hug. Stop beating around the bush and just tell me already."

She was right behind him as he leaned against the table, "I'm not beating around the bush. You automatically assumed you knew what was going on instead of hearing me out. So, tell me exactly what you think I've chosen."

He gripped the table tightly, looking down at his feet. He was trying not to snap or take out his frustrations on her. However, what little will power he had left vanished, and the words were coming out before he knew it.

"You chose the safe option. Thomas is stable, he's smart and financially secure. He has a semi-normal life and schedule. You chose the safety of having a normal guy instead of the fucked up rockstar. The fucked up rockstar with crazy fans, an even crazier schedule and who fucks anything that comes his way. Am I right? Tell me I'm right."

Zeppelin watched as her cheeks turned a dark shade of pink and her eyes hardened on him. He had seen Laurel mad plenty of times, but at that moment she was kind of terrifying.

"You really think that lowly of me? You really think I would simply choose the safe route rather than choosing who I really want to be with? That I would use Thomas by leading him on to think I'm one hundred percent in love with him when I'm not."

His head snapped up to say something, but Laurel was on a roll not letting him get a word in.

"I don't care about the fame or the money or that craziness of your life. If I cared about that then I wouldn't be out on tour with you right now. Hell, I wouldn't have stayed friends with you. I've been by your side through it all, Zeppelin. Every TMZ worthy night out, every fangirl who got to sleep with you before I did, everything."

His heart sank. She was right. Every moment, Laurel had been there to bring him back to solid ground.

"I told Thomas that yes, I have feelings for him. However, my heart belonged to you. It always belonged to you since the day we met in fifth grade."

"Laurel, I…"

"However, I'm starting to think that I shouldn't be with either of you. You both promised each other to protect me. Yet, both of you are the ones who have hurt me the most. First with you fighting and now, you thinking I would choose Thomas simply because he's the safest option."

Zeppelin tried reaching out for her, but she smacked his arms out of the way, "Don't. You're the one who taught me to live my life by following my heart. No matter how wild and crazy the path may be. Well, I guess I learned my lesson now, didn't I?"

Laurel headed towards the bus door, but he caught her elbow pulling her back to him. She pushed against him, but he held on tighter.

"Laurel, please don't leave."

"Why Zeppelin? Why shouldn't I?" She hit her fists against his chest, "I wanted to tell you that I chose you. That I love you. That I've always been in love with you and want to be on the crazy ride with you. I want you Zeppelin, but now… now I know how you really feel. I can't."

His arms went slack, and he watched as Laurel walked off the bus. His mind reeling with her confession. She loved him. She chose him. That kicked his ass in gear to chase after her.

"Laurel wait!" he yelled as his feet hit the ground.

"No, I'm done. You made your choice, Zeppelin." He ran up behind her and twirled her around into his arms, "Let go of me!"

He shook his head, "I'm never letting you go again. Laurel, I love you. I've always loved you. I told you there's only ever been one person to fill the void inside of me and that's you. I never felt good enough for you. You deserve the best of the best. You deserve someone who can give you the world and I've been working towards that goal my entire career."

Her body relaxed against his, "I don't need the best or the world. You're the only one I've ever needed; don't you see that? You're my world."

Zeppelin brought his hands up to either side of her face and pressed his head to hers, "And you're mine." He pressed his lips against hers gently.

"My world." He kissed her again.

"My heart." And again.

"My forever."

This time, she pressed her lips to his. Her hands went up into his hair gently tugging on it as their kiss deepened. He dipped down, grabbing her thighs and picking her up off the ground. Carrying her back to the bus. Zeppelin showed her how much he loved her until the last possible minute that he needed to go get ready for his show. Taking one last look at her lying on the bed, he knew for the first time exactly where his future was headed, and he couldn't wait to take that journey with Laurel by his side.

Laurel

Laurel woke up the next morning feeling like a completely new person. She knew there were still a lot of things to work out especially with Thomas. For now, she was enjoying the comfort and bliss of lying beside the man she loved. Zeppelin's arm rested along her side and his slow, steady breath against her shoulder brought goosebumps down her arm. For a split second, the tiniest hint of insecurity tried to rise out of her, grasping the sheet closer to her bare chest.

"Hmm…" Zeppelin shifted against her as a small gasp escaped her lips.

His hard length pressed against the curve of her ass and heat flooded her body. She felt his lips curve into a smile against her skin.

"I'll never get over your little reactions to my cock." He whispered.

"Trust me, I'll get used to it. Right now, I'm not used to waking up with a big dick next to me."

Zeppelin pushed himself up, letting her roll onto her back beneath him, "Awe, thank you."

"I wasn't talking about him," She reached between them stroking him gently, "I was simply talking about you."

He tried to act offended until a deep moan rumbled from his chest.

"Fuck, can't even be upset right now with you touching me." He leaned down, pressing his lips to hers, "I need you."

She smiled, "I'm yours."

By the time they arrived in Concord, California, Laurel and Zeppelin had made love, showered and ate breakfast. Zeppelin still had a couple of hours before he needed to head off to the venue making this the only opportunity Laurel would have to talk to him about everything. He was looking over some papers Jake had dropped off from Thomas.

"Everything okay?"

Zeppelin shrugged, "Thomas is wanting to take a leave of absence for a few months. He's going to go back to L.A. to find his own place. He's given me a list of potential replacements for him."

Laurel slipped into the booth next to him, "I'm sorry. It's going to be weird between us all now."

He nodded, "Yeah but we'll work it all out. For now, I'll enjoy the time I get to spend with you. You're coming back to L.A. after the tour, right?"

She took a deep breath to calm her nerves, "Actually, I need to talk to you about the rest of the tour. Do you want good news upfront or not so good news?"

"I really thought I was going to keep my little bubble of happiness for a little longer than a day." He looked over at her with a smirk, "Good news to keep the delusion alive."

She chuckled, "After the fight, I was talking to Raelyn about everything going on and she mention how it would make a great plot for a book."

"Oh no…" He muttered.

"It's not what you think." Laurel pulled out her notebook and started showing Zeppelin the outline she had come up with.

As she rambled on about everything she could see in this book, he kept reading each and every page. Finally, when she ran out of words to say he looked back at her with a wide smile.

"This sounds amazing, fangirl! You can tell you really love this story and want to tell it. I think you should."

"Good, keep thinking that because there is a little more." She averted her eyes from his, "I want it noted that this decision was made before everything happened last night."

"This must be the not so good news, but duly noted, continue."

"I told Leigh about my book idea, and she loved it. Her only concern was me being able to focus on getting my first draft written. So, she suggested for me to go on a writing retreat, and I thought what better retreat than with other writers.”

Zeppelin lifted her chin, “So, you’re leaving for your retreat after the tour.”

She shook her head, “I’m leaving when sound check starts. Jake is driving me to the airport. I’m flying home to get some things from my office and then to New Orleans to stay with Raelyn.”

His jaw clenched as he dropped his hand from her face, “You’re leaving today… well that’s just great.”

Zeppelin gently pushed her from the seat so he could get up. He walked towards the back of the bus as she followed him.

“Zepp, I honestly thought that I needed to leave so you and Thomas could patch things up. I didn’t know that you and I…” her voice trailed off as he turned around towards her.

“I know.” He ran his hand through his long hair, “I know and I’m sorry that I’m getting frustrated. I’m not used to being the one who is being left. Now, I have to finish out the last few cities without both of my best friends.”

She slipped her arms around his neck, “I think you should talk to Thomas before he leaves. See if you guys could come to a common ground for the last leg of the tour. I think if you two can just talk it out like you did when we were kids then he’ll stay.”

He hugged her tightly, “How long will you be in New Orleans?”

“I don’t know. Until I finish the first draft of my novel. Raelyn is working on her new book as well. Austin is going to be in Vancouver filming a movie for a few months and her daughter is moving away to college."

It had been the perfect situation for Raelyn and Laurel. Emerson had even texted them to say she would be traveling down south with the baseball team and would take a week off to hang out with them. It was truly the first time Laurel had felt like she had girlfriends in her life.

"Well, I hate to say this, but…" Zeppelin pressed his lips against her temple, "it sounds like this is the best thing for you and Raelyn. I can't be upset or mad if it's the best thing for you."

She looked up at him, "Really? You promise not to go off, drink your loneliness away and get with some fangirl."

His face scrunched up as he shook his head, "I've told you once and I'll tell you again. You are the only fangirl I want. I promise." He held out his pinky to her.

She hooked hers with his, "Good. Now, come help me pack quickly so we can spend what little time we have together."

A few hours later, Laurel was staring out the window of a plane, watching the clouds floating by. Zeppelin had been more of a distraction than help with packing and they ended up making out until Jake came to get Zeppelin for sound check. Their goodbyes had been filled with tears, kisses and promises of talking every chance they had. Now, alone with her thoughts and overwhelming feelings of heartache, Laurel pulled out her notebook to begin her rough draft by hand.

Thankfully, her mom met her at the airport to take her back

home. Walking into her house was like walking into a stranger's home. Nothing seemed the same because it wasn't. This was no longer her home. Now home was wherever Zeppelin was.

She went to her office to refill her writer's bag and grab her extra laptop charger. She passed by her bookcase when the picture of her, Zeppelin and Thomas at her book release caught her eye. Picking up the frame, she stared at the smiling faces in the photo. Everything was simpler then and part of her started to doubt that she had made the right decision in choosing anyone over keeping their friendship intact.

Her phone buzzed on her desk. She placed the photo back on her bookshelf then opened the text from Zeppelin. It was a photo of two whiskey glasses clinking together.

Laurel smiled sending him a text back immediately. She finished packing up what she needed, and her mom drove her back to the airport. As she waited at the boarding gate, her phone buzzed again with a text. Looking at the time, she knew it couldn't be Zeppelin since he was probably in the middle of their set.

> **Thomas:** There's always been one thing that Zeppelin and I can agree on and that's making sure you're our top priority. I'm staying on tour with him but will probably need some time to myself after that. Have a safe flight and have some fun with Raelyn. I'm here if you ever need me. I love ya.

> **Thomas:** Also, I threatened Zeppelin that I would kill him if he broke your heart in any sort of way. Just so you know.

> LOL! Thank you. I love ya too and I'm glad you two talked.

She put her phone away as they called her flight. Looking out the window once more, she couldn't help the smile spreading across her face. She finally felt like she had found her place in this crazy world, and it was in between two men that were crazy about her.

Laurel

July 2000 – 11ᵗʰ Grade

Her world was spinning. Swirls of green and blue flashing before her eyes. The smell of earth filling her nose. The loud crack of wood splitting ringing in her ears. Then came the pain. Every inch of her body screaming in agony. She couldn't move. Her arms wouldn't move. Her legs were in a tight vice. All the pain was washed away by shear, raw panic. An eerie silence closing in around her before an ear-shattering scream erupted from her.

Laurel's eyes snapped open, and everything was bleary. The light above her was as bright as the sun and a wave a nausea rolled over her. She was dead. This was the bright light she had read about at the end of her life. How did she die? Laurel couldn't remember anything. Driving. She was driving to Branson. Listening to her favorite mix CD from Zeppelin and enjoying to unusual cool July day. Then there was a truck… a big truck. Then her world went on a spin cycle.

"Oh, oh dear." A soft, kind voice brought her out of her memory.

An angel, it had to be an angel going to walk her through the gates of heaven.

"Let me go get the doctor." She said as Laurel's vision started to clear.

The light came in focus. Fluorescent, bright white like the ceiling titles surrounding it. Laurel thought it was weird that heaven would have ceiling tiles, fluorescent lights and a doctor.

"Well, well, Miss Adler we're glad to see you awake. There are going to be a lot of people happy to see you as well."

An older man in a white coat and a stethoscope around his neck leaned over her. He gently opened her eyes wider and flashed a pinpoint light in them. She tried to lift her arm up only to realize that something heavy was on top of it. When she tried to talked, her throat resisted, and another realization sent a wave of panic over her.

"Miss Adler, try not to talk or move. You've been in a serious accident and have been unconscious for several days. We'll remove the tube from your mouth, but it will be very uncomfortable."

She nodded eagerly, not caring how uncomfortable it would be. Slowly the doctor began pulling the tube from her throat and she began coughing uncontrollably. Fear spiked in her chest as the feeling of vomit surging up her blocked throat. Spit and vomit followed the end of the tube as the nurse rushed to her side with a plastic bin for her to heave in.

"Try to take a deep breath deary. You're alright." She rubbed Laurel's back as she kept dry heaving into the bin.

When the urge to throw up faded, she sat back in her bed completely exhausted. Her body aching in places she didn't even know existed on her. Looking down at her leg she found it three times the size it normally was by the hard, white plaster wrapped around it. She glanced at her right arm seeing it wrapped up the same way.

"You broke your arm at the elbow and radius. We think you locked your arm when you were hit which snapped your radius."

The nurse came over with a cup of ice chips and spoon fed her one. The moment the cool ice melted on her tongue she was desperate for more. "…'Ore, 'lease?" She rasped.

She smiled and fed her a few more as the doctor continued, "Your leg fared better slightly. The femur is broken near your knee but should heal fully in several weeks with physical therapy. Your arm will need more time to set and heal. You have a long road ahead of you but considering the alternative I think you'll be just fine."

Laurel let the ice chips melt down her throat then tried to speak, "M-My… m-m-mom…"

The doctor smile, "She's in the waiting room with the rest of your family including a young man that she threatened to have security kick out if he didn't go home and take a shower."

Laurel smiled imagining Zeppelin getting tossed out of the

hospital, "S-Sounds… about r-right."

"For now, I think you need to get some rest. We'll let them visit in a little bit. If you can keep your ice chips down you can graduate to broth and maybe jello."

She gave him a thumbs up already feeling her eyelids getting heavy. He gently patted her good leg and left the room. The nurse stayed to take her vitals and make sure her ice chips were in reach of her.

"That young man hasn't left your side in days. He even convinced one of our night security guards and head nurse to let him and your other friend in. You're a very lucky young lady."

Tears slipped down the side of Laurel's face, "I-I know."

"Get some sleep. I'm sure that handsome guy will be here soon enough." Laurel closed her eyes hearing the door shut as darkness consumed her.

Flashes of green spun in front of her. The sound of low voices speaking sternly at one another dragging her out of the green blur. Her eyelids were too heavy to lift open, but the voices were becoming clearer.

"You got some nerve being here now."

Zeppelin sounded angry, but she couldn't imagine who he could be angry with that was visiting her in the hospital. The other man spoke but she couldn't tell who it was still. Zeppelin asked him if her mom had told him she was her.

"Yeah, called me the night after the accident. It took me some time to get here from Vancouver."

Vancouver. There was only one person she knew in Vancouver. She was shocked that he would even care enough to come see her. Suddenly, her body was flowing with hot resenting rage that she had suppressed since the day he left.

"You had no way of knowing."

Her dad spoke, as the rage ringing in her ears distracted her from what Zeppelin had said. She felt his fingers laced with hers. His thumb gently running over her palm calming her in an instant. The burning rage went to a simmer and her body began feeling heavy again.

"I know, but that doesn't take away the feeling of guilt I have for not being here to protect her. I made a promise to her, to our friend Thomas, that I would protect her no matter what. I failed her."

Silence fell over them before her dad spoke again, "If you truly believe that, then what do you plan on doing about it?"

The darkness was starting to take over again. She tried to listening to Zeppelin's voice, but it was lulling her back to sleep. Soon it faded into nothing, and she was back in her car singing Blink-182. Instead of the endless spinning, she felt like something was pressing against her. Forest green flashed before her eyes. Or maybe it was someone.

Zeppelin.

She pushed her eyes open looking over to see an empty chair to one side of her. Then she felt movement from her other side and saw Zeppelin's mop of silky, dark locks covering his arm. She threaded her fingers through the strands.

"H-Hey, are you okay?" She asked.

His dark eyes snapped up to hers, "Laurel? Let me go get a nurse for you." He went to move but she reached out for him.

"Please stay, I-I don't want you to leave. Wha… what happened?"

Zeppelin brought her hand to his lips, "I promise we'll tell you everything, but please let me call for the nurse to come check on you. You truly scared the hell out of all of us."

She nodded as he left the room. Several things happened at once. The doctor from before came in to check in on her and get her more ice chips. Then her mom and Thomas came in fussing over her. Her mom was near tears as she kissed the top of her head. Thomas held her hand saying how worried he had been. Laurel couldn't help noticing Zeppelin standing by the door watching them.

The doctor cleared his throat, "Laurel still needs to get some rest. I think it's best to visit in small time frames."

"Baby, we'll be right outside. We're not going anywhere." Her mom whispered as she nodded.

"Could…" Laurel cleared her throat, "Could Zeppelin stay with me, please?"

The doctor nodded stating only for a few minutes then left the room. Thomas kissed the top of her head as her mom kissed her cheek. As Zeppelin was walking toward her bed, her mom stopped him saying something she couldn't hear.

She heard him say, "Yes ma'am."

Her mom smiled, following Thomas out of her room. He sat on the edge of her bed careful of her leg.

"What was that about?" she asked.

He shook his head, "Nothing, just me promising to never let you drive again."

Laurel rolled her eyes at him then patted the spot next her, "Would you lay with me?"

"Of course, fangirl."

Laurel moved over as much as she could to give Zeppelin more room. He was careful of her leg and made sure her arm was still propped up as it was. His arm slipped beneath her head and the other rested on her stomach.

"Better?"

Laurel yawned, "Much. Thank you, Zepp."

Zeppelin pressed his lips to her forehead whispering, "Anything for my girl."

Quickly she drifted off to sleep, no longer spinning endlessly in greens and blues. She was surrounded by the comforting forest green and a soothing melody of her song playing.

Laurel

The crowd was nearly as loud as the band playing on stage. Laurel watched her boyfriend bounce over to the opposite side of the stage from where she was standing. He was singing their newest summer hit, "No Quiet Songs (at Our Summer Carnival)"

We're all going to a summer carnival

No more reading for a week or two

Innocent clouds and shy parks at our summer carnival

No more quiet songs for me or you

For a week or two

Summertime, and the livin' is innocent

Clouds are singing and the parks are high

Oh, your brother's warm and your sister is wild

So hush my soft blossom, don't you cry

Oh the summer of 2000

He swung his guitar back in front of him and went into playing the chorus as Alec began singing. Beside Laurel was Raelyn. She had on a Heartstrings tour shirt and a pair of curve hugging jeans. Her head bopped to the beat Sam was hitting as her husband, Austin, stood behind her. Laurel chuckled when she found his hands gripping Raelyn's hips as he headbanged along with the song. Rock music had the same effect on everyone who listened to it live… it made them horny like rabbits.

A hand squeezed Laurel's shoulder as she turned to see Leigh motioning for her to follow her. She tapped on Raelyn's shoulder and yelled, "Be right back!"

She followed Leigh backstage to the green room where Thomas was pacing beside the couch.

True to his word, Thomas had moved out of the band house after last year's tour. Leigh had offered to get in contact with some friends of hers to help find him a place. As a thank you, he flew her out to L.A. to celebrate finding a quiet home on the coast. One thing led to another, and the next thing Laurel knew they were both texting her about the other and how much they were attracted to them. Laurel was over the moon for them to find one another.

"What's going on?" she asked.

"I think you should sit down for this." Thomas said, motioning to the couch.

She raised an eyebrow, "You're both scaring me. What happened?"

Leigh picked up her laptop, "Well you know your book came out a couple of weeks ago."

"Yes, I believe I was there for that."

"Well, the New York Times most recent bestsellers list came out today." Leigh slowly turned her laptop around, "Look at number seven."

Laurel scanned the list until she saw her book's title and her name, "Wh-What?"

Leigh nodded excitedly, "Congrats Laurel! You're a New York Times bestselling author!"

The room began spinning even with her seated on the couch, "I... I..." She looked up at Thomas, who was beaming with pride.

"Congratulations!" He leaned over the couch and kissed the top of her head, "You more than deserve this."

"I'm a New York Times best seller..." She muttered staring on the computer screen, "I'M A NEW YORK TIMES BEST SELLER!" she yelled.

She jumped up off the couch and hugged Leigh with tears of joy following immediately after that. There was a knock on the door before Jake walked in.

"Hey fangirl, your man is calling for you on stage."

Laurel's face must have reflected the panic consuming the joy that had been spreading over her, "What? Oh god..."

She quickly made her way back to the stage where Zeppelin was waiting for her, "Where the hell were you? Nevermind, come on fangirl."

He held his hand out to her which she took and led her on stage.

She hated it when he pull her out on stage, but dating a famous rockstar tended to put her in the spotlight more than she cared for. Sometimes, it was literally.

"I found her!" Zeppelin spun her in a circle as the crowd cheered, "Would you like to tell our amazing fans where you were instead of rocking out to some kick ass music."

She jabbed him in the side before speaking in the mic, "If you must know I was getting some news about my recent book release."

Zeppelin perked up before asking the crowd, "How many of you have bought my girl's book?"

The roar was deafening.

"How many of you have read it and loved it?"

The roar remained the same making her cheek burn as she took the mic from Zeppelin, "Well I would love to thank every single one of you because…"

She looked up at Zeppelin, "I reached number seven on the New York Times best sellers list! I'm officially a New York Times bestselling author!"

The crowd went wild as Zeppelin scooped her up and twirled her around, "Fangirl that's amazing! I'm so proud of you."

"I could have never done it with you and the constant inspiration you've given me every single day."

Zeppelin leaned down and kissed her hard. His lips on hers, her body against his, Laurel didn't care if thousands of people were watching them. She threaded her hands through his sweat, newly cut short hair as his hands beneath her butt and pressed her against him.

Suddenly, there were sweaty bodies surrounding them as the members of Heartstrings, her friends and the crew came out bringing them all into a group hug. Laurel never had felt more at home than at that moment.

After the show, everyone came over to her and Zeppelin's house. The band, now in their own places but still recorded everything in Zeppelin's home studio. Everyone was relaxing outside and chatting as they all wound down from their show.

Laurel was sitting next to Raelyn who clink her beer bottle against Laurel's water bottle, "Cheers to the newly minted New York Times bestseller."

"I don't think I'll ever get used to that." She chuckled, "So, what is this I hear about a convention we might all be doing?"

Raelyn smiled, "Ah yes, you've shared a little of your rockstar world with us and we've gone to a few of Emerson's baseball hottie's games. I figured it was about time I looped y'all into my world of fandom and conventions."

"This sounds terrifying, but please go on." Laurel glanced up to see Zeppelin and Austin talking with Rich and smiled.

Raelyn snapped her fingers in front of her face, "Hey, are you listening?"

"Sorry, admiring my rockstar from afar." She pointed to their guys talking.

Raelyn hummed, "Ah yes, they do look rather sexy over there

with their guitars."

Zeppelin and Austin each had a guitar in their laps as they strummed along the strings. Zeppelin's deep laughter flowed over her as she heard Raelyn sigh staring at Austin who was singing a few lines of a song.

"Okay…" Raelyn shook her head, "Back to this convention. Emerson has already agreed to it. It would be at San Diego after the Red Moon reunion panel. Leigh has a debut author that apparently matches all of our chaotic energy."

Laurel laughed out loud making Zeppelin look over at her and smile, "Oh boy… that says a lot about them. Is this the book we're all blurbing?"

"That's the one. Honestly, it's fantastic. Anyway, she's going to moderate, and we'll get to promote our fangirl books. You think Zeppelin will let you have a wild fangirl experience in San Diego?"

"I'm all for Laurel having wild fangirl experiences as long as they're with me."

She looked behind her to see Zeppelin and Austin standing behind their chairs. Each of them lifting their girl off her chair and sat down with them on their laps.

"I have to agree with Zepp. Wild fangirl experiences are only meant to be with your favorite celebrities."

Raelyn smirked, "I'm okay with that. Do you think Cali would be up for it and are you okay with Jax watching?"

Laurel swore she heard Austin growl before attacking her sides with his fingertips. A fit of giggles came from her friend and she leaned her head against Zeppelin's.

"What about you? Any other celebrities I should be worried about you wanting wild nights with?" He asked softly against her ear.

Laurel shook her head, "Nope, you're the only rockstar I want wild nights with."

"Damn right." Zeppelin pressed his lips against hers.

Laurel settled back against him, watching as Thomas and Leigh sat on the other side of Raelyn and Austin. Her heart was filled with so much joy that she thought it might burst.

"Whatcha thinking, fangirl?"

She lifted her head smiling, "Life could not be any better than what it is right now."

Laurel kissed Zeppelin letting the world around her fade into the background.

SNEAK PEEK

BOOK 3 IN THE FANGIRL SERIES

COMING OUT FALL 2025

Ending the call, all she could do was laugh at the two men in her life. Her dad, Will, was an amazing father even if he wasn't always there. For most of her and Everett's childhood, their dad played professional baseball for the Dodgers. They had lived in Los Angeles for most of their lives until one fateful night when their world changed forever.

Emerson shook the memories of that night out of her head, and she grabbed her camera. She couldn't think about her mom or the night she died. It had taken years of therapy to get her to where she was now in her grief journey. She wanted to keep herself from falling down that dark path again.

By the end of the third inning, Emerson was heading back to her car with some really great photos of Campbell High's varsity baseball team. A lot of the boys were talented enough to have scouts out in the stands. She was sure their names would be scrolling across her TV screen one day soon. She stopped by their normal diner for a takeout order. The old cook only chuckled when he saw her walk in.

"Your old man called it in about an hour ago." She thanked him with a generous tip and headed home for the night.

Emerson walked through the front door hearing her dad and

Everett cheering from the living room. Walking past them she made her way into the kitchen and started unloading their dinner. A louder groan came from them when she grabbed three bottles of beer from the fridge and set them on the serving tray with the food.

"How they looking?" She asked, sitting on her favorite chair beside Everett and her dad on the couch.

"Like they're two short of a World Series team." Everett grumbled.

"Sometimes, the players get a deal too good to pass up." Her dad took a beer and passed it to her brother then his plate of food.

Emerson looked at the screen to see the Dodgers were down 3-0 in the bottom of the sixth inning, "Wait… who got traded?"

Both men looked over at her conveniently taking a drink of their beers.

"No. You got to be kidding me?"

She pulled out her phone and started looking up the recent trade news from the Dodgers. Sure enough, three weeks ago her favorite player had been traded to the brand-new MLB team out of Vancouver, Washington.

"Oh, for fuc-" She started to say when her dad cut her off.

"Watch it…" He chuckled, "I really thought you knew already that Tucker and Knight had been traded to the Explorers."

She shook her head, "I've been busy and not regularly checking my MLB notifications. Honestly, I figured if any player was safe it would have been Tucker. He's been carrying the team for the last few years and Knight alongside him."

Her dad leaned over towards her, "I spoke to my buddy, Nick, you remember him, right?"

She nodded, "Yeah, he was team manager for the Dodgers."

"Well, he is now GM of the Vancouver Explorers. He offered Tucker and Knight a hell of a deal to lead his new team. They're going to be a little green with a lot of minor leaguers coming up and he needed some seasoned players."

"Well, I guess I need to look up their jersey so I can get a new Tucker jersey. Do you know will he keep his number?"

Her dad nodded, "More than likely unless he wants to change it. New team means he can have whatever number he wants."

Her dad turned his attention back to the pitiful game on the screen while Emerson looked up Pacey Tucker's Instagram account. He had no recent posts since the end of last season which wasn't unusual. One reason she liked him was because he kept his private life private. That and he was hot. She scrolled to one of her favorite pictures from last season. Pacey was standing in the on-deck circle getting ready to bat. He was mid swing when the photographer snapped the picture. Pacey was in perfect form and then she remembered watching him that game walk up to bat. Once again, he swung and hit a grand slam winning the game to get them into the Wild Card slot.

"Em, you're drooling." Everett chuckled as she threw a fry at him.

"And you're annoying as ever."

The next day, Emerson was thankful for there being no school due to professional development. This always gave her a day to catch up on any projects and edit photos for the social media pages. She was in the middle of going through comments on the high school page when her dad's name flashed on her phone.

"Everything okay?" She answered, hearing him laugh softly.

"Yes, everything is fine. I wanted to give you a heads up and let you know that there is absolutely no pressure to take what he's offering."

Emerson sat back in her chair, "What are you talking about?"

"My buddy Nick called me this morning about some issues arising with one of his players. He may be in the market to hire a social media manager for them. He asked me if I knew anyone and I…"

"You didn't…" She pinched the bridge of her nose, "Dad, please tell me you didn't offer for me to do it."

"All I said was you have worked in that field for many years in an educational setting. He asked for your number, and I gave it to him. Hear him out, he may be able to offer you a deal too good to pass up."

She sighed, "Fine, but I'm not making any promises that I'll take the job. You know how much I love my job."

"I know honey. Just after your mom's death, you stuck by Everett and me. I don't want you to miss out on living life."

Emerson's shoulders sagged, "I haven't missed anything, and I love my life. However, I will hear him out and truly consider it if the deal seems right for me."

He chuckled, "Thanks Em. I'll see you later."

The call ended and Emerson let her head fall back against her chair. She was in her late twenties when her mom died and her life had been put on hold. She had an entry level marketing job at a movie studio in Hollywood and had moved into her boyfriend's apartment. A year after her mom's death, her dad decided to move to Chicago to be closer to Everett and she moved with him. Never once had she regretted that decision or the life she built in Chicago. However, the closer to forty she was getting the more she realized how lonely she was.

Her phone chimed with a notification.

Pacey Tucker, MLB All-Star and first baseman for the Vancouver Explorers has been implicated by ex-girlfriend and actress, Lyn Dexter, in forcing her to have abortion months before their split.

"What the hell?" Emerson opened the link from her Twitter account.

Before she could read the article, her phone began to ring with a California area code, "Hello?"

"Emerson? This is Nick Steinberg; I'm an old friend of your dad's."

"Hi Mr. Steinberg, how are you?"

He let out a long sigh, "Well I've definitely been better. I'm sure you've seen the news about Pacey Tucker."

She sat up straight in her chair. Was it possible he wanted her to be Pacey's social media manager.

"Yes, just now but I haven't read the article yet."

"Well, that is why I'm calling you…"

SUMMER TOURS & HEARTS PLAYLIST

TOP 10 SONGS

1. City Grown Willow -Radio Company
2. Ramble On -Led Zeppelin
3. Numb -Linkin Park
4. Skeletons -Brothers Osborne
5. Dammit (Cover) -Alexandra Kay
6. Dangerous Night -Thirty Seconds to Mars
7. Restless Man -Radio Company
8. The Rock Show -Blink 182
9. You Shouldn't Kiss Me Like This -Toby Keith
10. Tuesday's Gone -Metallica

Check out the full playlist by scanning the QR below!

ACKNOWLEDGEMENTS

I want to thank my friends for always putting up with my crazy writer ways. You all have provided me with endless support and love. I'm forever grateful to have you all in my life. Paul, Megan, Kat, Zee, and Jen. I love you all.

To J.A. the man who inspired Zeppelin Foster, the constant joy and light you give to the world through the roles you play and the music you create is immeasurable. Thank you for sharing your many talents with all of us fangirls.

Finally, I want to thank the woman who gave me a love for music. From my earliest memories of listening to Metallica, Guns and Roses, Ozzy Osbourne and many others to rebelling in my teenage years by listening to Christian music. We went to numerous concerts and sat many of nights just randomly listening to music. Thank you Mumsie for making me into the woman I am today. I love you!

ABOUT THE AUTHOR

Nikki Rae resides in St. Louis, Missouri. She spends her days working as a library associate at her local library. She loves to read, attend concerts, travel to fan conventions and snuggle with any one of her three cats that deems her worthy of their time.